▶▶ACCEL WORLD 04

FLIGHT TOWARD A BLUE SKY

REKI KAWAHARA

ILLUSTRATION BY HIMA

DESIGN BY bee-pee

"This is the first time a mere week has felt so long...I want to go back to Tokyo and see you again already."

"...Me too."

KUROYUKIHIME

The Black King
Vice president of the Umesato Junior
High School student council,
controlling Black Lotus

"Long time no see, big brother. You're round as always, huh?! And you, Professor. You're gloomy as always!"

YUNIKO KOZUKI
One of the Seven Kings of Pure Color
The Red King, Scarlet Rain

"Follow me,
Silver Crow."

**BLOOD
LEOPARD**
Mysterious maid clerk
working at a cake shop

"It seems you came prepared in your own way. Well, maybe I'll get to have a little fun, then."

DUSK TAKER
Seiji Nomi's duel avatar

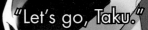

"Let's go, Taku."

"Okay."

SILVER CROW
Haruyuki's duel avatar

CYAN PILE
Takumu's duel avatar

LIME BELL
Chiyuri's duel avatar

"......"

KUROYUKIHIME is the...

"Black Swallowtail
Butterfly"
in the
Local Area
Network.

"Kuroyukihime"
in the
Real World.

"Black Lotus"
in the
Accelerated
World.

Kuroyukihime @
In-school local net
Black Swallowtail Butterfly

Kuroyukihime @
Real World
Kuroyukihime

Kuroyukihime @
Accelerated World
Black Lotus

▶▶▶ACCEL·WORLD 04

FLIGHT TOWARD A BLUE SKY

Reki Kawahara

Illustrations: HIMA

Design: bee-pee

YEN ON

NEW YORK

■ Kuroyukihime = Umesato Junior High School student council vice president. Trim and clever girl who has it all. Her background is shrouded in mystery. Her in-school avatar is a spangle butterfly she programmed herself. Her duel avatar is the Black King, Black Lotus.

■ Haruyuki = Haruyuki Arita. Eighth grader at Umesato Junior High School. Bullied, on the pudgy side. He's good at games, but shy. His in-school avatar is a pink pig. His duel avatar is Silver Crow.

■ Chiyuri = Chiyuri Kurashima. Haruyuki's childhood friend. Meddling, energetic girl. Her in-school avatar is a silver cat.

■ Takumu = Takumu Mayuzumi. A boy Haruyuki and Chiyuri have known since childhood. Good at kendo. His duel avatar is Cyan Pile.

■ Seiji Nomi = New seventh-grade student at Umesato Junior High. His origins are shrouded in mystery, but he uses Brain Burst in everyday school life and stands at the peak of the school castes.

■ Neurolinker = A portable Internet terminal that connects with the brain via a wireless quantum connection and enhances all five senses with images, sounds, and other stimuli.

■ In-school local net = Local area network established within Umesato Junior High School. Used during classes and to check attendance; while on campus, Umesato students are required to be connected to it at all times.

■ Global connection = Connection with the worldwide net. Global connections are forbidden on Umesato Junior High School grounds, where the in-school local net is provided instead.

■ Brain Burst = Neurolinker application sent to Haruyuki by Kuroyukihime.

■ Duel avatar = Player's virtual self operated when fighting in Brain Burst.

■ Legion = Groups composed of many duel avatars with the objective of expanding occupied areas and securing rights. The Seven Kings of Pure Color act as the Legion Masters.

■ Normal Duel Field = The field where normal Brain Burst battles (one-on-one) are carried out. Although the specs do possess elements of reality, the system is essentially on the level of an old-school fighting game.

■ Unlimited Neutral Field = Field for high-level players where only duel avatars at levels four and up are allowed. The game system is of a wholly different order than that of the Normal Duel Field, and the level of freedom in this Field beats out even the next-generation VRMMO.

■ Movement Control System = System in charge of avatar control. Normally, this system handles all avatar movement.

■ Image Control System = System in which the player creates a strong image in their mind to operate the avatar. The mechanism is very different from the normal Movement Control System, and very few players can use it. Key component of the Incarnate System.

■ Incarnate System = Technique allowing players to interfere with Brain Burst's Image Control System to bring about a reality outside of the game's framework. Also referred to as "overwriting" game phenomena.

▶▶▶*ACCEL·WORLD*

1

"Why...?"

Haruyuki had no choice but to listen to the cracked, broken voice that spilled from his throat. "Why would you...Chiyu...?"

The chill wind of the Purgatory stage ripped away his hollow question and blew it toward the yellow sky, but no reply came. Standing motionless on the school roof, the avatar the color of new leaves—Lime Bell/Chiyuri Kurashima—lowered her face to avoid Haruyuki's eyes. She slumped to the concrete beneath her with a soft *clack*, still clutching the iron railing with her right hand.

But instead of Chiyuri's voice, a deep, twisted laugh echoed a response.

"Feh...heh-heh...!"

Flat on his back nearby, arms and legs splayed, the dusk-colored avatar shook his lens-shaped mask back and forth. "Ehheh...heh. This...This is incredible...This is *restoration*...Truly a miraculous power! Heh-heh, ha-ha-ha!"

The avatar continued to laugh quietly, and his body—newly restored to perfect health—glittered a glossy blackish purple as if the incredible injuries he had sustained mere minutes ago had never happened. The healing didn't stop at his body; even the destroyed flamethrower of his right arm had been restored to mint condition.

After a fierce struggle on the field of Umesato Junior High, Haruyuki/Silver Crow and Takumu/Cyan Pile had crushed the twilight avatar Dusk Taker. Haruyuki had ripped his arms off in an air battle, and Takumu had impaled him with his special attack when Nomi/Dusk Taker crashed to the ground. Together, they had beaten him down to the point where a single hit with a normal attack would wipe out what little remained of his HP gauge. Now they simply stood frozen in place behind him.

Because Lime Bell had appeared out of nowhere to interrupt them from the roof. Her left arm sent a shower of light raining down on Dusk Taker, bringing his HP back up to full in an instant. Even his right arm was back in its socket, good as new.

"Why...*Why, Chi?!*" Haruyuki screamed as if to split his throat in two, turning his eyes back up toward the school.

Dusk Taker was the enemy. And Seiji Nomi, the new seventh grader behind the avatar, didn't appear on the matching list, despite the fact that he was in possession of Brain Burst. Instead, he made profligate use of his acceleration ability in kendo matches and on tests. He had even gone so far as to set a trap for Haruyuki, backing him into a terrible corner where he was on the verge of being expelled from school. And then, using his special attack Demonic Commandeer, he had stolen Silver Crow's wings in a duel.

Spirit shattered by this loss, Haruyuki had somehow managed to yank himself to his feet again and undergo an agonizing struggle to gain a new power to replace his wings. Broken and battered though he was from all this, victory had been within reach only moments earlier. So why, after all that, did Chiyuri have to interfere?

Plunged into a hell of confusion, Haruyuki could do nothing more than open his eyes wide beneath his silver mask and stare intently at Lime Bell.

Chiyuri didn't even open her mouth. She simply tightened her grip on the railing and kept her face hidden beneath the brim of her large hat. He could see her slender shoulders trembling—like she was fighting some impulse inside herself.

Why? It's obvious. The sudden insight struck Haruyuki, a bolt of lightning. *Nomi. Seiji Nomi probably talked to her during lunch today and demanded that she obey him.* Nomi had found her weak point, just like he had with Haruyuki, and was threatening her with something. That was the only possible explanation.

Yanking his gaze back to the field, Haruyuki watched Dusk Taker, still lying on his back laughing raspily, spread the black wings on his back. Cut from the cloth of darkness itself, the wings beat the air, and the slim avatar slowly began to stand, drawn up by invisible threads.

"Feh heh heh…Hmn, hn-hn-hn-hm…" The smug, throaty chuckling rapidly grew louder. Reddish-purple orbs flickered brightly beneath the illuminated compound eye of his visor. "Hm-hm, ha-ha-ha-ha! First flying. Now healing. Two very rare powers. And now both of them are mine."

After floating to his feet, the avatar drifted up another thirty centimeters and came to a halt. Throwing his regenerated arms out to his sides, Dusk Taker turned claw-shaped fingers skyward. An inky, dark aura gushed from his hands like a viscous liquid. "Aah…I feel so good! The delight of plunder! Taking someone's dreams, their hopes, their possibilities, and trampling them! This feeling of omniscience, I simply can't get enough of it!!"

The ugly joy in a young boy's voice became a physical pressure and radiated through the field, causing Haruyuki's injury-riddled avatar to reel. Paying no mind to this, however, Haruyuki forced himself to speak, his voice stained with a myriad of emotions. "You." He took a step toward the blackish-purple avatar floating high above him. "Nomi. What did you do? What did you do to Chiyu?!"

Dusk Taker languidly turned his head to gaze down at Haruyuki. Thin eyes within the half-closed spherical visor blinked with exaggerated slowness. A poisonous, deeply scornful smile grew wordlessly until it filled his face.

Haruyuki's field of view was suddenly dyed bloodred. All the confused emotion in his heart had snapped into laser focus upon a single point: an overwhelming loathing of all that was Seiji Nomi.

"No...miii...," Haruyuki growled, unconsciously arranging the remaining fingers of his right hand into the shape of a sword. *Veeeeen!* The squeal of resonance rang in his ears; a silver light flickered at his fingertips.

But the light wouldn't stabilize, as though the swirling hatred in his heart were static that prevented him from creating the image of his silver sword. Regardless, Haruyuki brandished his right arm and moved to slash Dusk Taker out of the sky.

"Unh...Aaaaaaah!!" A blue shadow streaked past Haruyuki's right side, together with a cry like vomiting blood.

Cyan Pile. The heavyweight avatar plunged forward, armor scorched and still smoking from the earlier fight, and the earth shook in his wake. "You...made Chi cryyyyyy!!"

Takumu never lost his cool, no matter what the situation. He was generally the one who kept Haruyuki's own violence in check, and yet here he was now, hurtling recklessly toward Nomi, screaming like a child.

Even with the equivalent of a tank charging at him, Dusk Taker didn't flinch. He casually raised a slender hand and spread the sharply pointed fingers. "Be gone," he spat.

Zzraa! At the strange vibration noise, his right hand was cloaked in a pulsing, glittering purple emptiness. The pulsation quickly changed shape to become claws—sickles slithering out from the tips of his fingers. Five of these long, curving claws lazily wrapped themselves around Cyan Pile's charging bulk and made contact in five places—both sides of the neck, the right flank, left shoulder, and the left flank—and then slid smoothly together. It was a fist clenching, as if Cyan Pile were nothing more than butter.

Haruyuki groaned silently as the blue, heavyweight avatar's torso was sliced into pieces. Head and arms flew off into space, terrifying cascades of sparks bursting from the stumps. They grazed past Dusk Taker and dropped heavily to the ground behind him, inert. Eventually, Takumu's still-sprinting lower half collapsed with a *thud*.

After a small lag—a lag that seemed to say, *The severing came before the system could even confirm the damage*—Cyan Pile's HP gauge slid into a precipitous drop. Halved, the bar turned yellow; at 20 percent remaining, red; and still it plummeted—

—to zero.

The remains of the divided avatar exploded into pale polygon fragments and scattered. Before Haruyuki's eyes, a system message popped up to the effect that Dusk Taker had destroyed Cyan Pile.

"…Keh…Keh-heh, hah-ha!" The voice that dripped from the twilight avatar sneered. "Losers…Why do you suppose they're just so funny? I mean, they don't even *attempt* to recognize defeat. They simply flounder as he did in such an unsightly fashion until, in the end, even their pride is taken from them. I really thought Mayuzumi was more intelligent. Quite disillusioning. Well, I suppose he was the muscle-bound, macho avatar, after all, right up to his brain. Hmn-hm-hm, heh-heh, ha-ha-ha-ha-ha!!"

Dusk Taker laughed loudly, a pronounced dark aura radiating from both arms.

Bathed in this sneering condescension, Haruyuki stared for a few seconds at the spot where Takumu had disappeared, and then looked up at Chiyuri, still crouched down on the school roof. As Haruyuki stood rooted to the spot, the silver light in his right hand flickered and disappeared.

It wasn't that he had lost the will to fight. Just the opposite, in fact. A ferocious destructive impulse ripped through his avatar like a raging fire, shaking Haruyuki to his bones.

I hate him. I want to break him. I want to beat the crap out of this duel avatar Dusk Taker—no, the consciousness of Seiji Nomi living inside the avatar. I want to slice it up, rip it to pieces, and dance on the remains.

This world was not a virtual game field anymore, the battle no longer an exchange of damage points. Until that moment, Haruyuki had never felt actual hatred toward an enemy who crushed him in any game, including Brain Burst, much less hatred toward the actual flesh-and-blood player controlling that enemy. But right now was different. The black loathing coursing through his veins burned far more hotly than the flame of regret.

THEN DESTROY HIM, someone whispered out of the blue, right behind him. *DESTROY HIM, EAT HIM. DEVOUR HIS FLESH, DRINK HIM DRY OF BLOOD, TAKE EVERYTHING.*

The voice was familiar. Haruyuki had definitely heard this twisted, low sound and its metallic overtones at some point, somewhere. However, before his brain could arrive at the memory of where exactly, he felt an intense cold, like being pierced with a needle of ice, in the middle of his back. Drilling deep between his shoulder blades, the ice penetrated to his heart before dissipating into a liquid-metal chill throughout his body.

A bone-chillingly cold hunger merged with his molten hatred, and his field of vision narrowed sharply. The metallic green ground of the Purgatory stage, the organic structure of the school, Lime Bell's head hanging on its roof—all disappeared beyond a swaying curtain of darkness. He could see nothing but Dusk Taker, still chuckling with his high-pitched scorn.

"Noo...mii."

A groan colored by the same metallic effect as the voice he had just heard crawled out from his throat.

"Nomi...You...bastaaard..."

Haruyuki dumped—forced—his raging emotions into the tip of his remaining hand.

Activating the Incarnate System—a technique allowing players to interfere with Brain Burst's Image Control System to bring about a reality outside of the game's framework—required a very deep mental focus. Appropriately, the "light sword" Haruyuki manifested with his will had disappeared the instant this loathing of Nomi had flooded him.

Nevertheless.

Zrrk! A long sword stretched from Silver Crow's right hand abruptly. But not in its former snow-white state: The blade in his hand was jet-black. It absorbed and thereby erased all light, a hungry darkness deeper than the midnight purple of the claws Nomi had materialized.

"Hmm?" Dusk Taker stopped laughing as he noticed the unusual change in Silver Crow. "Oh my. You're not still thinking of trying something, are you, Arita? Perhaps you plan to join in with your partner in solidarity and expose me to the same shameful sight?"

Haruyuki didn't have the mental leeway to respond to this sneering. His own thoughts were entirely swallowed up by the sword that was in his right hand. All that existed now was the singular urge to slice up and destroy the enemy before him.

YES. EAT HIM. EAT HIM. DEVOUR HIM, the brutal voice inside his head whispered.

Urged on, he staggered ahead, planting his forward foot. Immediately after, he kicked off the ground like a rocket.

"Unh...Aaaaaaah!!" Roaring, he brandished the dark sword high, high above his head. Putting everything—attack speed, his avatar's weight, his raging hatred—on the tip of this sword, Haruyuki slashed downward at the face mask of the floating Dusk Taker.

Kendo player that he was, Nomi should have had no trouble avoiding his completely obvious, head-on slash attack. But the purple avatar didn't even attempt to dodge. Instead, he simply opened his right hand and waited for the black blade, ready to grab it just as he had Cyan Pile.

The sword materialized by Haruyuki and the five sickles made incarnate by Nomi clashed in midair.

When they fought earlier, their Incarnate attacks had bounced back violently, fighting each other the instant they touched. This time, however, the exact opposite occurred: The moment the inky blade and the blackish-purple sickles collided, a darkness began swirling from center point, threatening to devour both weapons.

"Hngh." Dusk Taker let out a low groan. "An attack with the same attribute…?! How can this…?" He narrowed his eyes, as if observing the phenomenon intently.

In contrast, Haruyuki's mind was blank as he poured every ounce of his strength into keeping his blade from being knocked aside.

"Unh…Hng, graah!" Grinding his teeth below his mask, he roared, "*You* be gone, Nomi…Disappear! Get out of my… siiiiiight!!"

Vwaan!! The sword of his right hand shuddered, and the vortex of darkness at the point of contact grew more and more viscous. Nomi's long sickles crumbled at the tips, the gloom starting to swallow them.

"Tch!" Clicking his tongue, Nomi spawned oversize purple talons on his left hand as well and placed them over the sickles already clutching Haruyuki's sword. The darkness, a small black hole, twisted even more fiercely, sucking metal insects and fragments of objects up from the ground, which momentarily flashed before disappearing entirely.

"Such insolence!!" Dusk Taker cried, and the pulsing purple emptiness jetting from both hands grew.

"Hngaaaah!!" A beast-like roar surged from Haruyuki's throat.

Perhaps due to an abnormal gravity calculation where they stood, even the thick, hanging clouds began to spin slowly, drawn down toward the earth in a funnel. The school windows shattered one after another, a sharp light effect blew through the air, and concentric fissures rippled the ground with lightning-like sparks.

And then several things happened all at once.

"Stop! Stop already!!" Chiyuri's tearful scream echoed throughout the stage.

"Go awaaaaaaay!!" Haruyuki's thundering roar drowned her out.

The remaining time displayed in the upper part of his vision hit zero.

TIME UP!! The text blazed to life before his eyes, announcing the end of the duel.

After the Battle Royale mode results screen, when the acceleration was released and Haruyuki slipped through rings of radiated light to return to the real, he couldn't remember right away what he had been doing before the duel had started—or, for that matter, when or where he had been.

Stretching out before his eyes was the rubberized, reddish-brown track. Several boys in jerseys were running ahead of him.

And then Haruyuki himself was hitting the ground noisily with his own feet. His consciousness was unable to merge completely with the movements of his body; he was frustratingly sluggish, and he nearly tripped and fell. But he pinwheeled his arms madly and somehow managed to catch himself. The students sitting inside the track and the boy running alongside him burst out laughing.

Right. I was in the middle of the three-thousand-meter run. It's Tuesday, fifth period. The middle of gym class, he thought, dumbfounded, before suddenly becoming aware of a magma-like emotion erupting from the depths of his stomach. *What the hell am I doing? Gym class? Long-distance run? Who cares about all that?! Seiji Nomi...I have to destroy him! Whatever it takes!!*

"Unnh!" He couldn't completely suppress the low moan. He gritted his teeth, glared at the distant finish line, and poured all this newfound fury into his limbs. The plodding sound of his feet, scraping heavily on the track, increased in pitch. His body leaned forward.

A red letter *R* blinked next to the time clock displayed in the lower part of his vision, to let him know that he was breaking his personal record. Unaware of even this, however, Haruyuki put everything he had into sprinting the remaining ninety meters. He didn't actually overtake the students ahead of him in this last spurt, but he was clearly closing the gap, which caused a bit of a commotion among the boys in the class.

But Haruyuki was indifferent to their chatter, and to his new time flashing before his eyes, the instant he crossed the finish line. Without stopping for even a second, he just kept running in a straight line toward the doors.

"Heeey! Where're you going, Aritaaa? Bathroooom?" He heard his gym teacher's laid-back voice and the laughter of the other students, but he ignored them both.

He was obviously not headed for the bathroom. He was going to climb up to the third floor of the school and raid Nomi Seiji's classroom. He was going to pin Nomi's flesh-and-blood body to the ground, force him to direct, and make him unilaterally and unconditionally surrender, this time for sure. And if he couldn't do that, he was going to rip Nomi's Neurolinker off his neck, smash it into tiny pieces, and destroy the core chip.

This kind of barbarity was absolutely necessary, wasn't it? After all, this was the boy who had stooped to the most cowardly of blows: threatening Chiyuri to make her do his bidding.

Each time the intensely violent urge welled up within him, a point in the middle of his back throbbed. Almost like the urge was being created there, over and over again, endlessly.

"You just *wait!*" he spat, and pushed off the ground even more violently—until a powerful hand from behind clamped tightly down on his left shoulder.

"You have to stop, Haru!"

Haruyuki heard a stifled voice in his ear and reflexively put on the brakes. Unable to stop in anything remotely resembling the cool manner of his duel avatar, he pitched forward and was about to fall when arms grabbed on to him and yanked him back up.

"Taku, why are you trying to stop me?!" he squeezed out hoarsely, head hanging very low.

"If you get suspended for fighting now, the only thing that'll happen is Chi's life will get a whole lot worse!" Takumu Mayuzumi replied, holding Haruyuki's left arm with his own muscular right.

"Her life's bad enough as it is! Nomi—he threatened Chiyu and forced her to do what he told her! You just gonna let him get away with that?!" Haruyuki whirled around to look at Takumu and saw that the normally clear gaze in his eyes was twisted in agony behind his sport glasses. Haruyuki swallowed his breath.

Right. It wasn't like Takumu had no feelings. In his heart, he had to be even more worried about Chiyuri than Haruyuki was, and burning with rage at Nomi's tricks besides. But at the same time, his old friend was also worried about him—despite the fact that Haruyuki himself had been simply spurred on by anger, without giving the slightest thought to Takumu.

His back throbbed again, but this was the last time, and the violent impulse receded like a storm. After inhaling deeply and exhaling through his trembling throat, Haruyuki relaxed his shoulders and sighed. "But, I mean, you, you went flying at Nomi before I did."

Takumu let out a short, bitter laugh. "Seriously. How many years has it been since I lost it like that..."

Haruyuki felt the ill will that had hung between them melt away—the one that had been there since they'd argued at his house the day Nomi stole his wings. They stood in the corner of the schoolyard in the silence that followed for a while, but finally, with everyone apparently having finished their runs on the track behind them, the teacher clapped his hands to call the students all together.

"Shall we go back, Haru?"

Haruyuki nodded slowly at the words and added in a quiet voice, "You tell Chiyu. Tell her no matter what Nomi said to her, she definitely does not have to obey him."

"Yeah, I got it. I'll— No, *we'll* protect Chi."

They met each other's eyes for a moment and then turned on their heels.

Haruyuki glared up at the third floor of the school one final time and then murmured in the depths of his heart, *Nomi, you did something that should never, ever be done. From this moment on, the fight with you is a death match, no time limit. If it kills me, I will destroy whatever you are using to block accelerated duels. I will devote my life to hunting and fighting you until one of us has no more burst points.*

Grinding his teeth, Haruyuki began to walk back to his class alongside Takumu.

But a mere ten minutes later, everything skidded off the rails in a totally unexpected direction.

Fifth period was barely over before Haruyuki and Takumu were dashing over to the gym on the other side of the main school building. They spotted Chiyuri just as she was coming out of the hallway between the two buildings and beckoned her urgently from the shadow of a pillar.

Still in her T-shirt and shorts, she froze when she saw them. Which was only natural. Only a few minutes earlier, she had dived into the field of an actual battle for the first time and been forced to heal their enemy Dusk Taker. As a result, Takumu aka Cyan Pile had lost when his HP gauge hit zero, Haruyuki aka Silver Crow had lost by decision when time ran out, and both of them had had their points taken by Nomi.

However, they did their best to make their faces say that they didn't come to yell at her about it. Haruyuki kept moving his arms, while an awkward smile forced its way onto his lips. Chiyuri looked down as if to avoid his eyes, but finally, she said something to her classmates headed for the locker room and broke off from them, approaching Haruyuki and Takumu.

When he saw Chiyuri's cheeks pale despite the fact that she

had just been doing serious physical activity, his intense rage toward Nomi erupted in his heart again. Takumu, next to him, also clenched his fists tightly before taking a deep breath and opening his mouth.

"Chi. I think I already understand why you did what you did. Which is why I just came to say: You don't need to do what he tells you to."

"Th-that's right," Haruyuki added earnestly. "Right about now, he should be shaking in his boots at the power you have. I mean, with the power to not only recover HP but even destroy weapons, we could put up a real fight against him—no, we could win!"

Chiyuri furrowed her brow momentarily. It was her habit when she was thinking about something but unsure about that something. A few seconds later, she uttered her first words. "No, that's not it."

"Huh? Th-that's not it?" Baffled, he simply parroted her words back in question form, and Chiyuri changed suddenly, a fierce light glittering in both eyes.

"That's not it," she repeated, looking at Haruyuki and Takumu in turn. "Nomi's not forcing me to do anything."

"Chi...Th-then what...?" It was Takumu's turn to be stunned. He blinked rapidly as he took a step toward her.

Chiyuri pulled back, out of reach. "Nomi asked me," she replied, quietly but clearly, "to join him. He said I'd be his personal healer and he'd make sure I got a ton of points. And it's fine, right? Not like I'm in your Legion or anything yet." She took another step away from her friends, who were rooted to the spot in astonishment, before continuing. "From now on, *we* probably shouldn't have any kind of contact with Nega Nebulus. Because we're all out in the real to one another. Of course, the contract between Haru and Nomi is a completely separate deal."

His mind might have gone completely blank and been absolutely unable to grasp what was happening at that moment, but Haruyuki still understood what this "contract" was. It was, in other words, the agreement where Haruyuki paid Nomi ten burst points a week in tribute for two years, so that he could eventually get his flying ability back.

Chiyuri had no interest in fighting him and Takumu on the battlefield. But she didn't care about Nomi taking points from Haruyuki. That's what she was saying.

It was shocking, but Haruyuki was hit even harder by Chiyuri referring to herself and Nomi as "we." For all the years and years he had known her up to that point, when she said "we," she always meant Chiyuri, Haruyuki, and Takumu.

"'Kay, see you," she said curtly, avoiding their eyes. She turned adroitly aside and ran off toward the locker room.

All that was left of her presence was the sweet smell of milk, so familiar to him after so long together.

2

School had been unpleasant, to say the least, and Haruyuki trudged home, eyes on the ground, completely beaten down.

This experience was once a totally normal, run-of-the-mill thing for him. When a bunch of kids in his grade bullied him horribly and mercilessly last year, he'd counted the paving tiles of the sidewalk on the trek to his condo pretty much every single day. But having Takumu—*the* Takumu Mayuzumi—next to him, head hanging and dragging his feet in the exact same way, was a first.

Takumu had skipped kendo practice on the pretext that he wasn't feeling well, and they walked silently together on the road from Umesato Junior High to the condo where they both lived.

"Come over," Haruyuki said as they slipped through the front gate.

"…Okay." Takumu nodded listlessly, and they rode the elevator together to the twenty-third floor.

Opening the door to his empty apartment and heading into the living room, Haruyuki dropped his bag on the floor and sat at the dining table. Takumu sat down across from him, and for a while, the pair simply sat in silence.

We sat facing each other like this before, too, Haruyuki thought absently before finally realizing that this "before" had been a mere twenty-four hours earlier—i.e., the incident after school on Monday.

Haruyuki had fought Seiji Nomi for the first time the previous day, during a free period, and lost the silver wings on his back to Nomi's special attack.

Suspecting something was up with Haruyuki and Chiyuri, who had been there for the whole thing, Takumu came over after practice and sat down in that very spot across from him. Haruyuki was in a sadistic, self-torturing kind of mood and said some terrible things to Takumu. For his trouble, he received a solid fist to the face. After that, he jumped on a bus to Shibuya and despairingly threw himself into an accelerated duel. His old enemy, the bike-riding Ash Roller, cursed Haruyuki and his apathetic attitude before dragging him to the old Tokyo Tower in the Unlimited Neutral Field.

There, he was brought face-to-face with Ash Roller's guardian and former Nega Nebulus member, Sky Raker. She taught Haruyuki about the Incarnate System, a Burst Linker's ultimate power, and marched him through an extremely Spartan training regime so he could learn to use it.

For him to really grasp the first step toward the power of will, it took a full week in the Accelerated World, where his consciousness was accelerated by a factor of a thousand. Which is why, in a certain sense, it was only natural that he felt like the whole thing with Takumu and everything else had happened ages ago.

Unconsciously, Haruyuki raised his right hand and ran his fingers first over his lower jaw, where Nomi had punched him during the break the day before, and then his right cheek, where Takumu had hit him after school. There was hardly any visible trace of either anymore, but a convulsion of pain shot through him. He could accelerate his mental state and lock himself up in that other world all he wanted, but it wouldn't heal the wounds to his physical body—his actual pain.

This gesture as he replayed recent events caught his friend's eye. "Haru, I told you when I hit you that I didn't care who Chi was with, so long as she was happy," Takumu said with a self-deprecating laugh. "But I take it back. There's pretty much no way I can accept this. I mean, Chi partnering up with that Seiji Nomi kid."

"Forget accepting it," Haruyuki responded hollowly, dropping his hand to the table. "I can't even believe it. I mean, it's true there's no rule in Brain Burst saying you have to be on the same team as your friends in the real or anything, but...I just can't believe Chiyu's so focused on points, she'd betray us to join Nomi..."

"Well, from a points perspective, hooking up with Nomi's definitely going to be more effective than joining us. Now that he's got your wings, Haru, Dusk Taker's battle power's way over the top. And if he makes his duel debut with the healer Lime Bell on his team, there's not a midrange Burst Linker who could seriously take them on."

"Considering how depressed you are about it, that's a pretty levelheaded judgment, Professor." Now it was Haru with the wry smile playing on his lips, but a sigh soon pushed that aside. "But still, Taku...This is Chiyu we're talking about here. Chiyu, the girl who completely does not get games at all. I swear, she could even get her entire party wiped out in a story-mode battle in an RPG. You think she actually has any idea about the most effective way to get points?"

"I—I don't, not really. Dammit..."

As Haruyuki talked with his best friend, the shock of Chiyuri's declaration of farewell eased, if only slightly, and in a very muted way; slowly, he pulled himself to his feet and headed for the kitchen.

He took a frozen pizza box out of the large freezer and tossed it in the microwave before taking out a bottle of oolong tea and grabbing two glasses to go with it. He carried these out to the table, along with the pizza—which had finished defrosting and cooking in mere minutes—and set everything down.

"Thanks," Takumu murmured as he poured oolong tea in his glass.

Opening the box, Haruyuki grabbed a slice of the seafood pizza, and just as he was about to shove the tip, with its thin, dangling strings of cheese, into his mouth, he suddenly heard a voice.

Aah! You're eating this stuff again! Well, I guess I'll just have to get Mom to make you something.

But of course, it was not a real voice or even a PCM file played back by his Neurolinker. The flavor of the lasagna Chiyuri had brought over only a few days earlier came back to life on his tongue, and he took a huge bite of the mass-produced pizza to try and kill it.

As he chewed on the strangely salty pizza, head in his hand, he heard the sniffling back of snot. He raised his eyes slowly to witness Takumu, head also hanging, mouth also masticating pizza, rub his eyes intently beneath his glasses.

Abruptly, a completely different pain pierced his heart.

Taku's always so calm and collected, and so clever he runs circles around me. But he definitely can't take a real hit.

He tried to do everything he could to help me after my wings got stolen and I got reckless. So now it's my turn. It's my turn to cheer him up and have his back, Haruyuki murmured to himself. He closed his eyes, scarfed down the rest of his pizza, drained his glass of oolong tea, and slammed it back down on the table.

"Taku!" he shouted. Takumu's shoulders shot up and he turned red eyes on Haruyuki. Meeting those eyes squarely, he continued, "Taku, I believe in Chiyu! Which is why I don't believe what she said!"

"Huh?"

"I said it before, didn't I? Joining up with Nomi because she wants points? That's not like Chiyu at all. So we just scrap that possibility completely. Probably—no, I'm like ninety percent sure that our first guess was the truth. Nomi's threatening Chiyu to make her his partner, and he forced her to tell us that. That just makes so much more sense. Doesn't it?" Still holding his glass, Haruyuki laid out his thinking confidently.

Takumu considered this carefully. "Mm-hmm," he responded eventually, in a tone that was more or less back to his usual calm voice. "That does sound plausible. But, Haru, there's a bit of a contradiction there. 'Scrap completely' but 'ninety percent sure'? So then the remaining ten percent uncertainty is the possibility that Chi voluntarily went over to Nomi, right?"

"Yeah. But for a different reason."

"Reason? Are you saying there's something other than points that would make Chi turn against us?"

Looking up at Takumu as he cocked his head, Haruyuki instinctively shrank back. "That would be…," he whispered, "the leader of our Legion Nega Nebulus…Her…"

Takumu's eyelids fluttered rapidly, as if he had been caught off guard. But soon enough, the same uneasiness that was on Haruyuki's face descended upon his. "I—I see. If Chi thinks there's no way she's going to be subordinate to Master—Kuroyukihime…"

"Can you definitively say she wouldn't?"

At Haruyuki's question, Takumu shook his head from side to side, a fairly complicated expression on his face, and expelled a lengthy sigh. "But if that's the case," he added, almost groaning, "then we really do have to finally tell Master about everything and get her to help us fight. If she finds out that Chi betrayed us and healed Nomi all because of her…"

"She might totally destroy Lime Bell, along with Dusk Taker."

He knew only too well how severe she could be, Kuroyukihime, the person behind Black Lotus, the level-nine duel avatar who was the Black King and the leader of the Legion Nega Nebulus. Anyone she decided was the enemy was mercilessly cut down with the swords of her hands. It was pretty hard—no, impossible—to believe that she would not apply this same general principle to Chiyuri.

Haruyuki dropped his gaze to the surface of the table and then yanked it right back up to Takumu. "She's coming back from the school trip Saturday night, so we have four days," he said, like

he was trying to convince himself. "We just have to sort this out before then."

"Sort it out? How?"

"Either Chiyu's being coerced or she's actually doing all this of her own free will. But if we take Nomi down, if we push him to the edge and he loses Brain Burst, then everything ends. Right?"

Takumu took a deep breath at Haruyuki's words before a slightly bitter smile crossed his lips. "Easier said than done, Haru. Even if we somehow did manage to figure out what keeps him from showing up on the matching list, who knows how many times we'd have to win to get Dusk Taker down to zero points."

"Dunno," Haruyuki said shortly and began thinking out loud. "Nomi just started at Umesato, and he's been burning through points to build himself up, what with the test and the kendo matches. Especially in kendo with the 'physical acceleration' command. That costs five points. I mean, he's still at level five. Do you think he really has that many points to spare?"

"I guess not. Especially since he doesn't seem to be fighting any regular duels. His point supply should be limited." Takumu nodded, narrowing eyes, which, behind his glasses, had regained a bit of their former sharpness. He met Haruyuki's stare and continued quickly, "But, Haru, if that's true, then it's just a race against time, and Master's return to Tokyo has nothing to do with it. Now that Nomi has a specialized healer in addition to the flying ability, the time's totally right for him to make his duel debut. If he limits himself to tag-team matches, he won't be able to fight too often, but even still, he'll win the majority of the duels he does fight."

"So in other words, we have to cut the head off the beast before he starts racking up points," Haruyuki said decisively, after a quick glance at Takumu. "Okay. I'll figure out whatever trick he's using to block duels by myself, somehow."

"Wh-what are you talking about? We'll—"

"No, there's something I need you to do while I'm doing that." Clenching both hands on the tabletop, he lowered his voice dramatically. "Taku, you must remember, since he used it right on you. The way Dusk Taker made things disappear with his hands, basically nullifying whatever he touched."

"Y-yeah. I still can't believe it." Takumu shook his head sharply, as if doubting his own memory. "I mean, he was emitting that crazy light, but his special-attack gauge didn't go down. And I can sort of get how it would work with punches and kicks, but he even sucked in my nonphysical attack, Lightning Cyan Spark. I mean, that kind of top-level thing, it's impossible. What kind of ability could do that?"

"Um, it's not a system ability or special attack. I'm not sure how to put this…I can't really explain it well." Furrowing his brow and earnestly searching for the right words, Haruyuki clumsily tried to communicate to Takumu the knowledge he had only just gotten the day before. "It's like a superspecial attack and the energy source is the Burst Linker's own imagination. The proper name is the Incarnate System. It's the strongest attack power in the Accelerated World. You make things real with your heart and your will."

It took almost a full twenty minutes to finish explaining the main points of the Incarnate System that the recluse in old Tokyo Tower, Sky Raker, had taught him, and how he had managed to acquire the Incarnate sword of light.

As he spoke, Haruyuki was once again made aware of the fact that he himself still had a mountain of questions about the system. It could be a technique made possible by a bug, creating a hole in the program, like Sky Raker said, but then why didn't the administrator take care of it? If the admin was leaving it there deliberately, what was the point of that?

Brain Burst was, in fact, an extremely unfriendly game in that it came with no manual and there were no guide-type NPCs, but he felt like the existence of the Incarnate System just made the whole thing even more baffling. What exactly *was* this application…?

With these thoughts racing through his mind, Haruyuki somehow managed to explain everything he knew.

When he was finished, Takumu stared, dumbfounded, as Haruyuki gulped down oolong tea. "I don't know what to say," he finally murmured hoarsely. "Haru, you really reel in the older ladies, don't you?"

"Th-that's your first reaction?"

"It's just...To be honest, I'm having a hard time swallowing this Incarnate or whatever thing. Changing something as vague as the power of an image into an actual attack...I mean, I get what you're saying, but this goes beyond the domain of a fighting game."

"Well, yeah. And I can't explain how I get the sword to appear or anything." Staring fixedly at his round fingers, he kept thinking out loud. "But probably, what the will comes down to is something like, 'If you imagine it, you can make anything happen.' Maybe it's intimately connected to an avatar's attributes...or the nature of the Burst Linker themselves...or something. Like, my being able to get a sword to come out of my hand is because Silver Crow's arms were in a shape like that right from the start. I feel like it's maybe something like that."

"Hmm. So then, hypothetically, if I did the same training as you, I wouldn't necessarily be able to produce a sword of light the way you can?"

"Prob'ly not. But if that's the case, I think you would get a form of your will more suited to you, to Cyan Pile. The problem is, what do you have to do—what kind of training do you need to get it? When I think about it now, she—Sky Raker—made me climb that wall because she saw from the start what the optimal training for me would be. And this is just a guess, but I bet a high-level Burst Linker who had completely mastered the Incarnate System would probably also understand the way to train one's will."

Takumu bit his lip lightly, seemingly deep in thought. Finally, he opened his mouth, eyes still lowered. "In which case, even if I did dive into the Unlimited Neutral Field and blindly train, it's pretty unlikely I'd be able to grasp the Incarnate System on my own. So that means…you absolutely need the guidance of someone with a thorough knowledge of the System?"

"Yeah. I'm sure Sky Raker would teach you, too, but the problem is, I don't have any way to get in touch with her." Haruyuki sighed, and Takumu furrowed his brow.

"She's not an NPC," he murmured. "So the only way I'm going to get to see her is if I climb the old Tokyo Tower in the Unlimited Neutral Field. But we'd have to get in touch in the real, coordinate the timing, and then dive."

"That's just it. You'd probably see her eventually if you just waited at the top of the tower, but you're accelerated a thousand times on the other side, and who knows how many months or years could go by…There is just one way: We can duel Sky Raker's child Ash Roller in Shibuya and get him to make an appointment for us, but…dunno." Haruyuki cut himself off there and propped his fleshy cheeks up in his hands.

Takumu's face quickly turned serious. "Hey, heeeey, I don't owe you nothin', whiny babyyyy!" He skillfully imitated the bike-riding avatar. "That's what he'd say, no doubt about it."

The truth was, Haruyuki already owed Ash Roller an enormous debt from yesterday for bringing him to Sky Raker in the first place. He had to say that asking for his help—a member of an enemy Legion—on top of that was a pretty weak thing for a Burst Linker to do. He took another slice of the cooling pizza and racked his brain as he bit into it.

Normally, he would ask his guardian and Legion Master Kuroyukihime straightaway. She was the Black King; she would obviously be well versed in the Incarnate System. But she must have had her own reasons for not telling him about it up till now, which made him feel like she wouldn't tell him right away, even if he did ask her. And anyway, with her currently in the distant south of Okinawa, he had no way to meet her in the Accelerated World.

Then there was Takumu's guardian—or at least, that's where he wanted to go next. But he was a member of the Blue Legion and had already been retired from the Accelerated World via the Blue King's Judgment Blow for being the ringleader of the backdoor program incident six months earlier.

And there was really no other Burst Linker who would likely know all about the Incarnate System and also have a reason to lend Haruyuki and Takumu a—

"Oh...Oh!" Haruyuki chirped, having thought the problem through this far. He didn't notice the chunk of shrimp that tumbled from his mouth. "Right! Right! There is someone, a super-high-level Linker who owes us a huge favor, in an area just north of here."

The corner of Takumu's mouth spasmed faintly. "H-hey, hey, Haru. You don't mean..."

"There's no one else. Prominence Legion Master and Red King, Scarlet Rain. She's level nine; she has to have mastered the Incarnate System." He lowered his voice as he spoke, and the deep red avatar who occupied one of the seats of the Seven Kings of Pure Color sprang to life in the back of his mind.

The Red King. With the flame power of her enormous Enhanced Armament, a weapons array several times the size of her actual body, she set her enemies and entire fields ablaze. If, despite this incredible power, she had not mastered the Incarnate System, they would indeed be forced to push ahead in some new direction, something Haruyuki deeply did not wish to contemplate.

"And that's not all," Haruyuki continued. "You haven't forgotten the serious action we got into at Scarlet Rain...at Niko's request, right?"

"N-no, I definitely remember."

It had been a mere three months earlier that Niko, aka Yuniko Kozuki, had abruptly shown up in the flesh at Haruyuki's apartment. Her objective was to get Haruyuki to help her subjugate Chrome Disaster, a Burst Linker from her own legion who had gone mad. She came to Haruyuki after determining that Silver Crow and his wings were the only thing that could catch Disaster, who had been able to move freely through all three dimensions.

Together with Takumu and Kuroyukihime, Haruyuki accepted the mission, but before they could get to the real business, they ended up in a seriously tight spot, caught up in an unexpected series of battles when assaulted by a large group from the Yellow Legion. Or rather, in truth, it ended up being Takumu going blow for blow with a large enemy avatar.

"But, Haru, as payment for helping subjugate him, didn't Prominence agree to a cease-fire with Nega Nebulus? Wasn't that her way of paying us back as the Red King?"

But even Takumu sounded skeptical at his own words, so Haruyuki puffed his cheeks and rebutted, "Th-that's like repaying a meal of curry with a plate of SPAM!"

"Uh, I don't really know about that example."

"A-anyway, there's no other high-level Burst Linker we can contact in the real. And if we're planning to fight Nomi, we definitely need this power, if only to avoid his Incarnate attack. So... all we can do is bet on Niko being in a good mood..." Haruyuki trailed off, and his last few words were overlaid with the sound of Takumu taking a deep breath.

For a while, his tall friend, downturned face hidden by long hair, stayed silent. He loosely clenched his right hand on the table, and in that motion, Haruyuki understood that he was remembering the savage battle with Seiji Nomi.

When he finally lifted his face, the light in his strong eyes was different. And the voice he spoke with rang out in the dim living room. "Right, it's just like you say, Haru. In the battle against Dusk Taker, I thought we were evenly matched right until the middle of it, and then after he started to use the Incarnate, I couldn't do anything, which totally sucked. I could feel how we were just on totally different levels. If we're going to defeat him and get Chi back, then I can't be hesitating at a thing like this."

"Taku..."

"And, hey, Haru?" He stopped and stared right into Haruyuki's eyes over the rims of his glasses. "Your sword of light was just as—no, even more amazing than Dusk Taker's purple fluctuation. Even I could tell that you worked crazy hard to master that. You…A long time ago, you said it, didn't you? That time when we fought. You said you couldn't beat me in the real. I can't beat you in the virtual. So we're equal."

"Oh…N-no, that was…" Haruyuki was about to offer the excuse that it was just something he had said in the heat of battle, but Takumu rebuffed his objection with his right hand and continued.

"B-but, you know, I don't think that's real equality. We can get to be true equals by competing with each other and acknowledging each other in the real and in the virtual."

Abruptly, the look on the face of his childhood friend seemed somehow nostalgic for a distant past.

"When we were in elementary school, whenever I got a new game, I'd basically head straight for the walkthrough sites. And not just for action games. I'd even play RPGs with a chat window open, and then I felt like I was really adventuring. Which is why Brain Burst makes me so uneasy, I can barely stomach it. It doesn't have a manual, much less a walk-through. Thinking about it now, I wonder if that isn't why I turned to something like that backdoor program. But I finally get it now: This game doesn't go in for hand-holding. You have to stand up on your own and cut your way through. So an ability like the Incarnate System, that goes beyond the framework of even this crazy game…I want to master it. So that I can stick with you, with Silver Crow."

Even after Takumu closed his mouth, Haruyuki stayed silent, digesting his friend's words.

These last six months, Takumu had been so self-deprecating. He was convinced he had committed an unforgivable crime in giving in to the fear of losing Brain Burst and going so far as to infect Chiyuri's Neurolinker with a virus and hunting Kuroyuki-hime in dealing with that fear, and it was this conviction to an attitude of no forgiveness that led to him sacrificing himself over and over again in a variety of situations. And now, despite the huge blow he had been dealt by Chiyuri turning her back on them—whatever her motivation might have been—once again, he was trying to face his own weakness.

You really are strong, Taku. Stronger than me in every way. You can say it all you like, but I'm nowhere near your equal in the real world. Haruyuki kept this thought to himself and finally smiled.

"You gotta do it. Master some technique so that Nomi's pulsing thing's not a problem, take him out in a quick attack, and get Chiyuri back. Although Niko's training'll probably be a hundred times more brutal than Sky Raker's."

"I-I'm ready for it." Takumu returned a slightly stiff smile.

Haruyuki glanced away, at the time display in the right edge of his field of vision. With the frozen pizza break added in, the strategy meeting had taken a lot longer than expected, and it was already getting to be seven PM.

At level nine, the Red King Niko was one of the strongest Burst Linkers, but in the real world, she was still in sixth grade at a boarding school. Unfortunately for them, the place was fairly strict about going out at night, and it would be difficult to get her to meet them now.

"We'll call her tomorrow after school and go over to Nerima. Taku, will it be okay for you to skip kendo practice two days in a row?" he asked, and Takumu nodded right away.

"Yeah, I mean, I don't do kendo to make a good showing in the tournaments anymore. The coach and the captain will glare at me a bit, but whatever."

"Okay, it's settled, then." They met each other's eyes and nodded again as they stood up. Heading toward the entryway, an entirely different question jumped into Haruyuki's head.

Taku, right around the end of the duel today, did you hear a strange voice?

But no words came from his open mouth. When Takumu gave

him a funny look, he shook his head lightly and raised his hand in farewell. "See you at school tomorrow."

It was just my imagination, he murmured in the depths of his heart. *There were no duelers, and certainly no gallery, in that field. I couldn't have* actually *heard anyone's voice.*

After watching Takumu head off toward the elevator, he closed the door; once the automatic lock clicked shut, his apartment was blanketed by a deep silence. Suddenly, he was terrifyingly certain someone was standing right behind him, and he pushed his back up against the door before returning to the living room at a trot to clean up.

3

Wednesday, April 17.

At dawn on this day, the halfway point for the Umesato ninth-grade school trip, Haruyuki dreamed about Kuroyukihime for the first time in a while. But this one wasn't the type he had had so many times before, the kind that made him regret not being able to record it. It was, in a way, the total opposite.

In his dream, Kuroyukihime was adorned in her in-school avatar, complete with its spangle butterfly wings on her back, instead of looking like her regular real-world self. The lace hem of the avatar's black dress fluttered as she ran lightly through the trees of a deep forest.

Haruyuki was his pink pig avatar, and he pumped his short legs intently, chasing the black butterfly. Stretching out her left hand as if beckoning him, the fairy princess gradually grew distant as she bounded along, half flying.

Kuroyukihime! Haruyuki's shout echoed strangely in the depths of the forest. *Please wait for me!*

But Kuroyukihime did not stop. Once in a while, she turned, a mysterious smile on her red lips, but each time, his view of her was soon interrupted by a thick, moss-covered tree trunk. Finally, all he could see was the ruby-colored pattern decorating the obsidian wings. And even this glittering, these flickering flames, gradually melted into the gloom.

Don't leave me. Don't...Don't leave me behind! he shouted, but there was no reply. *It's because I lost my wings. That's why you're leaving me? You don't need me anymore?*

Still no reply.

Suddenly, a spot on his back throbbed in pain, a pain that quickly took actual form and squirmed violently. *Skrrrk!* He felt something piercing his avatar from the inside. It wasn't wings. It was something dark, thin and long like a tail, growing from his back. It twisted into the air, rose up over his shoulder, curving like a sickle, only to stretch out in a straight line like a lance.

From the depths of the woods came an ominous, wet sound.

Haruyuki chased his own tail and staggered around in circles. After he had gone around the umpteenth tree, the scene opened up before him. On the rough and bony surface of a remarkably large tree trunk, a black spangle butterfly was held by a thin pin. The wiry tail extending from Haruyuki's backside had pierced one of Kuroyukihime's large wings, fixing her in place, crucifying her.

His thinking curiously inhibited, Haruyuki stood before the butterfly and looked up. There was nothing that could be called an expression on the pale face, so ephemerally beautiful. The eyebrows were simply slightly furrowed, the eyes returning Haruyuki's stare.

Because you have those wings. Haruyuki heard the voice, twisted with a kind of darkness, slip out from his own mouth. *Because you have wings, you can just fly off whenever you want.*

His left arm rose on its own. His hand had at some point transformed from the comical hoof of the pig avatar to dark silver claws. His sharp fingertips, shining sinisterly, grabbed the edge of a jet-black wing as it flapped helplessly.

He put the tiniest bit of force into his glittering fingers, and the bottom right of the four wings was ripped out at the base. The wind immediately turned to dry black sand and spilled it from Haruyuki's hand.

Another.

And still another.

At some point, Kuroyukihime's head had dropped down heavily, and her limbs dangled loosely.

Now you won't be able to go anywhere, Haruyuki said as he reached out for the last wing. *You'll be locked in this darkness for all eternity. With me. Just like me.*

The instant he plucked the last wing, Kuroyukihime's slender body fell with a *thud* into his arms. He held her tightly with the blackish-silver talons.

But a second later, even the body pressed against his chest crumbled into inky particles, which flowed down with a quiet *shff*, forming a small mountain of sand at his feet—

"Aaaaah!"

Haruyuki bolted upright in his bed, screaming his throat raw. His heart was pounding like an old-school alarm clock, his entire body was covered in a cold sweat, and his mouth was parched.

Blinking sleep-blurred eyes repeatedly, he examined his hands in the gray light filtering through the curtains. Naturally, he found no ominous talons there, just ten plump fingers. Clenching them tightly, he pressed his fist to his forehead.

Unlike the nightmare after he had first gotten Brain Burst six months earlier, his memory of this one was crystal clear, right down to the smallest details. And even more frightening than that, he had taken his Neurolinker off before he'd gone to bed. Which meant the dream now was not due to any interference from the program; it was spun wholly from Haruyuki's thoughts and memories.

"Kuroyukihime," he murmured, husky, as he shook his head slowly. "I've never wanted to do anything like that. I—I just…"

I want to be together forever, that's all.

Haruyuki impulsively yanked his Neurolinker down from the shelf above his bed and slipped it around his neck. He turned it on, and once the initial connection was complete, he glanced up at the time display. Six fifteen AM. Way earlier than when he usually woke up, but he was no longer the slightest bit sleepy. The strength drained from his body, and he gave the brief "full dive" command.

"Direct link."

His dim bedroom disappeared, and a darkness spread out from the other side of a radiating light. Pulled down by the virtual gravity, Haruyuki fell and finally landed on a flat, cold gray surface. Several semitransparent windows with tags like PUBLIC UTILITIES and CONDO ASSOCIATION popped up around him with a crisp *ping*. This completely functional space was the main console for the Arita home net.

After staring for a while at the round right hand of his pig avatar, Haruyuki whispered a voice command. "Command: dive call. Number: zero one."

Before his eyes, a holodialog opened. A VOICE CALL WILL BE PLACED TO THE REGISTERED ADDRESS 01. OKAY? He shook off a moment's hesitation and pressed the YES button.

There were several modes of bidirectional communication using the Neurolinker. The most frequently used was a voice call, conversing vocally like the old cellular phones. Widespread use was also made of video calls, in which you removed the camera from the side of the Neurolinker and talked while your face was recorded.

In contrast with these, the dive call—in which both parties used their avatars to talk in a virtual space—was used only in exceptional circumstances. The reason was simple: It wasn't always the case that the person being called could immediately go into a full dive. At the very least, you had to mail or make a voice call in advance for an appointment, and the majority of business could be taken care of in such communiqués.

Thus, Haruyuki requesting a dive call at this early hour and completely out of the blue was relatively nonsensical. Even so, he wanted desperately to see her right away. And not just hear her voice or see a flat image, but touch her with all five senses. He felt as though a part of him would change into something else if he couldn't.

The CALLING in Mincho font blinked eight, nine times, and just before message mode kicked in, the word turned into CONNECTING.

All the windows around him disappeared with a *whoosh*. A drop of white light appeared in the inorganic gray space, followed by another and then a cascade of particles of white light shifting into the form of an avatar.

Klak! The toes of high heels touched the floor, and the fairy princess, black spangle butterfly wings on her back, blinked slowly two or three times before acknowledging the pig avatar a short distance away from her and smiling gently.

"Hey. Morning, Haruyuki."

Even after being greeted like this by her smooth, silky voice, Haruyuki couldn't manage to get any words to leave his mouth, afraid of the premonition that the slender figure before him would turn to sand and crumble. He rubbed his eyes hard.

But of course, no matter how many seconds passed, the avatar did nothing that would lead to her disappearance. Haruyuki came back to himself abruptly and hurriedly opened his mouth.

"Uh, um, good morning, Kuroyukihime. Uhh, I—I'm sorry. Suddenly dive-calling you, and so early..."

"It's fine. I just woke up and was trying to decide whether I should try to go back to sleep or not." She smiled again and then examined her surroundings. "And this, well, this is quite the simple place. Although it is like you to prioritize a lighter data load."

"Oh, uh, no, that's..."

The initial setting for a dive call meant that the person doing the calling brought their partner into the VR space they dove into. Because Haruyuki had called without moving from the main area of his home net, he'd ended up inviting Kuroyukihime into this world, a place without even a single chair.

"I-I'm sorry. I'll change the location right away!" Hastily, he pulled up a menu window and flicked through the object sets he had made and saved, but they were all emotionless places— the ruins of a battlefield, the deck of a battleship.

Kuroyukihime looked on wryly as he scrolled through the list, sweating profusely. Finally, she clapped her hands and said, "Maybe it would be a bit heavy data-wise, but perhaps you'll allow me to load a set I have? I want to try out one I bought yesterday."

"Oh! Sure! Please! Go ahead! Go ahead!"

Haruyuki nodded so hard he practically bounced, and Kuroyuki-hime smiled once more before moving her right hand. She navigated the menu with quick gestures, playing a virtual piano.

A progress bar popped up before Haruyuki's eyes. An object set was being sent from the Neurolinker of Kuroyukihime in far-off Okinawa, via the global net. Because it was a large file, it took five seconds for him to receive and two seconds to unzip and open. As the bar disappeared, powerful lightning—no, sunlight—poured down from above his head, and the cold emptiness around him evaporated.

Appearing in its place was a southern country scene with enough color to jolt him fully awake. Maybe it was a shrine: Hearth-protecting stone lion statues known as *shisa* were covered in moss and set on both sides of a short pilgrim's path. Windmill palm trees surrounded them, and at the end of that path were stone steps that led downward, while even farther off in the distance, he could see the azure sea.

When he turned around, there was a small vermilion shrine. Next to him, Kuroyukihime snapped open her parasol and held it above their heads. As if this were a switch, the chirping of countless cicadas closed in on them from all sides, and Haruyuki breathed deeply of air that smelled like the sun.

"Why don't we sit over there and talk?"

She pointed at the small stairs built directly in front of the shrine. He nodded his assent, and with gravel crunching beneath their feet, Haruyuki came to sit his avatar down next to hers. For a while, he just took in the scene spreading out before his eyes, both foreign and familiar at the same time.

Although this was, of course, a VR space built from digital data, it wasn't just an arrangement of ready-made polygons. The *shisa*, the palm trees—all the objects were created based on a real scene photographed with a special high-resolution camera. This kind of object set, reproducing in detail a picturesque scene, was currently the standard trip souvenir.

Haruyuki, who had never been off the main island of Honshu, much less all the way down to Okinawa, forgot that he had initiated the call, and kept staring almost dumbfounded at the scene around him. Kuroyukihime very patiently sat next to him as he did, but at last, she cleared her throat with a small cough.

"Although personally, I have absolutely no objection to just looking at the scenery like this with you…"

Haruyuki jerked his head to look up at the lovely face of the fairy princess beside him and finally remembered that this was the continuation of his thoughtless, early morning dive call.

"Oh, uh! I-I-I'm sorry!"

"No need to apologize. I just wondered if you didn't have some pressing business." She gazed at him, smiling.

Haruyuki realized an even more fearful fact. That is, he did not in actuality have a single thing that could be called business of any sort. Just that he had had a dream at dawn, and it had been a very scary dream…

Abruptly, the sensation of pulling the wings off of her back in the nightmare came back to life in his hands, and he screwed up his face, clenched his fists, and dropped his eyes.

His Neurolinker appeared to have dug from deep in his mind the words that then came out of his mouth, rather than from his brain's language center. "Uh…Um, I was lonely." Still not totally aware of what he was saying, Haruyuki let his duplicate self do the talking. "Not being able to see you. Being so far away from you for so long's been hard. So, uh…"

The virtual forest hushed around him. He didn't know if the cicada sound effect had actually stopped or if his own brain was blocking the environmental audio information. After a long silence, the reply he received was short.

"Me, too."

The shoulders of the pig avatar shook slightly, and he looked up ever so timidly to see her pale face frowning.

"I'm lonely, too, Haruyuki."

Unable to completely hold back a smile through her tears, Kuroyukihime raised both hands and held Haruyuki's cheeks firmly between them. "This is the first time a mere week has felt so long, despite the fact that I've done countless continuous dives in the Accelerated World for much, much longer than this. I want to go back to Tokyo and see you again already."

"...Me, too."

The instant he squeezed the words out, Kuroyukihime bit her lip hard. Between her arms, she yanked Haruyuki's head to her chest.

A sweet scent and a gentle, radiant warmth not possible in the Umesato local net (because an avatar's sense of touch was severely diluted there) raced along Haruyuki's nervous system. Normally, he would be panicking and turning into a stiff board-person, but right now, he was stirred by an overwhelming longing, and as if in a trance, he reached his hands out to cling to her slim body.

Please come home. That's what he wanted to say. *Please come home and help me like you always do.*

In that moment, Haruyuki became acutely aware of how close to his limit he had been pushed. No matter how desperately he fought, his enemy—Dusk Taker—continued to stand, as though a dark steel wall sneering at his efforts, a wall Silver Crow's slender fists could neither pierce nor climb.

But he couldn't say it.

It wasn't just for Chiyuri. For his own sake, too, he had to fight this enemy right to the end with his own power. Giving in to despair now and using Kuroyukihime as a crutch while she was on her school trip would be basically what he had done in the dream.

"We'll be able to see each other soon, right?" Haruyuki muttered finally in a hoarse voice. "Only three more days."

"Mmm. That's true," Kuroyukihime responded, and after

putting all her strength into her arms for one final squeeze, she released her embrace. Black eyes shining, she locked eyes with her junior, leaning in close.

"Haruyuki..."

She said his name anxiously, as if she had discovered something in those eyes.

But Haruyuki mustered every ounce of mental strength he had to put a smile on his face. "Um, I really want you to have fun in your last few days on the trip," he said, before she could say anything else. "I'm sorry for calling you so out of the blue like this."

"No, if you hadn't called me, I would've called you. I'm happy to see you, even if it is our avatars doing the seeing. I'll buy you the real thing for a souvenir, so look forward to that." Grinning, Kuroyukihime stood up and crunched onto the gravel. She twirled her parasol, closed it, and called up the menu window.

She pushed the DISCONNECT button, and even after her form had turned into particles of light and disappeared, Haruyuki continued to sit where he was. The cries of the cicadas, louder again, wiped away the lingering remains of the nightmare still in his heart.

After a breakfast of cereal and milk, he called into his mother's bedroom that he was leaving. Opening the door to his condo, he was greeted by a dull, cloudy, leaden sky.

Focusing his eyes on the icons lined up on the left of his virtual desktop, he pressed the weather report shortcut. The probability of rain was 72 percent after 12:40 PM. He took a step back, grabbed a light gray umbrella from beside the shoe cabinet, and went outside.

The tool known as an umbrella was probably one of the everyday-life accessories that had had the same basic structure the longest. At most, the fabric had changed to a nondegradable, water-resistant one, and the skeleton to high-modulus carbon.

Idly noting that rainy days would be a little more fun if his umbrella at least had an automatic closing gimmick like the one on the parasol Kuroyukihime's avatar was equipped with, Haruyuki walked down the hall and stepped onto the elevator. When the car, having begun its descent to the ground, stopped after a mere two floors, Haruyuki had a premonition that was a near certainty.

And, of course, standing on the other side of the doors as they slid open was Chiyuri Kurashima.

Meeting his gaze squarely, Chiyuri's large, catlike eyes wavered as if she were hesitating. Despite the fact that she would normally jump in with a hearty "Mornin'!" her black shoes now stayed perfectly aligned; she did not move.

Several seconds passed, and the moment the door began to move again, Haruyuki reflexively pushed the OPEN button with his left hand. He obstinately continued to stare at her face, hand on the button.

Just as the warning buzzer was on the verge of sounding, she lowered her eyes and quietly stepped in.

"Thanks. Morning," she said with a small voice as Haruyuki released the button.

"Mornin'," he replied in a whisper, looking sidelong at the light peach umbrella she held in her left hand as she stood a good deal farther away from him than usual in the moving elevator.

Long after he got off the elevator, the words that should have come next from his mouth filled his brain. *No matter what Seiji Nomi told you, you don't have to obey him. If he's threatening you and the threat is the hidden video from the shower room, he can't actually use that or anything.* Because the instant he destroyed Haruyuki with that video, Haruyuki could broadcast Nomi's real-world information in the Accelerated World and take Nomi down with him.

But it was also clear to him that Chiyuri probably wouldn't agree with this kind of "deterrence through mutual assured destruction." If it meant he would be expelled for an extremely shameful crime—there was even the slight possibility he would be arrested—she would do whatever it took to avoid that outcome. Even, for instance, be forced to be Dusk Taker's personal healer and stand against Haruyuki and Takumu in the Accelerated World.

Because they were friends. Because they were childhood friends who had spent a long, long time together in the real world. For Chiyuri, this was the most important thing, something to be defended above all else.

"Chiyu." Haruyuki said the name of his childhood companion in a voice so tiny it threatened to be swallowed up by the very modest sound of the elevator continuing its descent.

Her small shoulders twitched, but her lips remained firmly fastened shut. He dropped his eyes to her hand, the one that clutched the umbrella. He wanted to grab it and pull her toward him, but the words he would have said glommed together into a hot lump and stuck in his throat.

So Haruyuki stayed where he was, his body rooted to the spot as the weight of gentle deceleration enveloped him. The door opened, and Chiyuri proceeded briskly toward the entrance without looking back.

Having had his track team friend ripped away from him in what felt like the blink of an eye, Haruyuki trudged to school, head hanging, just like the trek home the day before.

Wednesdays, he normally went to buy the package edition of his favorite comics magazine at the convenience store, but today he just didn't feel like it and passed by without stopping.

Alternately feeling the delight of the dive call with Kuroyuki-hime and the pain of not having talked to Chiyuri about anything, he arrived on the road to the school—one-third less congested than usual with the new ninth graders off on their trip—and finally stepped through the Umesato Junior High gates, hunched into himself. His Neurolinker automatically connected to the in-school local net, and the attendance log time, the day's schedule, notifications from the school, and more were listed, *pop, pop, pop*, on the right side of his field of vision. At the end of this list, he saw the sentence IMPORTANT INFORMATION ITEM: PERSONAL in red characters and frowned.

After changing into his school shoes at the entrance, stifling the sense of something ominous approaching, he touched the row of characters with a finger. *Shp!* The message text opened, and stern Mincho-font characters lined up before him.

"Haruyuki Arita, student No: 460017, grade eight, class C: As soon as you arrive at school, report to the counseling office on the first floor of the general classroom wing.

—Koji Sugeno, class C homeroom teacher"

His heart stopped for a second. He wondered if Nomi had actually turned the video in to the school authorities. However, he quickly noticed that the message had been sent by his homeroom teacher. If Sugeno had such clear evidence as the video, the whole thing would be way beyond the level of a teacher interview; the administration would definitely be brought in. Sugeno was probably calling him in now based on his own personal hunch.

As Haruyuki tried to guess at what awaited him, he passed the stairs to his classroom, clenched hands drenched in a cold sweat, and headed toward the counseling office on the first floor of the building. As he did, he opened the local net's student database in a browser window and searched for something along the lines of "manual for when the teacher calls you to his office" as a kind of last-ditch effort.

And it turned out, there had been an article on that very subject in the school paper a few years earlier, which Haruyuki read, dumbfounded and grateful.

When he arrived in front of the counseling office, he quickly checked that there were no other students in the hallway around him, in line with the first part of the manual. He then took a deep breath in front of the gray door and pressed the entry button displayed in his vision. The system authenticated him, and the lock opened with a *clack*.

He opened the—not automatic, of course—door and looked

inside to see that Sugeno was already there in the somewhat small room. He was sitting at a chair by the window at a long desk, with his arms crossed in front of his chest, as if to show off their thickness.

"You're here? Come in." The welcome from the young Japanese instructor was not very friendly.

Resisting the urge to just shut the door again, Haruyuki cautiously stepped into the room and greeted his teacher with an indistinct "Good morning."

Sugeno sighed almost complainingly, but perhaps rethinking his approach, he closed his mouth and started over. "Good morning. Sit down here."

Unable to say, *No, I'm fine standing*, he had no choice but to obey and take the seat indicated, a mere chair length away from Sugeno.

"Arita." A single wrinkle carved deep into his suntanned face, his teacher turned a gaze on him that was more than looking but not quite glaring, and then abruptly and finally pulled the corners of his mouth up. "The truth is, I might look like this now, but back when I was in school, I wasn't popular at all with the girls."

"Huh…?"

"It's true. I was on the judo team, see? I used to be so jealous of the guys on the soccer team. They had one girlfriend after another."

He stared in mute amazement as Sugeno nodded in agreement with himself. *What he just said is totally not okay in at least four different ways*, he muttered in his head. *I mean, he's saying he looks hot now, no one in judo can get a girlfriend, everyone in soccer is a playboy, and on top of that, he's assuming girls don't like me.*

Even as he mentally added that he did have to concede that last point, Sugeno continued his monologue.

"Which is why I understand that sometimes, things get to be too much for a boy your age, Arita. I completely get it…Say, Arita?" Here the teacher called up a "you leave everything to me" kind of nuance in the vicinity of his thick eyebrows and nodded deeply. "If there's anything you want to tell me, anything you *need* to tell me, you can go on and do that right now, right here. I promise I'm on your side, Arita. How about it?"

"......" Further stupefied, Haruyuki simply stared at the man's face for several seconds. Finally, he somehow managed to collect his thoughts enough to form words. "Uh, um."

"Oh! What is it? You can tell me anything!"

"Uhh...Before I say anything, I'd like to record this conversation." Number two in the manual was to make sure you record, but the instant the words had left his mouth, Haruyuki seriously regretted having said anything.

Sugeno's eyes popped open, and his face—from neck to cheeks to hairline—turned red. When the trusty older-brother expression on his face finally peeled off and dropped away, Haruyuki could practically hear the *thud* of it on the floor.

"What's that supposed to mean, Arita?! Are you saying you don't trust your teacher?!" his now-menacing mentor shouted, eyebrows leaping up, and Haruyuki shrank with a yelp.

But there was no retreating. "No, it's got nothing to do with trusting anyone," he mumbled. "It's just that a student has the legal right to record a one-on-one interview with a teacher."

"What legal?! What right?!" Sugeno cried out in a voice that was a little inappropriate for a teacher, and slammed his hand down on the long desk. "Don't you understand that I'm talking to you now for your own benefit?! The longer this goes on, the worse things are going to be for you! Right now, there's still a chance of keeping the police out—"

Cutting him off midsentence was Haruyuki fiddling with his virtual desktop to activate Record mode, in complete desperation. Since he didn't work for the school paper, he needed his interlocutor's consent to record their conversation. In Sugeno's field of vision at that moment, there would be a button asking him to give permission to be recorded. If he pressed NO now, the log would record that he had rejected a legitimate request. Sugeno glared at a point in space, seething with indignation, but in the end, he lifted a finger and stabbed at the air.

In Haruyuki's field of view, the REC icon began blinking, accompanied by a message that recording had begun. He did not, however, have anywhere close to the nerve required to smirk at this, so he shrank intently into himself as Sugeno began to speak again.

"Arita, tell me one thing...please." Sugeno's voice was harder now, and quieter. "On the fourteenth, a Sunday, why would a guy like— Why did you come to school, when you're not in any clubs or teams?"

Seems like recording the conversation is more effective than I expected.

"To see my friend on the kendo team," Haruyuki answered immediately, albeit faintly, and Sugeno held his tongue. He had to know that Takumu (in kendo) and Haruyuki were friends, and the fact that Takumu had come to school on Sunday was registered in the local net. And the original reason Haruyuki had come to school that day was in fact to talk to Takumu.

But Sugeno doubled down, temples twitching. "Was it really just that? Can you tell me you had absolutely no other reason? Look into my eyes and answer me."

He's probably not a bad guy, Haruyuki thought. *Although I don't think we're going to reach any understanding here.* He looked up into Sugeno's icy eyes. "It was really just that. I can tell you that."

After letting out a long sigh that sounded like a large cooling fan, Sugeno said, "Okay, understood. In that case, you can go."

Haruyuki quickly stood up. "Yes, Mr. Sugeno!" he said, his voice the loudest it had been since he entered the room. He covered the short distance to the door, opened it the barest minimum required, and slipped out.

Having fled to the hallway, he took the deepest breath he was capable of before turning off record mode and checking that the sound file was properly saved as he trotted toward his classroom.

As long as nothing new came out, the recording was basically public acknowledgment of his innocence. That said, this little exchange had probably seriously soured Sugeno on him. There was not a single advantage in making an enemy of a teacher, and it wasn't the sort of thing Haruyuki liked to do, but confessing to being behind the secret camera just to keep Sugeno happy, when he hadn't done anything, was obviously out of the question.

Still, Haruyuki thought as he climbed the stairs. *This trap Nomi set, even if he doesn't use that fatal video, it looks like it's having a sort of seeping effect, like a weak poison. Because Nomi actually courted that danger and really hid a small camera in there.*

As a result, there actually had been an attempt to record secret video in the girls' shower room, and Haruyuki had ended up the prime suspect, coming as he had to school on a Sunday, even though he was not on any teams. Had Nomi seen this far ahead? No, impossible.

Shaking his head, Haruyuki opened the door to his classroom a minute before the first bell. Instantly, he got the sense that something wasn't right. It seemed like the chatter filling the classroom dropped in volume for the briefest moment.

"……?" He looked around, but it was already the same old morning classroom again. He wove his way through the students in groups of twos and threes, chatting animatedly about net shows and sports, and sat down at his own desk.

He hung his bag on the hook on his desk, and as he breathed a little sigh, the VOICE CALL icon began flashing in the middle of his field of view. The caller was…Takumu. Haruyuki resisted the urge to turn around and look at him sitting toward the back of the class and pressed the icon.

"Haru, we got trouble."

At this abrupt opening, Haruyuki very nearly opened his mouth to speak, but caught himself and replied in neurospeak. *"Huh? Wh-what's up, out of the blue?"*

"There's this weird rumor going around. About you."

The call was abruptly cut off. At the same time, a light chiming sounded in his ears. The bell ringing, which meant any real-time communication between students was now prohibited. The next time it would be possible to call would be lunch break. As an exception to this rule, he could send a text mail, but exchanges not directly related to classes were forbidden by the school regulations.

He thought he might just stand up and go over to Takumu to hear the rest directly, but then the front door opened, and Sugeno came in, so he was forced to abandon the idea. Although he really wanted to know the rest of the story, if it was something that simply had to be communicated to him right then and there, they could always talk in an accelerated duel. If Takumu didn't take it that far himself, then it wouldn't be a huge mistake to wait until the next break.

Having determined this, Haruyuki stood up with the other students and bowed to the teacher without meeting his eyes.

But immediately after that class was over, two boys came to stand in front of his desk as he raised a finger to mail Takumu. Reflexively stiffening, he lifted his face. Both were in his class, but he only remembered the name of the boy on the right. He was pretty sure it was Ishio and that he was a starting player on the boys' basketball team.

"Arita," Ishio said, jerking to the left the very adult-looking head he had sitting on a body so tall—it was hard to believe he was the same age as Haruyuki. "Sorry to bug you, but you got a minute?"

Before he knew it, the entire class had fallen silent. But this silence didn't have any sense of surprise to it. Rather, there was an air of approval, as if his classmates had even been expecting this scene.

Ishio turned toward the frozen Haruyuki, who was unable to grasp what was happening, and continued in a low voice that was nearly through the awkward breaking period. "I don't want to have an ugly conversation right here. And I know you don't, either, right, Arita?"

Haruyuki felt his stomach tighten abruptly. *Ugly conversation.* Hearing those words, only one thing leapt to mind. The secret video. Which meant that Ishio here and the boy next to him—no, everyone in class—had, without him even being aware of it, become deeply convinced that Haruyuki was the perpetrator of the whole thing.

"Ah…I—I…," Haruyuki muttered hoarsely. He groped for a lifeboat of some kind, and his eyes moved to the seat diagonally in front of him—Chiyuri.

His childhood friend was sitting there, head hanging low, eyes pinched shut, fists clenched tightly on her desk as though she were trying to endure something.

Despite the crisis he was facing, the instant he saw her, he thought, *Right now, the one making Chiyuri suffer is me, not Nomi. My stupidity got us into this. If I act all pathetic right here, it's just going to make this harder for Chiyuri. So the least I can do is be strong now. Even if it is just pretend.*

He took a deep breath and stood up, chair clattering. "Sure, let's go," he replied briefly, and one of Ishio's eyebrows jumped up. But he nodded, expression unchanging, and began to walk. The other boy followed, almost like Haruyuki was a prisoner with an escort.

He saw a student standing slowly in the back of the classroom. Takumu. His friend, rivaling Ishio in height, narrowed his sharp eyes behind his glasses and went to take a step. Haruyuki stopped him with his right hand and shook his head shortly.

I'm okay. I can get through this by myself.

They weren't on a voice call, so Takumu couldn't actually hear these words, but even so, he gritted his teeth and took his seat again. The sound of Ishio yanking open the door echoed loudly in the silent classroom.

They brought him to a place Haruyuki was intimately familiar with—the western edge of the roof. Given that first period had only just ended, there were no other students up there. When he was in seventh grade, Haruyuki had been forced to deliver bread and juice to some delinquent students in this place basically every day. Vivid memories of that time springing to life in his mind, Haruyuki started to head for the shadow of the antenna tower, the set location for any kind of bullying.

But Ishio stopped him. "Here's good."

"But this is still in view of the social cameras, you know," he replied, blinking hard.

"I don't care," Ishio spat. He shoved both hands into the pockets of his uniform and leaned back against the high steel railing before continuing. "Arita, you got called in by Sugeno, yeah?"

I knew it. The whole class already knows about it. So this is the "weird rumor" Taku called about. I was trying to be careful, but some other student must have seen me going into the counselor's office. But still, news of that has gotten around pretty fast. Almost like someone was deliberately spreading the rumor...

And then Haruyuki reminded himself that now was not the time for thinking outside thoughts, and he stared at Ishio and the other boy standing a little way off before nodding slightly. "Yeah."

"So then it was you? The one who put the camera in the girls' shower room?"

"No!" This time, his reply was immediate.

Ishio looked down on Haruyuki shaking his head and simply rubbed a hand over hair so short it was practically shaved.

"Well." The other boy spoke for the first time. "You can't exactly say, 'I sure did,' can you? But, look, I just don't think the school's gonna be calling a student in with no evidence. I mean, if it goes badly, they'd have a complaint against them instead."

It's just that hothead Sugeno! I mean, he actually got mad about rights and the law and whatever! He could insist on his innocence all he wanted, but he knew they wouldn't believe him, so his best option was to keep his mouth shut.

Ishio then took one, two steps to approach Haruyuki. "You got released after getting called in, so I guess they suspect you but don't have any proof?" he said in a near-whisper. "But here's the thing, I can't just let it go because there's no proof." Ishio suddenly grabbed Haruyuki's tie with his left hand and yanked him in. Haruyuki got a close-up taste of the other boy's rage-filled eyes. "Listen. My girlfriend was in the shower room when they found that camera. The whole thing hit her really hard. She was out from school yesterday and again today!"

At this point, Ishio's behavior was a clear violation of school regulations. But the starting player for the basketball team brushed off the other boy, who tried to stop him, and brandished his right fist in a showy manner. "There's no way I can let this go, Arita. I have to do this, no chooooiiiice!!" He thrust his fist forward awkwardly.

Haruyuki probably could have dodged the blow. Ishio's fist was clumsy and couldn't begin to compare with the punches from the students who used to bully Haruyuki, boys well acquainted with fighting. He could even go a step further—if he used the "physical burst" command to accelerate physically, maybe he could turn the tables and beat the taller boy instead. As it was, Ishio's face was twisted up into what amounted to a confession that he had never hit anyone before.

But, of course, Haruyuki did not dodge or retaliate, but simply took the punch to his left cheek. Winning a fight with the power of acceleration was the lowest of the low, even if it wasn't against the rules of the Black Legion. He heard a sharp *crack*, and for all its awkwardness, Ishio's fist made an impact that pushed Haruyuki's body back a few steps.

The Haruyuki of six months earlier maybe would have broken at this point and sniveled an apology. But he stopped after those few staggered steps and glared at Ishio as he felt the hot throbbing in his cheek. "I don't care how many times I have to say it," he shouted. "I didn't do it!!"

Ishio clenched his teeth and made another fist, but at last, he relaxed his hand. "If you can prove that," he replied, "you can hit me as many times as you want. But"—the basketball player with the shaved head thrust out a finger this time, rather than a fist, and declared crisply—"if it turns out you did do it, I'll smash that Neurolinker of yours and make it so you can't look at any images or videos or anything."

And then he whirled around and took long strides toward the stairs, rubbing his right hand with his left as if trying to wipe away the lingering sensation. The other boy followed suit, and Haruyuki was left alone on the roof.

This little bit of theater had to have been clearly recorded by several social cameras. If Haruyuki lodged a complaint about having been hit, regardless of the circumstances, Ishio would at the very least be suspended and probably lose his spot on the basketball team's starting lineup.

But, of course, Haruyuki had no intention of doing that. Ishio was just another person who'd gotten dragged into this mess. Into this lightless, heatless nihilistic vortex that the cruel villain Seiji Nomi had created.

Running a hand over his left cheek to check that he wasn't bleeding, Haruyuki trudged toward the stairs. As he walked, he opened his mail app and typed a short message to Takumu.

"It didn't turn into anything big. I'll explain everything after school. Sorry to make you worry," he wrote briefly, hit SEND, and then started to reach for Chiyuri's address. But on the verge of touching it, he yanked his hand back. He couldn't erase Chiyuri's fears with mere words anymore. The only way to get her back was to destroy Nomi, the source of all the problems.

A simple *"Got it"* soon came back from Takumu. He felt his friend's concern in that brevity, and finally relaxing his shoulders, Haruyuki trotted back to the classroom so that he could be on time for his next class.

Lunch break.

The bell had no sooner rung than Haruyuki was headed for the cafeteria by himself.

The cafeteria, too, with the missing ninth graders, was naturally a fair bit emptier than usual. Not feeling much like eating some bread up on the roof, where he had so recently had such an unpleasant experience, he lined up at the self-service counter. From the menu displayed in his field of vision, he selected pork curry with a boiled okra topping and checked that the holotag was floating in front of him. The lunch lady dished out the curry at superhigh speed, set the okra on it, pushed it onto the counter, and the bill was settled with a ringing sound. He grabbed the tray with both hands and looked around for a place to sit.

His gaze naturally moved to the lounge at the eastern edge of the cafeteria. But he didn't have the courage to charge into the space with its round white tables surrounded by plants and its obviously different atmosphere by himself, so instead he plopped himself down in a corner of one of the zillions of long tables. He picked up his spoon and glanced around. All the other students were enjoying their lunch, laughing and talking. No one was looking at Haruyuki. Or so he thought.

But he couldn't help feeling like everyone in the place was talking to one another telepathically. *The secret-video criminal is here.* No, that was impossible. He tried to shake the feeling off, but the indescribable weirdness of the moment he entered eighth-grade class C that morning had soaked into his skin.

To at least forget it, he started jamming curry into his mouth, but the blockage in his throat didn't seem to be going anywhere, even though just curry in his mouth was normally enough to make him unconditionally happy.

What if...

What if this thinking, this awareness of "Arita in class C's the one who did the secret video" thing, took root among all the students, whether there was proof of it or not?

Wouldn't it be hard for even Kuroyukihime, the student council vice president, to uproot it? In fact, she might be dragged down by Haruyuki and lose her current standing. Even if, hypothetically speaking, that did happen, she would never dream of abandoning him, but what if, because of him, they all gave

Kuroyukihime the cold shoulder, too? What if she was alienated within the school like he had been last year, or in the worst case, she ended up the butt of jokes?

Haruyuki felt goose bumps shudder up onto his ˙skin. He dropped his spoon onto his plate with a *clank* and grabbed his arms tightly with both hands. At that moment, he felt an abrupt presence and lifted his face.

A group of four or five people walking off in the distance greeted his eyes.

At the private Umesato Junior High School, there was a sports department scholarship system of sorts. The school wasn't particularly famous for sports, so the system was more on the level of a slight reduction in tuition for players who did well enough to make it to the intercity tournament level or higher. Even so, there was no doubt that there was a clear category of "scholarship student elites."

The group on which Haruyuki's eyes had landed was made up of a few of these sports athletes. A starting player on the girls' softball team, the hope of the boys' swim team, and a small student chatting away in the middle of them—

No mistake, it was a seventh grader from the kendo team, Seiji Nomi.

The kendo team at Umesato was definitely strong, but Nomi had just joined it that month; he hadn't been out to a real tournament yet. The earliest he'd be able to obtain scholarship student status would be in the latter half of that year, but they'd already welcomed him into their group, which meant that his win at the team tournament the previous week had made a real impact.

But you didn't even win that tournament with your own power!

Haruyuki unconsciously bit his lip, hard. At that time, as if sensing his eyes glaring from the corner of the long table in the distance, Nomi turned his gaze toward him with a casual gesture.

Haruyuki saw the cherubic smile on his feminine face instantly transform. Appearing from beneath the mask that peeled off was a cold, sadistically joyful grin, a thin razor sharpened to the extreme. Haruyuki felt as though he could hear his voice in the back of his mind.

What do you think, Arita? What's it like to be covered in mud, slipping endlessly down this hill? Having all your precious things taken from you one by one and smashed?

Nomi faced forward again to turn his original innocent smile upon the upperclassmen as he entered the brilliantly lit lounge without the slightest hesitation.

Even after the plants blocked him from view and Haruyuki could no longer see him, he continued to glare at the place where Nomi had been for a long time.

There was no doubt about it now. Nomi was the one who had spread the story of Haruyuki being interviewed by his homeroom teacher so fast to the class. Not only that, but given the situation, it was probably him who had tipped the school authorities off about Haruyuki having come to school on Sunday.

Abruptly, an enormous rage and an even greater terror erupted from the depths of his body, and Haruyuki desperately suppressed the urge to flip the table. No. He couldn't let his spirit be broken here. That would just be a return to his cowardly self of six months earlier. And not only that. If he lost heart now and sank to the bottomless depths of the bog that Nomi had created, he'd be dragging Takumu and Chiyuri—and Kuroyukihime— down with him.

It starts now, Haruyuki murmured in his heart as he robotically shoveled curry with his spoon. *I've faced this level of adversity a hundred times. I'll show him. I'll crawl back up one more time. No, I'll get up again a million times. I'm done looking at the ground.*

He opened his mouth wide, stuffed his cheeks with the curry piled high on his spoon, and chewed forcefully. The freshman girl sitting diagonally across from him gaped and stared in shock at Haruyuki cleaning his plate with incredible speed.

4

For the two hours of the afternoon, he wouldn't go so far as to say he was sitting on a bed of nails; the prickliness was more on the level of a cheese grater. The one thing that could be said to be lucky for him, if only just barely, was that now that Ishio from the basketball team had faced off with him, the classroom seemed to have put any further reaction on hold.

However, the girls' eyes were about 30 percent colder than usual, and some of the boys were already in the middle of deliberations on which nickname to present to Haruyuki. Before they could decide between what were apparently the final candidates—"Camerita" and "Papayuki"—Haruyuki grabbed his bag and umbrella and left the classroom.

He cut through the schoolyard in a straight line, the concrete wet and black with the rain that began falling in the afternoon just as the forecast had said, and breathed a sigh of relief once he had passed through the gates. With a TAKE CARE ON YOUR WAY HOME, he was disconnected from the Umesato JH local net. Global net information popped up in his vision, and he felt soothed in his heart, somehow, at this sense of connection.

He leaned against a wall twenty meters or so from the school gate and stared attentively at the headline news, the sound of the rain against his umbrella as background music. Finally, he heard familiar footfalls approaching.

"Sorry to make you wait, Haru," Takumu said, navy-blue umbrella hoisted in greeting.

Haruyuki returned his brief wave, and they fell in step with each other, walking east on the sidewalk.

A few minutes later, Haruyuki was the first to open his mouth. "Are you really sure it's okay for you to miss practice two days in a row?"

"It's fine; it's totally fine. The captain and the coach are both totally obsessed with the genius rookie; a transfer player like me isn't even on their radar."

"That's a mess, too, huh? But at least with everyone focusing on that jerk Nomi, you're free to move a bit more easily."

Bitter smiles crossed both of their faces, and they walked another minute in silence. When the intersection where Oume Kaido met Kannana Street came into view, Haruyuki finally broached the subject himself.

"Sugeno called me in today, about the hidden camera thing… Of course, I didn't do it."

"Obviously. Sugeno calling you in even though he has no proof of anything—" Takumu started indignantly, but Haruyuki stopped him.

"But I'm in a position where I could very easily be turned into the bad guy," he continued, almost groaning. "The whole thing was a trap Seiji Nomi set up for me. And I walked right into it…"

It took a lot longer than he had expected to explain the whole of Nomi's trap.

By the time they got on the electric-engine bus and settled down next to each other in the back, Haruyuki had finally finished giving Takumu an overview of the situation he had gotten dragged into. He left out only two things: the infection route for the visual masking program Nomi used on him and the fact that he had run into Chiyuri totally naked in the shower room.

However, the computational power of Takumu's brain was in perfect working order at a time like this, and he appeared to have immediately understood the program route. As soon as Haruyuki clamped his mouth shut, his good friend took off his blue glasses and pressed his hand firmly against his forehead.

"…Right." His voice was broken with a powerful sense of self-reproach. "It was that picture, huh? The kendo team photo with the new members that I sent you. So it was infected with a virus. Sorry, Haru. I totally forgot to check it—"

"N-no, it's not your fault!" Haruyuki hurriedly shook his head several times. "That virus was probably set to self-destruct the moment the photo was read in a system with a kendo team register tag. If anyone should have been more careful, it was me, the target. He's been gunning for me, not you, right from the start."

"But I should've noticed something was up when I saw the file was a little too big. Instead, I go and charge into your house, when you're having to deal with something like this. I said all those things to you…I even hit you on top of that!" Takumu shoved his glasses back on, grabbed Haruyuki's right hand with both hands, and yanked it up.

"Whoa! Hey! What—"

"Haru, hit me. You have to hit me or I'll never be able to forgive myself."

"I said it's fine! It's fine!"

Flustered, Haruyuki sent his eyes racing back and forth between Takumu's face and the front of the bus. The housewives and students on the bus with them were staring with wide eyes or giggling. If they couldn't hear their conversation, how on earth were they interpreting this situation: tall, handsome Takumu grabbing the hand of small, round Haruyuki and leaning into him?

But Takumu didn't seem to even notice the eyes around them. He gradually brought his face even closer, so Haruyuki was forced to whisper, "Wait, hold up, Taku! Uh, I…You have to hit me, too."

"Huh? What are you talking about?" Takumu furrowed his brow doubtfully.

Haruyuki returned his look and apologized—*Chiyu! Sorry!*—in his mind. She had told him that he was under no circumstances to talk about this, but with Takumu at least, Haruyuki was no longer interested in simply keeping quiet and letting things happen while he hung his head and stared at the ground.

"The thing is...When I was tricked by the visual masker and I went into the girls' shower room...Chiyu kind of showed up."

It took another two minutes to explain this incident.

Dropping heavily back into his own seat, Takumu pressed his fingertips between his eyebrows and sighed. "Is that it? So that's how Chi's involved in all this..."

"...It is..."

A totally different expression on his face, Takumu gave Haruyuki a sidelong glance and raised a single finger. "Anyway, let's leave this for now. I don't need to hear the specific details of what you saw, Haru. For Chi's sake, too."

"Right...You really are a gentleman, Taku."

"Thanks. Anyway, if that's the case, then I guess we can assume this is the basis of Nomi's threat. The secret video of you would definitely be an effective card against Chi, too...That has to be it."

"Yeah. If he's managed to see through Chiyuri like this to threaten her, Nomi is a serious genius at attacking other people's weak points."

Takumu let out a long breath and patted Haruyuki's knee lightly. "But that's also his own weak point," Takumu said in a slightly sharper voice.

"Huh?"

"I mean, it is, right? Taking, threatening, making people do what he says—that's not friendship in the real sense of the word. Even if he is making Chi, Lime Bell, obey him now, Nomi, Dusk Taker, is essentially alone. How can we lose to a guy like that?"

"...Yeah, I guess you're right."

This time, it was Haruyuki grabbing Takumu's hand, which was still resting on his knees. The cool, bony touch gave him more hope than he could say, and he was grateful from the bottom of his heart that Takumu/Cyan Pile was right there next to him.

They crossed Shinoume Kaido and got off the bus just as they were about to enter Nerima Ward.

They opened their umbrellas and watched the stream of cars flowing before them for a while. On the other side of the vehicles driving along, motors and hydrogen engines purring, was the territory controlled by the Red Legion, Prominence. Even though they had a truce with the Black Legion Nega Nebulus, that was only for the weekend Territory Battles. If they crossed the street now with their Neurolinkers still connected to the global net, there was no doubt that they'd be challenged to a duel in less than five minutes.

After meeting Takumu's eyes and nodding, Haruyuki took a deep breath and spoke the command. "Command: voice call. Number: zero five."

As he listened to the sound of the call being made, sweat oozed from his hands. He told himself to calm down, but he couldn't curb his nervousness. After all, the person he was calling was none other than the level-niner controlling the strongest long-distance duel avatar in the Accelerated World, the Immobile Fortress who struck fear in the hearts of those around her, the Red King Scarlet Rain.

"I haven't talked to you in ages, big brother Haruyuuuki!"

The high-pitched voice filled his brain, and Haruyuki's knees started to buckle. Somehow managing to stay on his feet, he replied out loud rather than with neurospeak for the benefit of Takumu next to him. "Oh, s-sorry I haven't kept in touch. Yuniko—"

"Ugh, Niko's fine, okay? So what's up, calling me out of the blue like this?" The Red King Niko was in angel mode, which was nothing more than a whim when she was in a good mood. But it did make things easier for him, so he spoke quickly to keep this chance from getting away.

"Uh, um, there's something I want to talk—or, I guess, get your advice on. If you can, it'd be great if we could meet now in the real. Uh, of course we'd come to Nerima."

"Hmm. It's raining, you know? Oh, but I was feeling kinda like having some cake. One with tons of strawberries!"

"M-my treat, my treat. You can eat as many pieces as you want."

"All right! In that case, meet me here."

A map whooshed up in his field of vision as she spoke. The flashing dot was in the neighborhood of Sakuradai Station on the Seibu Line, not far from where they were.

"O-okay. We can probably make it there in about fifteen minutes."

"Okay! See you soon!"

And then the call was disconnected. But they had pushed past the first barrier at least. He sighed heavily as he lifted his face.

"I have money," Takumu said with a slightly meek look.

"Nah, we'll split it."

"But we're getting her to meet us today because of me, so…"

While they were having this little back and forth, the next bus came, so they cut it short and jumped on. The moment they sat down, they disconnected their Neurolinkers from the global net. The bus raced along, large motor roaring, and crossed Shinoume Kaido to plunge into Nerima, the area reigned over by the Red Legion.

The shop they had been directed to was a cute little cake place tucked neatly among a row of shops on a small commercial street. Inside, half the room was taken up by chairs and tables, which he assumed meant that you could also eat in.

They had just closed their umbrellas and shaken the water off when they heard energetic splashing—feet jumping in puddles, approaching from behind. Haruyuki started to turn, only to find a small fist dug into his round stomach before he even had the chance to attempt a dodge.

"Hng!"

The grin looking up at the groaning Haruyuki from under a red umbrella belonged to a sweet-looking girl with large, greenish eyes, glittering in a small face full of freckles. Soft red hair was tied up in thin bundles on each side of her head, and she carried an elementary school backpack on her navy-uniformed back. The Neurolinker peeking out on her neck was the transparent red of a gem.

The girl took a step back. "Long time no see, big brother," she said, twirling her umbrella. "You're round as always, huh!" She turned her face to the left. "And you, Professor. You're gloomy as always!"

Stiff smiles rose up on their faces, and they bowed briefly in greeting.

"It has been a while. Sorry for calling you out like this, Niko—"

"Totes fine! Let's just get to the cake already!" The girl—ruler of the Nerima area, the Red King Yuniko Kozuki—shoved her umbrella into the umbrella stand and dashed into the store. The two hurried after her.

They sat at the table farthest back, and once they had a piece of cake outfitted with some serious strawberry resources and the somewhat frightening name "Strawberry Labyrinth," an iced milk, and the two coffees they had ordered before them, Niko immediately picked up her fork and used it to stab a large strawberry that was glittering and shining at the very top of the concoction. She popped it into her mouth, filling her cheek, and grinned happily.

She stared at Haruyuki, who had gotten carried away watching her and had started to move his own mouth sympathetically. "You can't have any!" she said, the purest of smiles on her lips.

"Th-that's fine."

"Aaw. Just kidding! Here, open up!"

She speared another berry and thrust it out in front of Haruyuki, so he reflexively opened wide. But with a heartless "kiiiiidding," she rotated the strawberry one hundred eighty degrees away from him and Haruyuki's teeth came down with a *klak* on empty air.

Thanks to a purposeful cough from Takumu, who was watching this play out from his side, Haruyuki returned to himself. *Right, this isn't the time for that.* He drew himself up straighter.

"A-anyway, Niko. What we wanted to talk to you about today…
We wanted to meet in the real like this because we had a little
favor to ask you."

"Fay-fer?" *Gulp.* "Ten strawberries and you got my ear."

"I—I don't know how that'll work exactly." He glanced at
Takumu, scratched his head, and got right into the meat of this
audience. "Um, we want you to teach the Professor here—I mean,
Takumu—about…how to use the Incarnate System."

Niko froze just as she was about to scarf down her sixth strawberry. Blinking her deep green eyes repeatedly, she cocked her
small head to one side, only to return her fork to her plate, strawberry still stabbed on its tines, and then leaned back in her chair.

Haruyuki could practically hear the snap of her circuits
switching, i.e., the sound of Niko's angel mode ending.

The innocent smile, so suited to the face of a sixth-grade girl, disappeared, and her eyes narrowed sharply. "What?" she barked in a
dangerous voice colored with fire.

Sweat dripping down his forehead, Haruyuki began to explain,
but she held a single finger up to silence him. Niko stood up. "Just
gonna borrow the back room for a minute," she called to the clerk
behind the counter.

The young woman in a grape-colored pinafore nodded silently,
and Niko started to walk briskly, the plate of half-eaten cake in
her right hand and the glass of milk in her left. Haruyuki and
Takumu looked at each other and, having no choice, grabbed
their coffee cups and followed her.

A thin hallway stretched out from the back of the eat-in corner, in the middle of which was a thick door with a sign that said
PRIVATE. Naturally, it appeared to be locked, but Niko raised the
hand with the glass up into the air and hit a single point, after
which came the sound of the lock opening.

On the other side of the door was a chic Western-style room
about nine square meters in size. The walls and the floor were
covered with a blackish paneling, a large sofa set sat in the center

of the room, and beyond that was visible a door to what appeared to be a bathroom.

Niko gently placed her plate and glass on the sofa set's coffee table, flicked a finger around on her virtual desktop to check something, and then turned toward them abruptly. "Idiots!!" she shouted. "You don't just start running your mouth about Incarnate in public!!"

"Ah! S—! Sorry!"

Haruyuki and Takumu stood ramrod straight and Niko glared at them both with eyes that looked like they might shoot fire. Finally, she heaved an enormous sigh, threw her small body down onto the sofa, and crossed her legs tightly.

"Well, I'll let it go this time. Sit."

"O okay."

They also placed their cups on the table and sat down on the sofa across from her. Niko grabbed another strawberry with her right hand and popped it in her mouth. "This room's sealed, so it's safe," she said in a low voice. "First off, tell me where you guys even heard about the Incarnate System. I know it wasn't your girl—Black Lotus. Because then you could just get her to teach you, and anyway, it's too soon for that. Way too soon."

Before he answered that question, Haruyuki had a few of his own. What was this shop exactly? Why would a cake shop in the middle of town have an electromagnetic isolation room?

However, the look on Niko's face indicated she was very much not in the mood for any detours, and he was forced to shelve his own questions. Taking a deep breath, he looked right at the Red King and began to talk.

"Umm, it's kind of a long story, but the whole thing started when a Burst Linker started at Umesato Junior High—the school we go to—as a freshman seventh grader…"

Working hard to summarize the key points with utmost brevity, Haruyuki continued his explanation: that although this new student Dusk Taker was connected to the in-school local net, he wasn't registered on the Brain Burst matching list. That he had toyed with them in the real world with a variety of tricks to back them into a corner. That he had used the special attack Demonic Commandeer to take Haruyuki's wings in the Accelerated World. That to fight back against this difficult enemy, Haruyuki had trained long hours in the Unlimited Neutral Field and studied how to use his will. That although they had been one step away from driving Dusk Taker into his own desperate corner thanks to this power, they had lost in an upset because of Lime Bell's sudden breakaway. And then, finally, that the Black King, Black Lotus, was on a school trip and would be away until the following Saturday.

He left out only Lime Bell's healing abilities and Dusk Taker's real information—i.e., the name Seiji Nomi.

The whole thing took nearly fifteen minutes, and once Haruyuki was finished, Niko still kept her mouth mostly shut. She stuffed her cheek with the final strawberry from the cake she had eaten as she listened, taking her time with it. Finally, she hummed nasally.

"Right, I get it. Dusk Taker...He's a duel avatar with a plundering ability. Add in the fact that he uses the Incarnate, and he really would be too much for you two to handle as you are now."

"Unfortunately, it's just as you say," Takumu said quietly. "Even in a situation where I should have the advantage, like close combat inside a building, once he started to use the Incarnate System, I couldn't fight back at all. I'm nothing more than baggage right now. I'm in the way. And...I hate that more than anything."

Niko shot a sharp look at Takumu as he pressed his clasped hands against his forehead in supplication, and then she let out a thoughtful sigh. "Which is why you came all the way to Nerima to ask me to teach the two of you—or rather, Pile—how to use the Incarnate System."

"That's exactly it, Red King." Takumu nodded deeply.

Niko deftly twirled her fork between her fingers and pointed the handle at each of them in turn. "Well, it's not like I don't sympathize with the situation you guys are in. But...to be honest, this is someone else's fight, another king's Legion's. And if I decided to, say, ignore this instead, Nega Nebulus'd be destroyed for me, and that's a future pain in my ass gone. That's the rational conclusion here, yeah?" Unable to contain himself, Haruyuki tried to butt in. But Niko still had more to say. "So let's say I say that. And then Crow there's gonna say something like, *How can you say that when you came to us for help when your own Legion was in trouble? I think you still seriously owe us one.* Or something. Right? That's the gist of it?"

Haruyuki had been about to say exactly that. Beaten to the punch, he simply flapped his jaw.

Niko returned the fork to her plate, pushed the whole thing to a corner of the table, thumped her rain-boot-free feet up in the now-empty space, and clasped her hands behind her head. "Aaah, I knew something like this would happen one of these days! Lecture on the Incarnate Systeeeeem, that's some pretty steep interest on that debt."

As he watched Niko sighing and shaking her head, Haruyuki leaned forward unconsciously. "What? So, so then…you'll do it?"

"Got no choice, do I? Pretty annoying to have people thinking I don't pay back my debts, right? Honestly, if I knew this was what was up, I would've gotten the Royal Palace instead of the Strawberry Labyrinth," she grumped, and Haruyuki couldn't suppress the warmth expanding in his chest.

He knew that people in the Accelerated World did not exist just to fight as duelers. Even if they stood against each other as enemies, there was something more important than that. There was friendship, bonds.

Not knowing how to express the emotions overflowing inside him, Haruyuki grabbed one of the bobby-sock-clad feet that had been thrown up on the table in front of him. Instantly—

"Eeaah!! Wh-why do you always grab my feet, you total perv!!" she shrieked in anger, and kicked with her other leg to bury that foot in Haruyuki's cheek.

Steam rising from her head, Instructor Niko's first command was, "Get the plugs from under the table and connect them to your Neurolinkers."

They twisted their necks and groped about to find that there were in fact several XSB plugs protruding from a hub-like contraption with a winding device. At any rate, although he pulled one out at the same time as Takumu, he felt a slight resistance to directing with an unknown connection.

"No tricks or anything in here!" Niko roared, casually inserting the plug. "This room's isolated, so the only way to connect globally is with an actual cable, all right?"

So he hurried to obey. The connection warning popped up in his field of vision and then disappeared.

After running the fingers of both hands through space for a while, Niko looked at each of them in turn. "All right, it's almost five," she said in a more severe tone. "I have to be back at the dorm by six, so the time I can spend with you two is thirty minutes, up to five thirty, five hundred hours in the Accelerated World...about twenty days. In that time, you'll learn an Incarnate technique you can use in an actual battle. And if you can't do it, well, I can't watch out for your sorry asses any longer than that."

"No," Takumu replied immediately to the Red King's cool words. "One week inside. That's enough."

"Oh ho! Big talk, Professor. I'll just see if you're as ready as you think you are." Grinning, Niko leaned her slim body, clad in a navy blazer and a pleated skirt, back on the sofa. "Okay, then. When I count to zero, we all dive into the Unlimited Neutral Field. Ready?"

Haruyuki and Takumu also pressed their backs and heads into the sofa. "Yes."

"Here we go. Ten, nine, eight, seven..."

He closed his eyes and took a deep breath. A second after he heard Niko's count reach one, he shouted the command to fly into the true Accelerated World.

5

The first thing he felt was a merciless cold, as if they had gone back in time three months.

Timidly opening his eyes, a gradient from white to blue and nothing else filled his field of vision. Snow. And ice. Every geological feature was built from thick ice, which was lightly covered by pure white snow. The sky was a uniform surface of milk-colored clouds.

"An Ice stage? Not happy about this."

At the sound of the voice, he looked to his right, where a girl avatar with ruby-red armor stood, long antennas swinging on her head. She was even smaller than Silver Crow. With her face mask and the round, cute lenses shining there, and her smooth body with basically no pointed edges, she looked like nothing more than a harmless mascot character. But this duel avatar was a long-distance fire demon who struck fear in the hearts of other avatars, the true form of the leader of Prominence, Scarlet Rain.

The Red King stared up at Haruyuki. "Hey, Crow!" she said, sounding dissatisfied. "That metal armor of yours, it good against the cold, too?"

"Y-yes, basically." He bobbed his head.

She had no sooner shouted, "No fair!" than she abruptly scooped up a pile of snow at her feet with both hands and rubbed it into his back.

"Eeyaaaha!"

"See! This body'll just rust! See! See?!"

"Jaaah! When I said *good against the cold*, I meant cold damage! The sensation of cold is still the same, you know!!"

Bouncing around to escape the ice attack, he heard an exaggerated cough at a short distance. Turning his gaze in that direction with Niko, he saw a large avatar with dark blue armor standing there, arms crossed. Of course, it was Takumu—Cyan Pile.

"O-oh, that's right, right." Scarlet Rain stepped away from Haruyuki, seemingly embarrassed, and coughed theatrically. "Anyhoooo, I'll just say welcome to my Nerima! Although if things were different, I'd be swooping in to chase your asses out of here!" She flung her arms out with a flourish, so Haruyuki looked around once again.

The first thing he felt was the immensity of the sky. He quickly understood the reason for this. Although the frozen intersection of roads where they were currently standing wasn't that large, there were basically no large-terrain objects that would obstruct his field of view. He could see a lone, tall ice palace in the northwest. He overlaid a map of the real world for comparison in the back of his mind and figured it was probably the Nerima Ward office. Other than that, there was just an enormous tower, hazy as though melting into the distant eastern sky. That was probably Sunshine City in Ikebukuro in Toshima Ward, where they had fought Chrome Disaster. There were no enemies or other Burst Linkers for as far as his eyes could see.

Haruyuki took in a chestful of the chill air. "It's so wide open! This area's great!"

Instantly, a snowball howling through the air hit smack-dab in the middle of Silver Crow's helmet. "S-so sorry there's nothing to show you! Your little Suginami's got nothing, either, you know!!" Niko shouted, antennas standing on end. She turned away before continuing. "Seriously! Introduction over! Lesson commencing immediately! Sit down over there, both of you!"

Guessing that his words were somehow an anger trigger for the residents of Nerima Ward, Haruyuki met Takumu's eyes and hurriedly took a formal kneeling position in the center of the intersection.

Scarlet Rain's aura abruptly changed as she drew herself up to her full height and paced briskly before them, arms crossed. The childishness that had drifted about her evaporated without a trace. The light emitted from within her lenses grew starker, and the physical stature of the avatar even seemed to grow.

"I'll just say this to start." Her voice was tinged with an echo cooler and crisper than the icy wind of the stage. "Before I teach you about the Incarnate System, there's one thing you have to swear to me." She looked at Haruyuki, who gulped loudly, and Takumu in turn, before announcing succinctly, "You absolutely must not use an Incarnate attack unless attacked with an Incarnate attack. Swear on your pride as a Burst Linker that you will always obey this rule!"

"Uh, um, is that because it's cowardly?" Haruyuki asked involuntarily, and Niko refuted him immediately.

"No. It's because in this game, the real enemy is you yourself. Because ultimately, Incarnate exists not for defeating enemies but for confronting your own weakness. So? You swear it?"

Pressed like this, there was no way they could say no. And they didn't want to study the Incarnate System so that they could use it to win in duels. It was just to fight the Incarnate user Dusk Taker. Haruyuki and Takumu glanced over at each other. "Yes!" they shouted in unison.

"Good. You break this promise, and I'll take responsibility and show you a serious world of hurt."

Bobbing his head up and down at lightning speed, Haruyuki timidly asked a follow-up question. "Uh, but, I mean, an Incarnate attack, at first glance, it's hard to tell apart from a regular special attack. I feel like you don't know until you're hit—"

"Look, you've at least learned the first steps, haven't you?" Niko said, slightly disgusted, and stuck out the index finger of her right hand. "Listen up. An Incarnate attack is different from a special attack in two big ways. One: When you use it, your special-attack gauge doesn't go down!"

"O-oh, th-that's true." Haruyuki nodded, but the next question soon popped into his head. "But then what are you supposed to do in the Unlimited Neutral Field, where you can't see your opponent's gauge?"

Niko threw another finger up. "Two! It glows!"

"I-it glows?" He parroted her too-vague words back at her. Although it was true, now that she mentioned it: Haruyuki's sword of light was indeed a white light, and Nomi's nihilistic pulsation also emitted a purple light, but was this a systemic phenomenon shared by all Incarnate attacks?

Niko heard the uncertainty in Haruyuki's voice, and a faint smile spread across her lips. "This isn't some wishy-washy thing like a battle cry or fighting spirit or whatever. Listen up. When you use an Incarnate attack, your consciousness and your duel avatar are connected through the Image Control System. When excessive imagination passes through this circuit, the irregular signals spamming the system are processed as a particulate effect with no real form—in other words, as light. Specifically, it's...like this."

Niko clenched the right hand still thrust out in front of her. Suddenly, red flames rose from her fist up to her elbow. Or rather, they weren't exactly flames, but a red light wrapped around her arm, flickering.

"It depends on the strength of the will, but if the image's strong enough to use in a fight, it'll definitely glow this much at least. We just call it 'Overlay.' Get it? And the one and only time an avatar continuously emits light like this is when the Incarnate System has been activated. Even if a special attack does glow, it's only for a second."

The flames disappeared as abruptly as they had arrived. "In

other words," Niko said, summing up, "if the enemy avatar glows with an aura like the one I had just now, and their gauge doesn't go down, it's an Incarnate attack. But, look…even if you do get in that kind of sitch, if you can run, run. Responding with Incarnate to Incarnate is only for those fights when there's literally no other way. Got it?!"

The question of why the system had to be so tightly restricted was a natural one. However, Niko, waiting for the pair before her to respond, had an intensely menacing air about her befitting a king, and Haruyuki couldn't bring himself to ask anything else.

"Yes, understood!" he shouted as one with Takumu, and the Red King finally nodded, as if satisfied.

"Good. Then that's it for the preliminaries." She crossed her arms in front of her flat chest and cleared her throat. "You guys're prob'ly thinking like this right now," she commented unexpectedly. "That the Incarnate System must be incredibly powerful if using it's so seriously restricted, and if you master it, you'll be able to do anything. But that is a huge mistake."

"…Huh." His surprise at this won out over the intimidation emanating from the Red King, and Haruyuki unthinkingly spoke. "B-but…doesn't the Incarnate System make the impossible possible—"

"No. Listen, Incarnate's not a cure-all. Get that in your brain right off the bat." After she refuted him, her tone inferno hot, Niko continued with the faintest of smiles bleeding onto her lips. "You seem unhappy, Crow. You don't agree?"

Swallowing hard, Haruyuki nodded hesitantly. "Y-yeah. I mean, I-I've experienced myself how amazing the power of the will is. Both getting hit with that power and hitting with it."

"Hmm, you seem pretty sure of yourself. Okay. Stand up."

He obeyed the flicking index finger gesturing him to his feet and pulled his body up nervously. Feeling Takumu's eyes on him, he took a few steps forward.

"So now show me this power of yours."

Haruyuki had been expecting her to say this, so the instant he stood, he had readied himself for it. Responding with a simple "Got it," he walked over toward a large block of ice that had fallen nearby.

I know my Incarnate attack's definitely not going to be anything from King Niko's point of view, but still. Although a layer under this thought there definitely existed a feeling of *Okay, I'll show you!* After all, Haruyuki had pierced the nihilistic fluctuation of his formidable enemy Dusk Taker with a sword of light he had spent a week facing off with the three-hundred-meter-high precipice of old Tokyo Tower to master.

He stopped about a meter and a half in front of a transparent blue ice block the same size as he was and dropped his hips into a ready stance. He definitely wouldn't be able to reach across this distance with his normal succession of punches. He folded the thumb of his right hand into his palm and lined the remaining four fingers up in a row. Twisting his torso to the right, he pulled his sword-shaped hand into his side.

My hand is a sword. A sword that moves at the speed of light to pierce anything.

The sound of arctic wind blowing through the stage receded and disappeared. The scene around him sank into a dim gloom, and only a single point in the center of the blue ice block floated up, vivid.

Fine vibrations passed through his body with a whine, and the white light, Niko's Overlay, appeared at the tip of his sword hand. This finally spread out from his wrist and up to his elbow.

"Sha!" With a brief battle cry, Haruyuki thrust his sword hand straight out, using the thrust of his rotating hips.

Shkeeeeng! Together with the high-pitched, crisp sound, a sharp white light surged more than a meter from his extended right arm and was swallowed up by the center of the ice block.

A heartbeat after the light disappeared, the ice creaked, and then the enormous lump split into two pieces along the vertical crack, which then fell off to the sides. At the weight of the impact, a thin layer of snow danced up in a plume.

Haruyuki exhaled, pulled himself back up, and turned around to be greeted by two sets of applause. Takumu was intently bringing together his left hand and the Pile Driver of his right, while Niko slapped two normal hands together.

"Wow, that's more serious than I was expecting. Pretty decent."

Haruyuki started to scratch his head in a "no, it's no big deal" kind of way at the Red King's assessment, but her next comment stopped him short.

"For a first step of a first step."

"...F-first step?"

"Obviously! What you used just now was one of the basic Incarnate techniques, Range Extension."

"...B-basic?" Haruyuki repeated, stunned, and Niko gestured for him to come back. When he was sitting in his original spot again, she cleared her throat and continued.

"Listen, we call it a fancy name, *Incarnate*, but in the end, it's just one more logic executed in the Brain Burst program, okay? The main idea of it is the 'overwrite.' Which is basically something the diver does with image power. To put it another way, a powerful thought causes the system—the god of this world—to mistake it for fact." She paused for breath, and then said slowly, as if to carve her own words into her two students, "But, look, to actually make something happen, you need an image so strong that it tricks *you* before it tricks the system. Way past the level of imagination, all the way to conviction. And to have this conviction live in your heart, you need two things: experience built up over an overwhelming amount of time and desire, sourced from a missing necessity. An image that doesn't have both of these backing it will not become fact."

"...Experience and desire...," Haruyuki murmured hoarsely, and Niko nodded slightly.

"So here's a little something for you," she said as she took a few steps back and let both her arms hang down. "I'll show you the real thing, just once, so watch closely."

Haruyuki and Takumu twitched and sat up straighter. To keep

from missing anything, they opened their eyes so wide beneath their helmets that the orbs almost popped out.

The small, girl-shaped avatar spun around toward the south side of the intersection. Just like before, an aura of thin red flames shot up around her left fist. "This is one of the four basic techniques: Range Expansion."

With no fighting yell, she shot her left arm forward so fast it was nearly smoking. The air cracked as if whipped, and a line of fire was etched in space.

Instantly, a wall of ice some thirty meters away hissed and erupted in snow-white water vapor, which was dispersed by the wind, and they saw an enormous hole, big enough for a person to crawl through, piercing the center of the wall. The smoothed interior went from blue to black, and they couldn't tell how deep it went.

The two boys, eyelids peeled back in amazement, heard her pick up where she had left off. "And this is the second basic technique, Movement Expansion."

The flaming aura wrapped itself around her small legs this time. The avatar quickly sank down, and then she completely disappeared.

No. Haruyuki's eyes could just make out a hazy, blurred shadow—from behind him. He whirled around and there was Niko, hands on her hips. She had moved nearly twenty meters from her original position. When he looked more carefully, he saw a thin rut etched into the surface of the ice, melted and smoking white.

He didn't even have time to take a breath before Niko vanished again, leaving nothing but a soft echo behind. A circular rut enclosed Haruyuki and Takumu, and she was back in her original position.

It was overwhelming. The range of her long-distance attack was far beyond Silver Crow's sword of light, and the speed of her sliding dash easily put the charge of Ash Roller's bike to shame.

Clenching both hands tightly to control his immense surprise,

Haruyuki waited for the next performance, so as not to miss a single thing.

However...

The bright red avatar spread her hands out lightly. "The end."

"B-but..." It was Takumu who spoke. "Before, you said that there were four basic techniques—"

"There are. The third is Attack Power Expansion. And the fourth is Armor Strength Expansion. But, look...*I can't use either of them.*"

"Y-you can't?! Basic techniques...You, a king?!" Haruyuki shouted reflexively, and Niko glared at him hard. Still, she explained without losing her cool.

"That's right. Because...I personally know I'm not that strong. And that's because of the mental scars that power this duel avatar, Scarlet Rain."

The cherubic mask was turned up to the snowy sky directly above. "I'm afraid of the world," the Red King, one of the strongest people in the Accelerated World, a ruler with terrifying long-distance firepower, said as if talking to herself, in a voice that made him feel sad somehow. "Because the closer I get, the more it hurts me in every possible way. Brain Burst ate up my longing to get away from the world and made this avatar. Scarlet Rain's long-distance flame power's like the spines on a hedgehog. Inside all that, I'm just a weakling of a little kid with no power at all. Which is why I can't use my will to enhance the attack or defensive power of the main body of this avatar. Understand, Crow? Pile? This right here is the absolute limit of the Incarnate System."

For a while, the only sound in the icy world was the reedy whisper of the cold, wintry wind.

Haruyuki dropped his head and digested the Red King's words in his heart. He couldn't say he knew very much about Niko— Yuniko Kozuki—in the real world. Not knowing her real parents, she attended a full boarding elementary school that doubled as a welfare facility. That's all she had told him. But this history was harsher than Haruyuki could even imagine, and Niko must have been hurting all this time. So much so that even disguised as an avatar in the virtual world, she could no longer believe in her own strength.

In which case, Haruyuki thought, *it's clear, actually too clear, that my avatar reflects my longing to run away from this place. Hands to reach for something beyond reach. Wings to flee to a place where there's no one. That's why I could master the Incarnate Range Expansion and why I could recharge the gauge for the Gale Thruster with the Incarnate Movement Expansion. And for the same reason, I probably won't be able to use the Armor Expansion, which would raise my defensive power.*

But even if that is how it is, I want to believe...her. Believe her telling me over and over and over again, You can change.

"So then is this how it is?" Takumu's quiet murmur broke the long silence. "The Incarnate abilities you can obtain are limited to those that conform with the duel avatar's essential nature? Or to put it another way, even if you master Incarnate, you can't do what you can't do."

"Right," Niko declared shortly, and turned her eyes on Haruyuki. "Like that Range Expansion Crow demonstrated before. To be perfectly honest, with the speed and flying ability that Silver Crow has, you don't really need that technique. Although that was probably the optimal training for you to get how to use the Image Control circuits. And you can say the same thing about the techniques I showed you. I made a big deal of making that huge hole in the ice, but even without focusing on the image, I got this." She patted the holster on her hip. "If I had used this, I could've made a bigger hole way easier. So then why do you need an Incarnate attack?"

Haruyuki stared at Niko as she stopped talking, and cocked his head to the side. But Takumu, being Takumu, sat up very straight and answered crisply, "Because Incarnate attacks can only be defended against with Incarnate attacks, right?"

"That's exactly it. Because the Image Control System determines the results of offense and defense faster than commands given to the system by Movement Control. It's like you have swords and shields and clubs, and the enemy has a laser rifle. And, Professor, you were on the receiving end of an Incarnate attack from this Dusk Taker guy, without knowing anything about anything. You totally get how absurd that sitch is."

"...The way it sinks into your bones. The way Dusk Taker scrapes away everything with those claws probably belongs to the Attack Power Expansion group. It felt like trying to punch a sword with my bare fists."

Niko hummed nasally and placed her hands sharply on her hips. "Ultimately, you're definitely going to need to learn at least Attack or Defense if you're going to fight Dusk Taker for real. And so we finally arrive at the big purpose of diving here." Here, an unusual, albeit slight hesitation crept into the Red King's tone. "Just like I said before, if the Incarnate's at odds with the avatar's attributes, there's basically no chance of mastering it, no matter how hard you train. So now there's something I really have to ask you here. Pile, is that avatar of yours close-range or long-distance?"

"Huh?!" It was Haruyuki who cried out wildly. After looking alternately at Niko and Takumu, he produced a dumbfounded voice. "H-he's obviously close-range...right? I mean, an avatar this vivid of a close-range blue, you almost never see them in the Shinjuku area."

"That's what I thought, but if that's the case, then that Enhanced Armament..."

"Oh." Haruyuki fixed his eyes once more on the enormous Pile Driver taking up Cyan Pile's right arm, up to his elbow.

This Enhanced Armament shot out the built-in, meter-long steel spike at a ferocious speed. So fast, in fact, that it had once ripped the arm of the metallic Silver Crow clean off in one blow.

If it was just that, Haruyuki thought it might just barely still be a close-range weapon, but the issue was Cyan Pile's strongest special attack, Lightning Cyan Spike. That technique transformed the spike into a beam of light before firing it. The range easily exceeded fifty meters, setting it firmly in the category of long-distance attack.

After staring unconsciously for several seconds, Haruyuki jerked his head up and cast his eyes far away.

Duel avatars were created with mental scars as the source. Cyan Pile's appearance and the Enhanced Armament of his right hand were an expression of Takumu's hopes and fears. And Haruyuki had decided in his heart that he would not do anything to pry into that.

However...

"It's okay, Haru," Takumu's soft voice insisted.

Haruyuki timidly raised his face. "T-Taku..."

"Ever since you told me about the Incarnate System last night, I've kind of known. That to learn it, I'd have to confront my scars head-on."

"Th-then I'll just drop out now."

"No, I want you to hear this, too. The truth is, I should've told you a long time ago..." Straightening his seated posture, Takumu looked directly at first Haruyuki, then Niko, and said, "I think that Cyan Pile is essentially a close-range type. So then why was it created with this long-distance-type initial equipment? That's probably because my fear is expressed here."

"...Your fear?" Haruyuki asked, stunned. What on earth could Takumu—*the* Takumu Mayuzumi, who seemed to have looks, brains, and everything else—be afraid of?

Takumu uttered the following words at his friend. "I was horribly bullied from third grade to fifth. I even thought about jumping from the roof of our condo once or twice."

"......!!" Haruyuki's entire body froze in shock. *No way, impossible*, the *Takumu being bullied*. The thought whirled violently in his brain.

"You couldn't have known," Takumu continued gently, almost as if consoling Haruyuki, when it should have been the other way around. "It didn't happen at school or at the condo, but at the kendo school I was going to back then. I…I mean, I'm not trying to brag or anything, but I do think I had an affinity for kendo. Ever since I started learning it in the spring of third grade, it's like I just naturally understood the techniques. My rank went up pretty quickly, and I started winning against the older kids, too. But…I guess it was around the end of the second semester. When our teacher left us alone for a while at the dojo, a bunch of older kids said, *Hey, let's practice piercing techniques.*"

"P-piercing? B-but…"

"Of course, you're not allowed until high school. And I said I didn't want to. But practicing was just an excuse. They pinned me down from behind and stabbed my throat over and over and over and over again with the wooden *shinai* sword. I was completely terrified. I screamed from under my mask, *Stop it, please.* After a while, I couldn't scream anymore…When they finally let me go, even protected by all my equipment, I had these insane bruises. Even now…" Cyan Pile lifted his right hand and traced it along the left side of his neck. "The scars here don't disappear; they're still there. The same kind of stuff happened more than a few times after that. But I didn't quit taking lessons. It was more like I *couldn't* quit. I totally couldn't tell my parents, or you or Chi. I couldn't say to you, *I'm quitting kendo because of bullies.*"

"Taku…I didn't…I didn't know…" was all Haruyuki could manage to squeeze out.

Takumu shook his head lightly, as if to say it was okay. "Naturally, I had the option of talking to my parents or the teacher. But there were no social cameras in the classroom, and it was the teacher's policy that we take our Neurolinkers off, so I had no proof…and more than that, I think I even lost the will to fight back. Walking to the dojo, I don't know how many times I wished I would just disappear…The bullying kept up until the ringleader started junior high and quit taking lessons. You have no idea how happy I was when he was gone." The last bit was uttered as if it were riding on a sigh.

Haruyuki empathized so hard it was like he was the one talking.

But Takumu's story didn't end there. Following a muttered, "But the thing is," there came an extra, unexpected confession.

"Not long after I started sixth grade, I noticed I'd developed this habit. I'd be fine during practice, but when I got to a tournament, if my opponent turned his *shinai* toward my throat, I'd reflexively try to guard with my own *shinai*. It was a fatal weakness. I tried so hard to get over it, but the more I focused in a tournament, the worse it got...The terror of the vicious attack on my throat that day had seeped into my bones. Right now, the rules still don't allow piercing techniques, so I fake my way through it, but once I get to high school, I probably won't be able to make any kind of serious showing in tournaments. I totally can't handle being hit with a piercing technique or using one myself."

He stopped there and looked at Niko, who had said nothing all this time, then at Haruyuki beside him, and finally at the Enhanced Armament of his own right arm before quietly bringing his story to an end.

"This Pile Driver is the incarnation of my terror of piercing techniques...and my anger. It's saying I'd like to line up those guys who bullied me back then and slam this stake into their throats one after the other. Which is why I'm a close-range duel avatar who also has a piercing weapon rather than a sword, Red King."

The final words were directed at the crimson avatar silently looming over them.

The long monologue finished, Niko finally nodded. "Okay, I hear your scars. So that's the reason the majority of your potential was poured into an Enhanced Armament that's the opposite affiliation of your avatar. In that case, what you need to confront, Pile, is your own stake. If you can overcome that terror, your avatar should be able to gain the Incarnate Attack Power Expansion as a true close-range type," Niko declared severely, turning back to Haruyuki. "So the professor and I are going to get into the actual training now. What are you going to do, Crow? Hang out?"

"Uh, um." Haruyuki blinked fiercely before answering so they wouldn't see that his eyes under his silver mask were full of tears. "No. I think it's probably better if I'm not here. I can't...really explain why, but..."

"Thanks, Haru," Takumu said and nodded, so Haruyuki smiled awkwardly and stood up.

He looked back over at Niko again and added, "And there's something I want to check into a bit on my own. The mechanism that keeps Dusk Taker from showing up on the matching list."

"Yeah, you seriously can't ignore that part. Actually, that's a bigger problem than the Incarnate attack. And I feel like I heard something similar recently."

"What?! R-really?!" He unconsciously sidled up to her and the Red King shoved him back.

"Why does that mean you gotta get so close?!" she cried. "It's just a rumor! A rumor, geez! I don't know all the deets; go ask the person who does!"

"Huh? Wh-where?" He looked around instinctively, but, of course, there was no one there.

"Log out and you'll see. There's a portal on the first floor of the Nerima Ward office, over there."

"O-okay."

Niko waved a curt hand as if to say she was done with him, so Haruyuki started walking.

But—

"Oops! Hey, wait!" she called out to stop him, and he turned around once more.

"Wh-what?"

"Aah, that Range Expansion Incarnate technique of yours before. You give it a name?"

"A-a name?!" Haruyuki raised a shrill voice at the unexpected question.

Niko thrust out her index finger. "It's not for some dumb kid reason like it's cooler like that or something!" she shouted quickly. "The heart of an Incarnate technique is whether or not the image is firmly fixed in your mind. Ideally, you wanna be able to call it up as naturally as you do the abilities and special attacks you had from the start. You were concentrating for nearly three seconds from the time you crouched down to the time you moved. That's way too slow! So first, you give your technique a name, so then you superimpose over the image with you shouting the name as the trigger. C'mon, name it! Name it now!!" she exploded.

Haruyuki hurriedly racked his brains as he looked at his hands. "Umm...Sword...Swooord...Light...th-then." He raised his eyes. "L-Laser Sword."

"Pft! Weak sauce." She immediately laughed off the name he had so desperately thought up, the name that was so cool by Haruyuki standards.

"Th-then what's the name of your Range and Movement attack from before, huh?!" Haruyuki retorted instinctively.

"Like I'd tell you, stuuupid!"

Here, they heard a familiar throat clearing.

Haruyuki looked over at Takumu and scratched his head. "Oh, uh, that's...Umm...Taku, g-good luck!" He awkwardly thrust the thumb of his right hand up.

Standing, Cyan Pile returned the gesture. "You, too, Haru. But please don't do anything too dangerous."

"Got it. I'll report back to you tonight."

They nodded at each other, and then Haruyuki ran a few steps toward the Nerima Ward office rising up in the west before turning around one final time to shout, "Niko! Thanks!!"

The voice that came back to him was the same energetic abuse as always.

"Shut up and just go already!!"

6

Via the leave-point set in the lobby of the Nerima Ward Office, Haruyuki returned to the real world. Taking a deep breath, he sat up on the sofa. As he pulled the XSB cable out, he looked to his side and saw Takumu breathing evenly, long eyelashes lowered beneath his glasses.

Right now, his good friend's consciousness was in a different time stream from Haruyuki, entirely devoted to a desperate training. No, the simple word *training* couldn't quite encapsulate it. Takumu was at long last confronting psychic wounds he had likely spent years pushing to the bottom of his heart and trying to overcome them.

"You can do it, Taku," Haruyuki whispered, and then stood up.

On the opposite side of the table, he saw the innocent sleeping face—although she wasn't in fact sleeping—of the girl clad in an elementary school uniform. She really almost *was* an angel like this. "Thank you," he said to her, and he meant it from the bottom of his heart. Then he went to step out of the electromagnetic wave isolation room, opening the thick door into the hallway.

"This way. Hurry." A voice came down from above his head, and he jerked his eyes upward.

Standing there was, no mistake about it, the clerk who had brought their drinks and cake earlier. Jacket puffed up at the shoulders, long skirt, both in a dark cherry color, topped by a snow-white apron decorated with conservative lace over. The Alice band on her head and the thin ribbon on her chest were both a brighter red than her clothing. In short, she looked the maid in every way. Seen up close, she was younger than he had thought; she was fairly tall, but she was probably still in high school. Her fringe was parted perfectly in the center and the hair in the back was gathered into a braid that fell below her shoulders. Her face was angular, and her narrow, upturned, single-lidded eyes reinforced the impression of sharpness.

Does she mean hurry up and get out? Are Niko and Takumu gonna be okay like this? Haruyuki wondered. He bowed, in any case, and tried to slip through the hall to the shop. But...

He heard her say, "Not that way," as the collar of his blazer was yanked from behind, knocking his head back. The shock he felt that a cake shop clerk, and one dressed as a maid to boot, would act so aggressively grew several magnitudes larger with the words that came next.

"Go out the back. Follow me, *Silver Crow*."

"Wh—?!"

Oh crap, I'm outed in the reeeeeaaaal! he screamed in his mind and instinctively tried to run away, but she had a firm hold on his collar, so he only ended up strangling himself again. She was slim, but she had a seriously powerful grip.

"No need to run. And anyway, it's too late for that," she told him in a husky voice that was almost a monotone, and he had no choice but to give up on thoughts of escape. He turned around.

The maid looked down at him completely expressionless and finally let go of his collar. "Scarlet Rain told me to help with your investigation," she informed him with extreme nonchalance. "My name's Blood Leopard. If you're going to call me by name, go with Leopard, not Blood. If you need to shorten it, go with Pard, not Lep."

"Hey...uh...Please hold on a minute." Haruyuki managed to

get that much out somehow, while he earnestly set his brain to work to try and understand the situation.

I don't know all the deets; go ask the person who does! the Red King Niko had said right before he'd logged out. However, he had naturally taken that to mean within the Accelerated World. But it seemed that that maid, exposing her real self in the real world, was the "person who does" Niko had mentioned: a Burst Linker in the Red Legion Prominence, and at the same time, a clerk in this shop. In other words, this was no ordinary cake shop but something along the lines of a Prominence base.

He had muddled this far when the maid, Blood Leopard, nickname Pard, said as if growing impatient, "I waited two seconds. Think about the rest as we move." And then she whirled around, long skirt fluttering, and started toward a door visible at the end of the dark hallway.

Haruyuki no longer had any other options. He followed the mysterious older girl's order.

The door was apparently the back exit, and where it came out was next to a garage behind the cake shop.

The maid moved her fingers, and the shutters facing the road began to open automatically. Blood Leopard seemed to be a fairly impatient type for some reason, and she thrust a finger out at Haruyuki, as if she couldn't waste time waiting.

"This is all Master told me: You got a Burst Linker who doesn't show up on the matching list, even though he's connected to the local net. You want to figure out how. That's the end, 'kay?"

She sought his assent with half of the word *okay* carved away, and Haruyuki nodded. "R-right, that's exactly it."

"I've heard of list interception, but lately there're rumors of a local net troll."

The maid's assessment was sudden, and Haruyuki, flustered, unconsciously leaned forward. "L-local net troll? What's that?"

"Don't know the deets. Apparently, on a certain net, this Burst

Linker challenges you, but when you go for a rematch, the Linker's already gone from the list."

"Wh-where is this 'certain net'?!"

"Akihabara."

Haruyuki recoiled at the concise reply. "A-Akihabara? That's the Yellow Legion's territory, ri—"

"Yup." Haruyuki watched the maid nod as if it were no big deal. He swallowed hard.

It was a mere three months earlier that, due to the evil machinations of the Yellow King, Yellow Radio, ruler of the Legion Crypt Cosmic Circus, the Red King Niko had, without warning, ended up in serious trouble, ambushed by dozens of people. Haruyuki and the other members of Nega Nebulus had been dragged through that hell with her, so it would be fair to say that currently, of the six major Legions, Haruyuki was the most vigorously opposed to Yellow.

He wanted very much to go and collect information, but not quite having the courage to head off into such an enemy's territory, Haruyuki bit his lip. *But this isn't the time for me to sit here freaked out. I mean, just her telling me there's a clue in Akihabara is a lucky break. If I just go and hang out in a normal duel gallery there and ask about any rumors, I should be able to get in and out without too much trouble...*

These thoughts running through his mind, Haruyuki tried to muster what little courage he had.

Blood Leopard, similarly silent for several seconds, finally said with utmost brevity, "'Kay. We'll go now."

"Huh?"

...Go? To Akihabara? With her? Dressed like that on a train...? His eyes opened so wide, his eyelids threatened to peel right off.

She grabbed his collar, almost as if to say she wasn't interested in talking anymore, and strode into the garage, short boots *clacking* on the concrete.

Enshrined there, radiating an overwhelming sense of presence, was an enormous electric bike at least two meters long. A completely different beast from the electric scooters zipping along peacefully with their lilting engines, the body was enveloped by a sleek red-and-black cowl, and the motorized front and rear wheels were astoundingly thick, maintained by an active suspension arm so tough it looked like armor. The streamlined body was low, practically crawling on the ground.

"W...ow..." He let out an involuntary sigh of admiration.

Pard grabbed something rounded from the rack on the wall and shoved it at him. He took it reflexively and looked down to find an open-face red helmet in his hands.

"Huh?" He simply stood and stared, not understanding the meaning of this. Blood Leopard approached on quick feet and picked it up again—and then popped it on Haruyuki's head. She deftly buckled it on under his chin with one hand.

She slipped a full-face black helmet over her Alice band, and after a quick shake of the braid poking out from under it, she grabbed Haruyuki's collar again and plopped him down in the passenger seat of the large bike.

...*No way. No. Wait. Wait a minute.*

The older girl didn't even leave him the time to groan. She straddled the bike, still in her maid's clothing, and grabbed the handlebars firmly, slender hands in leather gloves.

"Start," she murmured, apparently a voice command, since the bike's dash subsequently flashed to life. The fully extended front and rear suspension arms whined with preloading.

Haruyuki's Neurolinker also automatically connected to the bike's CPU, and windows appeared for speed and battery gauges and other things one after another before his eyes. Meanwhile, he heard Blood Leopard's voice—not her real voice, but one communicated wirelessly.

"*Hold on.*"

"Huh? Uh, no, but...," he cried, but two hands immediately stretched out from in front of him and took hold of his arms. She yanked his forward and forced them around her slim waist to lock over her apron. This girl was apparently not the type to give an order twice.

Thinking escape was likely impossible, he half gave up at this point, but he couldn't fully let go of the dream of freedom. *"Uh, um, are you going to drive dressed like that?"*

"Waste of time to change."

"A-and what about the shop?"

"My shift was till five. Any other questions, ask them all at once."

"...That's it."

"'Kay." And the maid casually opened the throttle.

The massive machine slipped smoothly out of the garage attached to the cake shop, the noise of its motor the eye of the storm made by its bottomless torque.

The clock display in the lower right of his vision read 5:08 PM. At some point, the rain had stopped, and the gaps in the clouds streaming westward were dyed a spectacular orange.

Ah, I left my umbrella in the shop. Oh well, Taku'll probably grab it for me.

Haruyuki idly wondered about this and other escapist thoughts while the electric bike silently and slowly slid through the Sakuradai neighborhood. Blood Leopard seemed to be as safe a driver as she was impatient. But just when he had started to relax, the bike turned right at a large intersection onto Kannana Street.

Krraaaaa!! The internal motors in the front and rear wheels roared and the needle on the hologauge jumped up. In the periphery of his vision, he could see her long skirt flapping and fluttering. The wind pressure slapped his face through the shield of the helmet.

"Aaaaaaaah!!" Haruyuki screamed with his real voice.

The enormous bike with the driver dressed as a maid and the passenger a junior high boy in his school uniform moved from Kannana to Mejiro Street and raced hard to the east.

Although these days, the legal speed limit for motorcycles and passenger vehicles couldn't actually be broken. Control systems were equipped with limiters, which were automatically set to the maximum speed for a given road. If you wanted to break the speed limit, your only choice was to illegally mod the vehicle or order emergency mode and temporarily shut down the control AI. Naturally, it was against the law to turn off the AI without good reason, so either way, you had to be ready to face the police.

Blood Leopard's bike was naturally neither modded nor in emergency mode, and the limiter was, in fact, set at Mejiro Street's legal speed limit of eighty kilometers an hour, but they went from zero to the speed limit in an exceedingly brief period. Huge Gs slammed into Haruyuki's round body, the likes of which he had never experienced in the real world, and he nearly shrieked. And as if that wasn't enough, he wasn't sure about this whole thing where his stomach was glued to Pard's slim body.

Way better that I'm sitting in the back. If we were the other way around, it wouldn't be her back, but the feeling of her front. Agh, the other way could totally never, ever happen.

As his mind raced, the bike turned onto the outer ring road at Iidabashi, which was fairly busy, as you might expect at dusk in the city center. The drivers of the electric cars and scooters around them opened their eyes wide when they saw Blood Leopard's motorcycle. Which was only fair, given that you hardly ever saw a large bike like this these days, much less one ridden at twilight by a dazzling maid in a snow-white apron, with a roundly plump junior high school student on the back, to boot.

Unable to stand the many eyes concentrating on them as they waited at the light, Haruyuki shrank into himself. *"Uh, um, I feel like we really stand out?"* he said in neurospeak.

"Yes." Pard sounded like she didn't care, and maybe she really didn't.

Haruyuki kept himself from flinching and continued, *"A-and we're charging into CCC's stronghold; it's a little dangerous."*

This time, her answer was somewhat longer. *"No prob. We won't stand out."*

"Huh?"

But he got no further response; she opened the throttle all the way the instant the light turned green. Lightning from the motor. Haruyuki suffocating.

After the bike pulled into a parking garage adjacent to the western edge of the Akiharaba district and they had walked for a few minutes, he finally understood what she meant.

The instant they stepped onto the main street that cut north-south through Electric Town, at least three women in maids' uniforms leapt into Haruyuki's sight. They were, of course, not real maids—although, that said, neither was Blood Leopard—but rather seemed to be doing promotion for some store, handing out holopapers to passersby with sparkling smiles. The only difference between them and Pard was the presence/absence of a smile.

"I get it." He nodded his complete agreement and looked up again at the majestic city that never slept.

Due to redevelopment in the early 2000s, this area had once been redesigned as a new kind of stylish neighborhood. However, as the center of electronic sales shifted to Ikebukuro and Shinjuku, property values dropped, and in the recession of the time, the banks got spooked and pulled out completely. This led to a subdivision of the land rights, and by the twenties, the former chaos of the previous century had once again descended on the area.

Now, in 2047, countless tiny shops jostled up against one another for any and every business related to electronics and networks and subcultures. Because the windows of the buildings lining the streets glittered with as much neon as people could pack in, there was nothing in the way of uniformity of color. Standing in Electric Town at night was like standing in the middle of a galaxy with dense formations of primary-colored stars.

If Haruyuki connected his Neurolinker to the global net now and allowed unlimited ad information, his field of vision would no doubt be so full of holopamphlets for sales on Neurolinkers and standalone custom computer parts and all sorts of applications software, he wouldn't be able to see.

"Nice." The edges of his mouth relaxed at the informational disorganization that was far more virtual world than real one when he was abruptly choked by the collar of his jacket yet again.

"This way." Blood Leopard seemed entirely unaffected as she started walking north on a sidewalk overflowing with shoppers, dragging Haruyuki along with her.

She took him to a remarkably noisy building a little off from the main street. At first glance, he had no idea what kind of place it could be. A neon sign at the entrance read QUADTOWER, but beyond that, the lights were turned down, enshrouding the place in a gloom. Loud electronic noises leaked out, an infinity of machines.

"Quadtower? What is this place?" Haruyuki asked, a little freaked out.

"Arcade," Pard replied, aiming for the building without the slightest hesitation. They descended a short staircase and the instant they stepped out onto the dark floor, the meaning of that single word became clear.

The bare concrete floor was jammed with prehistoric game machines, old CRT monitors and joystick control panels embedded in enormous cabinets. The sounds of punches and explosions and background music flowed unimpeded from the many speakers, while players sitting on long chairs pounded and banged single-mindedly, all *clacks* and smacks, on the panels.

He watched in mute amazement from the wall as one player, at a console backed up to another of the same kind so that they were in mirror position, struck a victorious pose, and the audience behind the player burst into cheers. On the opposite side, a young man stood up, looking regretful. Players apparently fought each other on the two machines.

A member of the audience soon slipped in to take the losing

player's place. The girl, flamboyantly dressed as if she herself were a game character, plucked a silver hundred-yen coin from her pocket and dropped it into a slot in the middle of the panel.

"O-oh, right," Haruyuki murmured with a dry mouth. "*Arcade* means video arcade…and these machines, they're those arcade games from way back!" he continued excitedly, but Blood Leopard simply replied, "Yes," with her standard brevity and started walking again.

While he understood the reason they had come to this neighborhood and the seriousness of the situation he had gotten dragged into, he couldn't help thinking how much he'd like to sit down at that fighting game, just once. He had never touched that sort of large controller, but when it came to game pad–controlled 2-D fighting games, he had played so many on consoles at home, it was sick.

However, the real kicker here was that he did not have a single piece of old-school material money like a hundred-yen coin in his pockets or in the bag on his back. If he poked around in the arcade, he'd probably find an electronic money changer somewhere, but if he got separated from Pard in this expansive, dim place, he'd be screwed—or more to the point, she'd get mad at him—so he regretfully abandoned the idea.

Finally, belatedly, feeling doubts about why she had even brought him to this place, Haruyuki chased after the plait swinging against the maid's back and arrived finally at an elevator in the wall farthest in. They stepped into the cab of the terrifyingly ancient machine, and it started to lurch and *clack* its way upward, stopping at the fourth floor.

The other side of the opening door was pin-droppingly quiet, a world apart from the ground floor. Instead of game cabinets, this room was lined with narrow booths, divided by solid-looking panels. The wall to the right was taken up by a row of drink machines.

This sort of place Haruyuki was familiar with. A so-called "dive café," a place that provided private rooms for full dives, both in the middle of town and at a low price. You could lock the booths, so compared with leaving your real-world body in an open space like a family restaurant or a coffee shop, a dive café was far and away the safer choice.

That said, if they were just headed to a dive café, he was sure there were several near the garage where they had left the motorcycle. He wondered why they'd had to come all the way to this building. Pard quickly finished up at the deserted front counter and walked briskly into the café, leaving him no choice but to chase after her again.

"Get in."

He was ordered into what was clearly a single-person booth, but Blood Leopard came in after him, as if it were the most natural thing in the world. This time, he couldn't keep his questions to himself.

"Uh, um, there's only one chair."

"No pair seat booths open. We can squeeze in," she responded expressionlessly, closing the sliding door. The sturdy-looking lock fell into place with a sharp *clack*.

Gathering up her long skirt, she sat on one side of the recliner. When she slid her slim frame right to the edge, there were actually about forty centimeters of space left on the chair. But that was just barely enough for his plump self. He'd have to jam himself in.

"Um." He was about to continue with, *I'll just get another room for myself*, but the maid beat him to the punch.

"No prob. I'm fine with a kid stuck up against me."

But I am totally not fine!! And anyway, considering the first requirement for a Burst Linker, we are at most three years apart!! he yelled in his heart, but still, he resigned himself to let things be what they would be and set his body down next to Blood Leopard's, stammering, "E-e-excuse me," as he did. He did his best to cling to the armrest, but there was still only a gap of about two millimeters between her aproned chest and the tip of his nose.

A soft, sweet scent wafted up, and the moment he realized

it was the smell of cream and strawberries, he nearly lost consciousness. But he managed to hold it together somehow, and he heard her murmur so close to him he could feel her breath on his forehead.

"First, set up a full-dive avatar that's not connected to the real you."

"Huh? Ha, yeah." Cranking his decelerating brain back up, he did some quick manipulations of his virtual desktop and changed his avatar from the pink pig he used in the Umesato local net to a green lizard he had never used. "I-I'm done."

"When you do the full dive, dive into the access gate with the tag 'Akihabara BG.'"

"G-got it."

"'Kay. Countdown. One, zero."

Normally, you start from three at least!! Simultaneous with this thought, the same command was released from both of their mouths.

"Direct link!"

With a *whoosh*, his consciousness and real-world body were separated, and Haruyuki fell into the darkness.

Several access gates approached from below. Since he was currently disconnected from the global net, they should all have been via the local net operated by the Quadtower building. Among glittering and sparkling text like ALL-YOU-CAN-READ COMICS! and FREE ONLINE GAMES, there was indeed the inconspicuous tag AKIHABARA BG.

When he reached an invisible hand toward it, his vision was pulled in and the moment he was sucked into the circular gate, he felt the slightest of lags—the sense of something being verified. But the sensation of moving soon came over him again, and eventually, the soles of his feet touched the ground with a hard metallic *clank*.

When he raised his lowered face, he couldn't tell if he was in an enormous bar or a club or what. All the floors and walls were made of steel plates and chain-link mesh rusted red. The center of the square space was a sort of atrium, and on the first and mezzanine floors enclosing it, rough, naked steel tables were lined up equidistant from one another. He could see a few avatars at the tables in the gloom who appeared to have dived into the bar at the same time as him. They sank into the shadows, but the instant he saw their silhouettes, something clicked in him.

This was not the Accelerated World. It was a normal virtual space. Even still, Haruyuki knew these people were all Burst Linkers. And he realized only people with Brain Burst in their Neurolinkers could connect to this Akihabara BG net. He gulped his green lizard throat several times and let his eyes roam farther.

The next thing he noticed was the large four-sided monitor suspended on chains from the ceiling in the center of the expansive space. The bar was dimly lit, so he could clearly make out the text on the virtual screen.

Displayed at the very top was TODAY'S BATTLE in a gothic font. Below that "18:00," probably a time. And then FROST HORN, LV5, 1.57 VS SLATE BOTTLE, LV4, 3.22. Definitely a notice for an upcoming duel. But he didn't really understand the numbers after the levels, the ones with the decimal.

"Um, where..." Haruyuki finally stopped looking around and started to talk, hushed, to Blood Leopard, who was standing next to him.

Her avatar was—justifiably but perhaps surprisingly—no longer wearing the maid's uniform. Her entire body was covered in a skintight black leather riding suit. But topping this body was not a human head, but a catlike beast with sleek, dark red fur. Here, for the first time, Haruyuki remembered the Japanese meaning of the English name *Leopard*.

The feline-headed female rider glanced down at Haruyuki's lizard avatar with eyes that glowed a faint gold. "Akihabara Battle Ground. The Burst Linker duel Holy Land."

"H-Holy Land...?" he repeated before a thought struck him.

"So, Akihabara? Does that mean this is a Yellow Legion base or something?"

"No. This is the only neutral place in Akihabara. Follow me." She walked away, boots ringing out against the hard floor, so he started after her.

At the very back of the bar was a counter, naturally made of steel plating. Blood Leopard slid down into the center of a stool in a single, smooth motion. Haruyuki climbed up onto the one next to her with a heave-ho of his lizard body.

"Evening, Matchmaker."

An avatar popped its face up on the other side of the counter at Pard's quiet voice, and Haruyuki immediately shouted to himself, *A dwarf!* Stout and short of stature with a scraggy beard, wire-rimmed glasses over sunken eyes and a huge bow tie around his neck...He looked so much the dwarf it was strange he wasn't holding an ax in his sturdy hands.

The dwarf avatar first looked at Pard's leopard head and hoisted a single eyebrow before looking next at Haruyuki's lizard head and humming nasally. He looked back at Pard and grinned.

"Well, here's a sight for sore eyes. How many months has it been, Leopard?" An incredible baritone, the perfect dwarf voice. But the person connected to this net and controlling the avatar had to be a Burst Linker, too, which meant that even if he was one of the most senior ones, he couldn't have been more than seventeen. But it was probably rude to be noticing things like that.

Pard shrugged lightly. "Eight months."

The dwarf, who apparently went by the name Matchmaker, laughed and his beard shook again. "Guess you're missing the shoots here. Or you just looking to earn a little pocket money?"

"Sorry, I didn't come to duel today. Or bet."

At this, Haruyuki reflexively asked, "B-bet?!"

The dwarf raised an eyebrow and indicated the huge central monitor with a jerk of his beard. "You saw those numbers, yeah? You saying those look like anything other than odds?"

"Odds..." Now that the dwarf mentioned it, that was exactly it.

The 1.57 and the 3.22 after the duelers' names were nothing other than the stakes for a bet. So then this place was like a bookie for Burst Linker duels.

"Wh-what on earth could you bet? N-n-not burst points?" he asked in a hoarse voice, and the dwarf snorted loudly.

"Idiot. You let people bet points, some jerk gets carried away and ends square at forced uninstall. Bets are in real money, obviously."

"R-real money..." That was still plenty risky. This kind of privately operated gambling hall was completely illegal. Haruyuki flapped his mouth open and shut, and the Matchmaker grinned suddenly.

"Kid, you got any idea how much the leopard-headed lady here's earned?"

"Don't give him the wrong idea. The only thing I earned here was money from fighting; I've never made a bet, and even if you win, it's five hundred yen a match. Way less than what I get at work."

"...F-five hundred yen," Haruyuki repeated, dumbfounded.

The dwarf laughed gleefully. "Well, that's how it is. Betting, max is three hundred yen a match. Pretty much the best you could do on a student's allowance."

"...R-right..." Haruyuki finally relaxed the slightest bit, and then Blood Leopard put him back on the edge of his seat.

"Enough small talk. Let's get straight to it."

"Impatient as always, Leopard. If you're not here for a match or to bet, then why'd you come?"

"Came for information. Wanna know about the local net troll...the Burst Linker who can block the matching list even when connected to a net."

His reaction was striking. The instant he heard Pard's request, a sharp light came glinting into the dwarf's eyes, and he quickly looked up and down the counter. After checking that there were no other divers within hearing range, he squeezed out an even lower voice. "Where'd you hear about list blocking? The rumors running around now aren't so detailed as that."

This time, it was Blood Leopard's brow that furrowed. "I'm asking the questions here."

"Hmph. Guess so. In that case, you don't need to pay me for this story, just tell me yours in exchange."

"'Kay, as much as I can."

The Matchmaker nodded sharply, leaned into the counter, and began to talk in a voice like a groan from deep in his beard. "The Burst Linker blocking the matching list. He's a huge problem behind the scenes here right now."

"So listen, kid," the dwarf said, turning toward Haruyuki, who was visiting this place for the first time. "Akihabara BG's a local net. You can only connect to it from inside the Quadtower arcade. If you want to be a betting match here, you gotta come here and register as a player at the counter. Then the system weighs level and compatibility to select the optimal duel opponent and displays the match time and odds in the center of the monitor.

"If you wanna bet, you put a maximum of three hundred yen on one of the two right up to the cutoff time. After that, immediately before match time, one of the players accelerates, selects their opponent from the matching list, and the duel begins. That's the basic structure. Simple, yeah?

"The biggest rule on this local net is, only the players who've been matched up are allowed to duel. Break that rule, and a very competent bouncer will take down the better or whoever it was who went and challenged someone to a duel—in a duel, natch—and chase you out. This place is the dueler's Holy Land. Even the ruler of Akihabara, the Yellow King, can't touch anyone in here."

"So anyway." After taking a gulp of the liquid in a tumbler that had at some point appeared on the counter, the Matchmaker continued. "About a week ago, this rude bastard shows up and challenges one of the duelers right before the announced match was supposed to start. Without registering as a player. Akihabara BG's set up so that all the divers have to show their ID when they connect initially, so the moment the guy showed up again the other day, the bouncer accelerated to send him packing. So then, see? He was definitely connected to the local net, but…his name wasn't on the matching list."

Haruyuki inhaled sharply. The situation the Matchmaker was describing. It was exactly the same as what was happening on the local net at Umesato Junior High.

Draining the glass of the amber-colored liquid, the dwarf set it down on the steel plate of the counter. "That day, too, the bastard jumped into the match, took the player down, and then logged out cool as a cucumber. And then the next day. And the day after that. Right now, I'm explaining it away to the players and the customers as a glitch in the match registration system, but I'm at the end of my rope here. And rumors of the 'local net troll' are spreading like wildfire. If I can't stop this guy running wild like this, it could mean the end of Akihabara BG."

"Uh, um." Gulping hard, Haruyuki asked timidly, "What's the name of this Burst Linker who doesn't show up on the list?"

The name the dwarf uttered with annoyance was "Rust Jigsaw."

It's not him. Haruyuki sighed unconsciously, but if it wasn't him, then he had a different problem. Because that meant that there was more than one Burst Linker with the ability to block the matching list like Nomi could. In the Brain Burst system, this privilege was too huge.

The Matchmaker whispered similar misgivings. "You don't get to pick your duel opponent. That's the fundamental principle of the Accelerated World. You might wanna pick out only guys you're good with, but you never know when one of them's gonna show up on the list. And while you're waiting for your perfect match to show, you get sucked into a duel with someone you're bad with. Happens all the time. That's why all us Burst Linkers polish our special skills and work hard to overcome our trouble spots."

"That's exactly it."

"So this Rust Jigsaw is using the Akihabara BG system right

now to pick out whatever opponent he wants. You just look at that monitor there and you know which Burst Linkers are gonna be connecting at what time. All that's left is to pick someone you're sure to win against and challenge them right before the match starts. Bastard's already earned more than a hundred points in duels here alone. As the Matchmaker...and as a Burst Linker, I definitely can't let this stand." Concluding his painful story, the dwarf glared round eyes behind round wire frames at Haruyuki and Blood Leopard. "And that's the long and the short of it. So now it's your turn to tell. The only ones who're supposed to know about Rust Jigsaw blocking the matching list are me and my bouncer, so where the hell'd you hear about it?"

"Um." Haruyuki glanced up at Pard and then moved his lizard mouth haltingly. "It's not got anything to do with this place. On a local net I usually connect to, another Burst Linker with the exact same ability showed up. And I just thought maybe someone in Akihabara would know..."

"What? At the same time, another one?! That can't be a coincidence." The dwarf groaned lightly before asking the obvious question. "Where's the local net?"

"I-I'm sorry. It's connected with my real info, so..."

"What? Then I'm basically the only one talking here, ain't I?!"

"Matchmaker," Pard said abruptly in a quiet voice. "What's this Rust Jigsaw's level and type?"

"Hmm? Level six, same as you. Color's just like the name says: rust. So you got that in common, too, but his fighting style's different. Guy's hunting short-range types, leaving the mid- to long-distance ones, so you being mainly close-range, to be honest, pretty poor compatibility."

Pard's a close-range type? Even though she belongs to the Red Legion, and the name "blood" seems pretty red, too?

Blood Leopard's next words blew this momentary question away. "'Kay. Then instead of paying you for the info, I'll do this. Me and the kid will register as players for a tag match and restrict opponents to long-distance-type teams. If on top of that, you cancel all the remaining matches, Rust Jigsaw'll have no one else to attack, so he should pick us as today's prey."

"Wh-wh-wha—?!" Haruyuki nearly fell off his stool and hurried to grab on to the counter.

The dwarf turned suspicious eyes on him once again. "Leopard, your name's more than enough to be decent bait. Just who is this new kid already?"

"Maybe more famous than me." Pard let slip the faintest hint of a smile and whispered into the dwarf's ear, "This kid's the shining crow of the reformed Nega Nebulus."

Hyoo! The low sound was the Matchmaker half whistling from behind his beard.

Haruyuki and Blood Leopard opened their Brain Burst option menus and registered each other as a tag team. This way, when one of them was called into a duel, they would both automatically be connected to the stage. You could check on the matching list whether or not a Burst Linker was joined up in a tag team, and a solo Linker could challenge a tag team, but the converse—a tag team taking on a solo Linker—was naturally not possible.

When the names Blood Leopard and Silver Crow appeared as a team on the large monitor in the center of the bar, the floor erupted into commotion. Cries like "Hey! Promi's Leopard's fighting!" and "Why is she teaming up with NN's crow?!" rose up all over the place, and the odds numbers immediately started to move.

They shifted from the counter to a dim table in the corner, and Haruyuki decided to ask a few questions while they were waiting for the match to start. "Um, why a tag match? The problem Linker, Rust Jigsaw, he's a solo act, so he's not gonna charge in on two opponents, is he?"

"Not necessarily." Pard shook her head briefly, after touching the cocktail glass to her leopard mouth. "The level difference is calculated from the tag-team total, not the average, so if you challenge as a solo, you're not out that many points if you lose, and if you win, you get a ton of them. Rust Jigsaw seems to be focused on points, so there's a very good chance he'll think we're very tempting prey. My name's fairly well known as a close-range type, and Jigsaw seems to specialize in close-range hunting, so there's no disadvantage for him compatibility-wise. And…" Here, she flicked golden eyes toward Haruyuki and closed her mouth once, before opening it again to continue. "Pretty big rumor has it you can't fly anymore. If Rust Jigsaw knows that, the chances he'll attack are even better."

The concern Blood Leopard had shown, even if it was momentary, over the fact that he had lost his wings was hard to bear, but it also made him happy. He hurried to say something. "Right. If he kills me right away, then it's just a regular one-on-one with you."

Nodding slightly, Pard brought her glass to her lips once more, and Haruyuki followed suit, gulping down his virtual cocktail. He scowled at the bizarre taste as he thought.

Hypothetically, if this Rust Jigsaw were connected with Dusk Taker, he had no reason to be worried about Jigsaw learning anything about Silver Crow here. Dusk Taker was, after all, the very person who had taken his wings and weakened him like this.

He checked that they still had a while before the start of the match and voiced his next question. "Also…maybe I'm getting ahead of things, but…even if Rust Jigsaw isn't showing up on the matching list, the fact that he's connected to this local net means that he has to be somewhere in Quadtower in the real world, right?"

"Yes."

"Then can't we do something to find this real self?"

Pard shrugged her leather-clad shoulders lightly. "It's an arcade from the ground floor to the third floor and a dive café from the fourth to the sixth. At this hour, there are hundreds of people here, very high density, so identifying him would be difficult. But…"

"B-but?"

"There might be a way."

"H-how?!"

"I'll explain later. More importantly..." Pard's body next to him on the sofa moved fluidly, bringing her leopard mouth near Haruyuki's lizard ear. So quietly, it would be impossible for any other diver to overhear, she whispered, "As long as your enemy doesn't use it, you can't use the Incarnate System."

He flinched and nodded. "R-right," he couldn't help but add. "That's what the Red King said. But...but why is that? I do think it's not fair for just one side to use that power. It's way too strong. But if your opponent's breaking the Brain Burst rules—"

"No, it's not for your opponent's sake. It's for yours."

"Huh?"

Now that you mention it, Niko said basically the same thing, didn't she? he thought.

Pard brought her body even closer, and she stared into Haruyuki's eyes from an extremely short distance. "The Incarnate is born from the hole in your heart. When you pull power from it, you also get pulled into the hole bit by bit. If you ever lose that tug-of-war, you'll be swallowed up by the darkness at the bottom."

"D-darkness?"

"The will of the first Chrome Disaster, the Incarnate running wild, was what produced the cursed Armor of Catastrophe you fought. And the kings know that, which is why they've been trying for years to keep the existence of the Incarnate System quiet."

Haruyuki stiffened once again. The Incarnate, the will was generated from hope with a missing necessity as the source—the Red King Niko had said that, too. And that you couldn't learn Incarnate unless you faced your own mental scars.

"But," Haruyuki said slowly, as if talking to himself rather than Blood Leopard, "the person who first taught me about Incarnate said that what generated the will was the power of the wish. That the other side of those mental scars was hope."

"That's also true, I think," the red leopard murmured, exhaling softly. "But just like Brain Burst itself, the Incarnate System also has two sides. The other side of hope is despair. When you chase after that power, you absolutely lose something as payment. Your teacher's probably no exception."

Instantly, in the back of Haruyuki's mind, an image of Sky Raker sitting in her silver wheelchair floated up. The legs she had lost, that she would never have again. He blinked his avatar's eyes hard before speaking, half in thought. "Even still, I want to believe. In the will...In the power of the wish. No...In Brain Burst, which saved me."

Blood Leopard, strangely for her, stayed silent for a long time, seemingly on the verge of saying something. Finally, she relaxed her fierce gaze and murmured in his ear, nearly kissing it, "I get it. It's just like Rain said. You...This Accelerated World, maybe you can—"

However, he didn't get to hear the rest.

Just more than a minute before the official start time noted on the monitor, Haruyuki's ears were filled with the dry sound of a lightning strike. Then the text announcing the appearance of a challenger burned red to fill his field of vision.

7

Haruyuki, as the duel avatar Silver Crow, found himself standing on a water tank sticking out from the roof of a building. The city unfolding in all directions around him was colored with countless neon lights, similar to the scene he had witnessed before diving. Lights and lasers from the ground illuminated the clouds hanging low in the night sky, an airship with enormous glowing advertisement panels passed over his head, and commercials in a bizarre language popped up here and there in the town. But this was of course not the Akihabara of the real world. It was a 3-D file re-created from the images in the social camera net. The affiliation was "Downtown."

Haruyuki quickly crouched down and checked the HP gauges in the top of his field of vision. His gauge was on the left, and right below that, the gauge of Blood Leopard, his tag partner, was displayed slightly smaller. And under the gauge glittering in the top right was, as expected, the name Rust Jigsaw.

He caught his breath under his silver mask and stared at the small light blue cursor floating in the center of his vision. The enemy should be in that direction. Luckily or maybe not, as in the Century End stage, entry into buildings was not permitted in the Downtown stage, so he had apparently gotten some distance and relocated himself.

Okay then, first, I gotta hook up with Pard—

As soon as he had this thought, he heard a still voice from behind and whirled around.

"'Kay. We got a bite." Although he heard no footfalls or even sensed her presence, the tall, lean avatar had, in the blink of an eye, popped up right behind him.

Her overall form was very similar to the leopard-headed rider she'd used in the bar. However, rather than the leather, a dark red matte armor covered her whole body. Her mask was bullet-shaped, protruding in the front, with something like ears sticking up on the end on both sides, making her look not unlike a wild feline of some kind. The most conspicuous part of the sleek, smart silhouette was her bulging thighs.

The very nimble-looking avatar crouched down next to him, and Blood Leopard, level six Burst Linker, member of Prominence Legion, continued, "You and I are both close-range types; our enemy, in contrast, is a mid- to long-range. He'll first try to split us up here with a range attack, and then come to take you out. So don't launch any reckless counterattacks; make not getting separated from me your top priority."

"...R-roger." Haruyuki nodded.

Half a second later.

Zzzeeee! An earsplitting vibration approached rapidly from the direction of the cursor, and Haruyuki reflexively leapt back.

After a slight delay, the water tank he had been standing on until then split completely in two. The water gushing out spread out on the roof, and, careful not to step in it, he ran over to Leopard. She had leapt much farther than he had and had her back pressed up against the ventilation tower.

"That just now should have been his long-distance attack Wheel Saw," she explained, words coming almost too fast to hear, and, remembering what the Matchmaker had told them about Rust Jigsaw's abilities, Haruyuki also responded at high speed.

"The technique where he sends a saw blade flying, right? But it's so dark, it's basically impossible to see the actual blade, huh?"

"Our only hope's the sound. It doesn't seem like he can shoot them off in succession, so after we dodge the next one, we go hard."

"'K-kay." He didn't have the time to nod before the whine came at them again.

Straining his eyes—or rather his ears—at the source of the noise, Haruyuki jumped out ahead and to the right. An extremely thin ring spinning incredibly fast whirred by to his immediate left, slicing through the ventilation tower and sending it crumbling to the ground.

Haruyuki had no time to watch it, however; he was desperately trying to keep up with Blood Leopard bounding ahead of him. The red leopard avatar was definitely more than moderately quick. She reached the edge of the building in a few steps, almost as if she were flying instead of running, and threw her body into the sky without a moment's hesitation.

It was nearly twenty meters to the edifice on the other side of the wide road wedged in between the lines of buildings. The leopard flew light as a cloud through the neon-colored air.

She wants me to jump, too?!

Don't think, just go!

Haruyuki pushed this transient thought into his right leg and pushed off with everything he had. The air whistled past his ears, and the roof of the building on the other side raced toward him. His feet dug into the structure a mere ten centimeters or so from the concrete edge. But he didn't get the chance to breathe a sigh of relief. The outline of his enemy was already visible on the roof of the next building over, which was flush against the one he was standing on. The linear silhouette caught the lights of the town and glittered a rusty red.

Rust Jigsaw! Haruyuki shouted in his mind. *Are you Nomi's— Dusk Taker's friend?! Are you blocking the list the same way?! What the hell is your secret?!*

Almost as if laughing at Haruyuki's frustration, Rust Jigsaw spread his hands very broadly and turned deftly aside, retreating to a building behind him with unexpected speed.

"As if I'd let you get away!" Haruyuki cried in a low voice, and he stepped into a fierce dash. He might not have his wings, but he could still catch a long-distance type with his speed—

"Stop."

If he hadn't eased up on the gas pedal the slightest bit at her sharp call, his head would no doubt have gone flying.

Suddenly, something hit his throat hard. Something thin and biting. Then a whining vibration assaulted him, and orange sparks scattered like blood. His HP gauge was crunched down, together with his neck armor.

"Ngh!" Clenching his teeth, Haruyuki twisted his body as far as he could to escape whatever it was that was cutting into his neck. Pitching backward, he could definitely see something: an extremely thin line floating horizontally in the air right where Rust Jigsaw had spread out his hands a few seconds earlier.

A jigsaw.

He crashed to the roof on his backside and Blood Leopard grabbed his arm. She had no sooner yanked him to his feet when a round blade came flying from off in the distance to slice through the very place where he had fallen.

After dragging Haruyuki to the shadow of a massive billboard, the leopard said, astonished, "Good thing you're a metallic color."

"S-sorry, I forgot. That was his other technique?"

"Steel Saw. Fixing a jigsaw in midair." Her gold eyes glittered sharply beneath her pointed mask, and Leopard continued, "He keeps us at a distance with the fixed saw and attacks from far off with the round one. He really is the natural enemy of close-range types."

"Wh-what should we do?"

The big cat thought for a moment. "Give me your special-attack gauge." Without giving Haruyuki the time to react, she snapped open the mouth hidden behind her mask and bit hard into Silver Crow's shoulder with needle-sharp teeth.

"Eeah?!" Haruyuki shrieked and was even further astounded by what happened then. His special-attack gauge, down to

30 percent or so thanks to the earlier damage, quickly drained, while Blood Leopard's increased at the same pace.

Once she had stolen every pixel from his gauge, the leopard released him and shouted, "Shape Change!!"

On both hands on the concrete surface, the avatar shone a momentary deep red before transforming from a human being on all fours to a completely quadrupedal beast. Her back was long and slender, her shoulders swelled with strength, and her rear legs were folded in a Z shape, hiding enormous power.

"Wh-wh—"

"Get on," Blood Leopard said to the thrice-stunned Haruyuki, in a voice with stronger animal effects applied to it.

Since the only thing he knew for sure was that she would bite him again if he stood there all spaced out, Haruyuki jumped onto the back of the massive beast as if in a dream. The leopard crouched down, and, avoiding the next Wheel Saw that came flying at them from the side, she leapt off in a straight line into the night sky glittering with neon.

"Ngh!" Haruyuki unconsciously yelped in his throat. Her dash was beyond fast. With each push of her powerful legs, they leapt a solid ten meters. Countless decorative lights melted into thin lines and flowed past on both sides of his visual field.

Suddenly, when they had run over too many rooftops to keep track of, Rust Jigsaw's black shadow rose up before them. He twisted around and opened both hands, a gesture he repeated over and over as he ran. The space in which he did so was likely frozen with lethal jigsaws, but moving at this speed, Haruyuki noted with apprehension that he couldn't see them.

Abruptly, the leopard bounded in a huge leap to the right. Landing on all fours behind a billboard illuminated by a spotlight, she then took off toward the left to kick down the neon tower there and head to the right again. They were definitely closing in on the enemy, despite the fact that he was running in a straight line, while at the same time avoiding the spaces where Jigsaw had probably placed Steel Saws with his large jumps.

When they were only another three—no, two jumps away, Rust Jigsaw turned around and showed them something new. He drew a large circle in the air with his right hand and waved it directly at Haruyuki and Blood Leopard.

Zzzeeee! The same vibration noise. Wheel Saw. But in the middle of a jump, there was no way Blood Leopard could avoid it—

"Take care of it."

Haruyuki heard her voice from below him, and he reflexively responded, "'Kay."

The circular saw was an immensely powerful cutting weapon, but even still, it had its weak points. If it was like the ring that had nearly taken Silver Crow's head off, there should be no teeth on the inside. And more importantly, it was slower than a bullet.

Of course, if he hadn't seen Jigsaw launch it, he wouldn't have been able to get the timing right. But his eyes picked up the extremely thin line slicing through the primary colors of the night sky in the nick of time. Just as it was on the verge of hitting Blood Leopard's right shoulder, he thrust his hand into the ring from the side as hard as he could.

Shhnk! came the sharp metallic squeal, and sparks scattered from his fingertips. But his slim fingers were not cut off, and he yanked the ring of fifty or so centimeters in diameter and changed its trajectory so that it flipped off into the distance behind them.

His attack sidestepped so daringly when it was so close to its mark, Rust Jigsaw took on a faintly agitated air.

"GJ," Blood Leopard said simply before taking off in one final bound.

They swooped down on Rust Jigsaw from the front as he had his arms spread out, trying to place a jigsaw in the air. Blood Leopard buried her open jaws deeply in his shoulder.

At the intense impact, Haruyuki was knocked off and fell on his backside, where he watched in amazement the battle/hunt unfolding before his eyes.

"Guh!" Rust Jigsaw—an avatar that looked like a collection of steel frames—let out a low groan as he intently beat at the red leopard hunched over him. But the giant teeth biting deep into his right shoulder held fast like a vise.

If Rust Jigsaw had been a close-range type, he might have been able to turn the situation around. Each time he landed a punch, Leopard's HP bar did indeed go down, but his was disappearing at a much faster rate. A light effect generated by the damage periodically gushed from the bitten shoulder, red so that it looked almost like real blood. Jigsaw twisted and struggled, but even when he did manage to break free of the teeth, Leopard immediately leapt up to sink them right back in, clearly having no intention whatsoever of allowing him to escape.

After one such attempt—

"Unh...Aaah!!" Rust Jigsaw couldn't suppress the scream that welled up from below his mask. At the same time, Haruyuki heard an unpleasant metallic *snap*, and Rust Jigsaw's right arm was ripped from the socket and fell to the ground.

And with all the damage from that loss, he blew through the rest of his HP gauge. The avatar exploded into a million pieces in that familiar, glass-shattering effect. The text You WIN!! flamed to life in the center of his visual field, but Haruyuki could not stand up.

...Holy shit, she's strong!! This was the only thought swirling in the back of his frozen brain.

The enormous leopard, who had just slaughtered their enemy with her teeth, abruptly raised her head and looked at him with golden eyes. "GG," she said.

And then the acceleration ended.

Enduring a momentary vertigo as the sensations of his body returned, Haruyuki couldn't immediately remember what his real-world self was doing, and where.

Thus, as he was about to open his eyes, he couldn't even begin to guess at what the deeply elastic something was up against his face. He reflexively squeezed his eyes shut again, his body stiffening as he wondered just what it was, when his collar was yanked.

"Get up," a sharp voice commanded.

His eyelids instantly flew open. He was, of course, in the recliner in the one-person booth in the dive café on the fourth floor of Quadtower. The default setting for Brain Burst was to release a full dive along with the acceleration once a duel was finished, so they had returned to the real world, instead of the bar in Akihabara BG.

The girl in the maid's outfit who had dived with him from the same chair was already standing and unlocking the booth door. The instant it was open, she poked her head out slightly to check in each direction.

Wondering what she was doing as he slid out of the chair, Haruyuki felt his consciousness chill all at once at the words that followed.

"Let's go. We might be able to identify him still."

Identify. Who? No, it was obvious. *Rust Jigsaw in the real. But how on earth...*He shelved the question and chased after the now-familiar plait swinging against the back of the maid's uniform.

Briskly but cautiously, Blood Leopard headed for the elevator. She pressed the DOWN button, and they had barely even gotten in the cab before she was talking and talking at tongue-twister speeds in a low voice.

"I did consecutive damage to the right side of Jigsaw's neck earlier. With that kind of pain stimulation in one spot over a long period, the effect remains for a short time even once you burst out. Look for someone near the entrance looking like that spot is causing him pain."

"R-roger." That was a seriously terrifying way of marking someone. But it was probably the only way to make some kind of mark on the real-world body of an enemy in the Accelerated World.

When the elevator stopped at the first floor, Haruyuki swallowed hard as he walked through the boys and girls acting out their fights on the game machines in the real. He shot his eyes around with the bare minimum of movement, but he didn't see anyone doing anything with their neck. They were all just staring in a trance at the flat, old-school monitors.

Slipping through the floor, Haruyuki and Pard stepped from the building into the throng of the street. They exchanged glances and then wordlessly split up. Heading down the left side of the street, Haruyuki concentrated all his mental powers on the dozens of passersby entering his field of view.

The girls dressed as game characters handing out holopamphlets. The three young people standing at the end of the road, engrossed in conversation. The guy walking restlessly, weighed down by multicolored paper bags—

Haruyuki's eyes were drawn to the back of a boy he glimpsed on the other side of this crowd. Because he could see the pale neck with no Neurolinker attached to it. With a start, he strained his eyes and saw that the boy's raised left hand was firmly pressed to the right side of his neck.

Is that him?! Quickening his pace, Haruyuki chased after the boy as he grew distant. Gray team jacket. Faded jeans. Leather cap on his head. Dark brown hair sticking out. Head hanging, the boy was hurrying toward the station. With his left hand still on his neck, he pushed his right hand through space, as if to shove aside the passersby.

Wondering if he shouldn't call Blood Leopard, Haruyuki turned around for an instant, but her maid's outfit was lost in the crowd and he couldn't see her. Giving up on that, he turned to face forward again—

"I hope you'll join us!" a cute voice chirped, and a hand was thrust in front of him, blocking his way forward. Lifting his face with a start, he was greeted by the smiling face of an older girl advertising some shop. She was probably handing out holopamphlets, but not connected to the global net, Haruyuki couldn't see anything. He shook his head in apology and slipped by her hand. But...

"H-huh…" He couldn't see him. The gray-team-jacketed back had disappeared.

Dammit! Biting his lip, he quickened his pace and scanned the area intently. But maybe the boy had turned a corner somewhere because no matter how far forward he went, Haruyuki couldn't find him. He hurried to retrace his steps, peeking in the narrow alleys to the left and right, but the boy was indeed gone.

"Ngh!" Out of options, he simply stood there, still biting his lip, while the people on the street pushed by looking annoyed at the obstruction. But their irritated faces didn't register with Haruyuki, either. Only bitter regret and self-reproach filled his heart.

You let your hard-won clue get away.

"Pretty great just seeing his back," Blood Leopard said when they met up again, but Haruyuki, leaning against the wall of a building, couldn't look her in the eye.

"I'm sorry. You worked so hard for me." Self-hatred at his use-lessness during the duel and in the chase afterward weighed heavily on his shoulders.

"You worked hard, too." He felt a hand on his unkempt hair.

"Huh…" He raised his face unconsciously, and something remotely resembling a smile bled onto the lips of the older girl, whose face had until then been perfectly blank.

"You fought wonderfully," she whispered. "I'll tell the Match-maker what you saw of the guy from behind. If we can pick him out in the real the next time Jigsaw shows up, we might be able to learn the secret of list blocking by monitoring him after that. As soon as the logic's clear, I'll send you the information."

"O-okay."

So maybe, just maybe he could still cling to a thin shred of hope? He comforted himself with this thought and at last returned her smile, although his was likely full of self-pity.

Pard shifted her hand from his head to his shoulder, and her expression returned to its normal nothing. "Jigsaw definitely won't show up again today. And it's getting to be time for children to be getting home."

Pard was at most in eleventh grade, but she compelled him to nod obediently somehow. "Okay."

Blood Leopard put an end to the night's adventures in her usual clipped way. "'Kay. Let's go."

They left the increasingly busy Electric Town as the clock struck eight, and, immediately returning to Kannana from Mejiro Street, Pard took him straight to Suginami.

"Here's fine," Haruyuki told her right around the time the elevated Chuo Line came into sight, and got her to let him off. Returning the helmet, he once again bowed his head deeply. "Um, thank you so much. Really. Spending this much time on another Legion's problem…"

Here, Pard took off her own helmet and shook her head lightly. "Akihabara BG's an important place to me, so it's my problem, too, now. Besides—" She cut herself off and averted her eyes for a moment, a somehow bashful look coming over the face of the Burst Linker in the maid's outfit. "I wanted to say a proper thank-you to you. You protected Rain—my king—when Chrome Disaster happened. Thank you."

"Huh…"

"I hope you stay friends." And then Blood Leopard smiled her first clear smile since they'd met, before pulling her helmet back on. The motor roared as the large bike spun around in a U-turn into the opposite lane, and she raced off to the north at an incredible speed.

He watched until her taillight got lost among the lines of vehicles, bit down hard on his lip at all the feelings belatedly welling up in him, and bowed his head deeply, even more deeply, one more time.

Returning to his deserted home, Haruyuki dropped his bag on the floor in his room and practically threw himself down on his bed.

Wonder how Taku's doing. The thought was in his brain, but it was too much to move his hand to make the call. A physical and mental exhaustion exploded in him and then settled heavily on his back.

He stayed still like that for a while, eyelids gradually growing heavier and heavier, so he shook his head hard and yanked himself up. He couldn't go to sleep now. He needed to talk to Takumu while his memories of Akihabara were fresh, and he hadn't even touched that day's homework yet.

He took off his uniform, and after using that as an excuse to have a shower, he warmed up a frozen seafood casserole in the microwave. While he waited for it to be done, he connected his Neurolinker to the global net and placed a voice call to Takumu.

"Hey, Haru." The voice that replied seemed to be the same as always, and he breathed a sigh of relief.

"'Sup...You okay? You remember all the stuff up until today?" Haruyuki asked nervously in neurospeak, but the air of a wry grin came through the connection.

"Hey, hey, I wasn't under for as long as all that. Although I did dive for a full week."

"A-and your Incarnate training was good...?"

"Yeah." A short groan of a voice. *"Although the Red King's call was that I still have a long way to go before I can use it in a real fight. But I got the trigger at least."*

"You did? You're such a perfectionist, though. Don't go diving all by yourself in the Neutral Unlimited Field and spend however many years training!" Haruyuki said, breathing a second sigh of relief, and Takumu laughed again.

"I definitely don't have the energy left for that. Anyway, what about you? You get anything on Dusk Taker and his list-blocking secret?"

"That turned out a whole lot different than I expected."

Haruyuki told him the series of incidents from the moment he left the isolation room at the cake shop, summarizing and simplifying the parts related to Blood Leopard as much as possible. Even still...

"Hmm. So while I was all sad and alone doing my training, you

were on another date with an older girl, huh?" was Takumu's first comment.

"I-it wasn't like that at all!" Haruyuki hurried to protest. *"A-and anyway, you were with Niko for a whole week—"*

"Sorry to say, she only instructed me at the beginning and at the end. For the rest of it, she said something about how she had come all this way, so she might as well hunt some Enemies to earn points and disappeared."

"Sh-she did, huh?" Before the conversation veered into even stranger directions, Haruyuki wrestled it back on topic. *"Anyway, about the list-blocking mechanism. Because I flubbed up and lost sight of Rust Jigsaw's real self, all we can do now is wait for news from the manager of Akihabara BG."*

"The Holy Land of duels? I've heard the rumors. So it really does exist, huh, the underground stadium?"

"Although the amounts you bet and the fight money aren't really any kind of underground prices."

"If we weren't dealing with all this, I'd want to go hang out there." Takumu paused for a moment and then sent a voice that sounded consoling. *"Whatever the results, I think you did great, Haru. Nice work. Let's just hope now that the manager over there gets something on that mechanism soon."*

"Guess so. Thanks."

"I brought your umbrella home, too, by the way. Okay, see you tomorrow at school."

The connection ended, and taking a deep breath, Haruyuki pulled the now-warmed casserole out of the microwave and ate it by himself. He then cleared the table and started in on his homework in his room, but he couldn't concentrate right away the way he usually could.

Today, he would crack Nomi's list-blocking system; tomorrow he'd attack and they'd duel, and with Takumu, who would have mastered Incarnate, they would destroy him together. Somewhere in his heart, that was the way he had expected—no, assumed—that things would play out.

Unfortunately, that was now impossible. Leaving the situation as it stood another day meant Nomi got to spend that much more time with Chiyuri. It was too much to bear when he imagined the two of them talking, even just a single conversation.

Haruyuki shook his head several times and tried to turn his focus on nothing but the holowindow before his eyes. But even as he struggled to translate the English text, the weight pushing heavily on his heart didn't seem to be going anywhere.

Almost as if to mock his impatience, in the evening of that day, April 17, the tag team Dusk Taker and Lime Bell made their real debut in the Accelerated World. Haruyuki heard it from Takumu's mouth the following day.

Instead of Suginami, the pair invaded the Shinjuku area, the western Tokyo dueling mecca. A tag team putting Lime Bell's healing ability with Dusk Taker and his ultimate combo technique of flying and long-distance flame power was the very definition of *invincible*, and the team thoroughly decimated any and all comers.

Nomi's tactic was entirely rational: actively use Chiyuri and her inferior attack power as bait, and then slaughter the enemies coming in to cut her down with his flames. This ruthless strategy had no drawbacks for him, since he wasn't worried about his partner occasionally getting dragged into a ranged attack, and all the Burst Linkers facing them for the first time were turned into piles of ash.

Given that they even came up underdog-style to defeat the two top Blue Legion members who challenged them last, the Accelerated World now thundered the name Dusk Taker, much more loudly than it did at the appearance of Silver Crow six months earlier.

8

"A-a hundred percent win rate?!"

The next day, the eighteenth, Thursday, lunchtime.

Haruyuki raised an astonished voice on a bench that sat upon the roof of Umesato Junior High. "That's…not like a metaphor or something? They really haven't lost once?"

"Yeah." Takumu, seated next to him, nodded, the sandwich he had bought in the cafeteria resting on his knees. "I heard it from someone I know in Shinjuku. She says she watched every duel Nomi and Chi were in right from the first one, so I guess it's true. Once Dusk Taker's gauge is full and he takes to the air, no matter what the duel avatar, he doesn't let them do anything."

Haruyuki stared in amazement for a while at the hamburger he had just bitten into before nodding slowly. "Right, I get it. Close-range types can't get near him in the first place, and with long-distance types, it's a shooting match. It'd be impossible to take out Dusk Taker when he's got a healer."

"Yeah. It sucks for you, Haru, but flying's basically such a huge power that you can't materialize it without throwing away all other potential. But by taking it, Nomi's got the perfect match for his long-range techniques. Right now, he's deviating in unexpected ways from the principle of 'same level, same potential.' On top of that, tactically, he's got no weak points." Peeling back the plastic wrap of the sandwich half automatically, Takumu added in a heavy voice, "Yesterday, it seemed like the high rankers at level seven or eight were watching to see how it played out, so I don't know what'll happen when they show up on the field. But if Nomi ends up winning against even them, the situation's way more serious than we were picturing."

"Wh-what do you mean?"

"Haru, somewhere in our hearts, we've been thinking that no matter how strong Nomi is, once Master—once Black Lotus comes back...she can solve this in a single decisive stroke. But..."

Haruyuki very nearly dropped his hamburger. Reflexively, he gripped it as tightly as he could, and paying no attention to the sauce squeezing out to drip down onto his hand, he cried hoarsely, "T-Taku! Are you saying she'll lose?! Kuroyukihime to Nomi?!"

"It's not like I want to think that! But at the very least, we have to acknowledge that that's Nomi's plan."

Haruyuki realized that Takumu's hand was trembling slightly as he tried to farther peel back the plastic wrap. "Right," his good friend said, almost groaning, pale face turning even paler. "That's probably been Nomi's plan right from the start. He'd chase us into a corner during the week Master's away, hit us where it hurts, and line his ducks up in a row to take her down. It's not even about fighting her. He...*he's trying to hunt the Black King, Black Lotus.*"

"H-hunt?"

"Yeah. I got interested in targeting the Black King way back then precisely because she only had the fighting power of her dummy avatar. I figured if I could just take a few of her points, that kind of thing. But Nomi's different. I know he thinks he can defeat Black Lotus in her true form and take this school—no, even the king's throne..."

"Impossible." Haruyuki shook his head vigorously, as if to chase away the cold sensation crawling up his spine. "As, as if Kuroyukihime would lose to that guy!"

For Haruyuki, the gorgeous jet-black avatar was the lone

absolute presence in the Accelerated World. He sincerely believed there was no way she could lose to any Burst Linker, even another king. It was impossible for his Black King to be defeated by an acceleration user who broke the rules like Nomi. It was impossible, but...

If I were dragging her down...

If an idiot who gets infected with a virus, has secret video taken of him, and even gets his wings stolen were to dull her blades... Or, in the worst case, to have that effect in reality as well—

"Haru." Takumu abruptly clasped Haruyuki's shoulder firmly. "Haru. No matter what Nomi's planning, there's one thing we should do. Before Saturday, we have to do everything we possibly can."

"Everything we can...So what's that? As long as he's blocking the matching list, we can't touch him," he muttered hollowly, and scowled fiercely. "Are you saying we should go to Shinjuku? You want the two of us to challenge Nomi's team and take Chiyu down with him?"

It was Takumu's turn to be silent. Finally, he took his hand from Haruyuki's shoulder, closed his eyes behind his glasses, and whispered, "Don't make me say it."

"...Sorry," Haruyuki apologized after a long sigh, hanging his head. "We can't try to choose between Kuroyukihime and Chiyuri...Let's just believe that right now the people at Akihabara BG and Blood Leopard will get to the bottom of the list-blocking mystery for us."

These words were closer to an entreaty to some god than an actual expectation, but the truth was they didn't have any other options left to them. Even if they went to Akihabara again, all they'd be able to do was basically wander the streets at random.

Haruyuki took a big bite of his crushed hamburger, and as he chomped away, he stared up at the slightly overcast sky.

Haruyuki made it through the two hours of the afternoon somehow, and after he slipped away as always, practically fleeing the chilly air of the classroom, he changed his shoes and gave everything he had to a dash off school grounds. With a feeling like praying, he connected to the global net and checked the anonymous mailbox he had given Blood Leopard, but—

"...Still nothing..."

He knew the situation was not as simple as all that, but that didn't stop a tidal wave of disappointment from crashing over him, and his shoulders fell.

The day after tomorrow, Saturday evening, Kuroyukihime would already be back from Okinawa. He should have been excited for that moment, but right then, that excitement was perfectly matched by the desire for her to stay safely away, if even for just another day.

Forty-eight hours left. In that time, they had to discover Nomi's secret, delete the video, and get Chiyuri back. But the only thing he could do right now was wait eagerly for information.

Tortured by a burning impatience, Haruyuki hung his head as far as it would go and arrived at the road home alone. Takumu definitely couldn't skip practice for a third day, so he was at kendo.

Haruyuki trudged back to the condo under a sky that intermittently dropped rain on him, entered the spacious lobby, and looked up. At that moment, he saw the back of a girl in the uniform of his own Umesato Junior High, standing in front of one of the two elevators at the opposite end of the lobby.

Short hair down to her shoulders. Sports bag slung across her body. Even from behind, Haruyuki immediately knew it was Chiyuri. But why, at that hour? Chiyuri was on the track team, and she normally spent every day after school running around the track until the teachers kicked her out. She shouldn't have been home until a full two hours after Haruyuki, himself a member of the "Go Home" team. And as far as he could tell from seeing her in class that day, she didn't have a cold or anything like that.

Once the familiar back disappeared into the elevator and the door closed, Haruyuki finally got it. She was skipping practice at Nomi's instruction. To duel in Shinjuku this evening, just like yesterday. To keep using her own avatar as bait to lure in the enemy and heal Dusk Taker, who sat safely up in the sky.

"...Chiyu," he murmured, and unconsciously clenched his hands into tight fists. He didn't know what this feeling was, welling up with the heat and density of molten metal from the bottom of his stomach. But, agitated by it, he ran to the elevator and flew inside the instant the door opened. There, he impulsively struck the button for two floors below his, the twenty-first.

When he got out of the elevator car, he ran once again and stopped in front of the Kurashimas' door. Unhesitatingly, he pressed the doorbell button displayed and listened to the tinkling sound effect. Chiyuri would already know through her home server that the visitor was Haruyuki. He waited stubbornly, and finally, he heard the sound of the lock, and the door opened.

Perhaps her mother had gone shopping, because it was Chiyuri herself standing there on the step into the apartment. She looked as though she had been in the middle of changing; her blazer was off and the blue ribbon hung undone from the collar of her shirt.

To all appearances totally calm, Chiyuri tilted her head slightly and uttered a single word. "...What?"

"I came to talk," Haruyuki replied immediately. In truth, he hadn't practiced what he would say, but nonetheless, his mouth moved automatically.

"...That so." Clipped again. Chiyuri whirled around and headed back down the hallway.

Haruyuki held his breath and stepped over the threshold. He quickly took off his shoes and chased after her.

Six months earlier, Haruyuki had also been struck with a similar impulse and come to her house. That time, it was to direct with her and try to see whether or not she was Cyan Pile, the mysterious Burst Linker who was attacking through the Umesato local net at the time.

This time, too, Brain Burst was at the heart of it. Despite the similarity, the situation now was completely different. Chiyuri was the Burst Linker Lime Bell, and on the surface, she stood in opposition to Haruyuki and Takumu of her own free will.

She flopped down on her bed, clutching one of the many stuffed animal cushions laying around—probably a sea creature of some kind—to her knees. "So what's there to talk about?"

Haruyuki stayed standing near the door, and words came out as his mouth moved. "You skipping practice?"

"Yeah."

He met her eyes with an unusual firmness as she gave him the bare minimum of an answer, and further asked, "Did Nomi tell you to?"

"...And if he did?"

"If he did, quit it. It's wrong to put Brain Burst above real life."

Here, for the first time, the expression on Chiyuri's face changed. Her brow furrowed slightly, and she replied in a sour voice, "You're one to talk. Haru, the only thing you ever think about is Brain Burst."

"Th-that's not true. I'm not on any teams, and because of that, I never forget to do my homework."

"And you put the rest of your time into the game."

He held his tongue and Chiyuri suddenly grinned.

"Just stop. It's only a game. Don't get so serious." Her face was cheerful and smiling, but Haruyuki, who had spent a lot longer looking at that face than he had at his own, could see a clear, albeit faint, awkwardness hidden in her expression. But Chiyuri smiled even more broadly and made a peace sign with her right hand.

"It's pretty amazing. Just yesterday, I went up two whole levels. The people in the Gallery said that going from level one to level three in a day might be the fastest ever in Brain Burst. And, I mean, I've got a bazillion invites to Legions."

"...Chiyu." As Haruyuki said her name in a voice that caught in his throat, he took a step forward.

"I'm only skipping practice just right now, so don't worry about it. Once I'm settled enough so I can fight on my own, I'll slow it down. I've already got a pretty good feel for how the duel—"

"Chiyu!!" he half shouted, and words escaped from his throat like they were fleeing his body. "Chiyu, you obeying Nomi, it's because of that video, isn't it?! He told you he'd turn the video he secretly took of me in to the school, didn't he?! If he did, you don't have to worry about threats like that! Nomi can't use it. If he does, I'll reveal his real info to other Burst Linkers, and he knows that. That...He can only use that video to threaten you, not me! So just forget about it!" Even as he spoke, he knew it wouldn't make a difference, no matter what he said.

If Nomi did expose the video, Haruyuki would almost certainly be expelled. Not only that, it was possible he would be arrested and sent to juvenile detention after a family court trial. As long as that possibility actually existed, Chiyuri would continue to obey Nomi. Because she was Chiyuri. Because she was Haruyuki's childhood friend who had always and forever tried to protect him.

She lowered her eyes and stayed silent for a long time before smiling once more. "It's not like that, Haru. I just want to hurry up and get points so I can level up. I told you that the other day, too."

"That's...that's not like you at all!" Haruyuki shouted, eyes at some point starting to well up with tears. "It's me, it's all my fault! Being made to dance like a puppet by Nomi, all my weaknesses uncovered, and on top of that...if he takes you from me, too, what am I supposed to do...?" Dropping to a squat on the floor, Haruyuki hung his head and Chiyuri's voice, similarly wet, reached his ears.

"You don't get it, Haru." He raised his face with a start to see his childhood friend still had a smile on her lips but two thin tear trails dragged down her tanned cheeks. "You don't get anything about me."

"Huh..."

"Nothing...You don't understand anything at all!!" Suddenly

shrieking tearfully, Chiyuri started to do something wholly unexpected. With the fingers of shaking hands, she began to undo the buttons of her shirt, starting at the top.

Frozen before her, Haruyuki swallowed hard as Chiyuri, after a moment's hesitation, ripped her shirt off. Her torso, clad in nothing more than a simple undershirt, was revealed to Haruyuki's gaze without any obstructions of any kind.

A few days earlier, when Haruyuki had been tricked by the visual mask and charged into the girls' shower room, he had seen Chiyuri completely unclothed, but for some reason, seeing her like this in front of him now hammered into his brain with overwhelmingly huge implications.

"...Will you get it if I do this?" Chiyuri whispered, her voice wavering. "Even if my avatar in the Accelerated World is following Nomi, the me in the real world is here...where you could touch me if you wanted to. Do you still not get it? No one's taking me away from you or anything like that." She stared at Haruyuki with tears spilling out of fiercely shining eyes and said, measuring each word, "I move of my own free will. I always have; I always will."

Haruyuki—

—did not get it.

Chiyuri moved of her own free will. What was that supposed to mean? That just like she had been saying, she had determined that, as a Burst Linker, it was more to her advantage to go along with Nomi rather than Haruyuki and their Legion and join up with him to get even more points?

Instantly, Haruyuki realized the burning emotion that had propelled him from the condo entrance to this spot was jealousy. He was supposed to like Kuroyukihime and want Takumu and Chiyuri to work everything out, but just thinking about Chiyuri at Nomi's side, something endlessly black welled up from deep in his heart.

But Haruyuki brushed this feeling aside and simply hung his head. "I'm sorry. Please put your clothes on." He didn't understand Chiyuri's intention. But he decided to trust her. She was probably fighting, too, trying to get out of a bad situation under her own power. He had to believe that at least. If he couldn't believe that after everything she'd said, he didn't deserve to call himself her friend anymore.

He stood up, taking care to not look at the motionless Chiyuri, and turned back toward the door. "I believe you." He said his last words firmly. "So please believe me, too. Nomi's not going to beat me. I'm going to take back everything he's taken." And then he opened the door and took long strides toward his own house.

Stepping out of his living room onto the balcony, Haruyuki placed both hands on the railing and stared out at the urban center of Shinjuku rising up in the eastern sky. Catching the angled sunlight, the government center, which stood more than five hundred meters tall, glittered and sparkled among the other skyscrapers in the herd. Duels were no doubt well under way against the backdrop of these giants. Dusk Taker was steadily increasing his fighting abilities, and there was nothing Haruyuki could do right now about the Accelerated World shouting his name from the rooftops.

As if he would give up now. "…There's still one thing I can do," he murmured, clenching the rail tightly.

And that was *think*. Scrutinize all the information, investigate, hypothesize. No robber could take just this weapon from him. Still in his uniform, Haruyuki felt the cool wind blowing across the twenty-third floor as he began to recall the particulars of how this situation had come about—every single event from the moment Nomi Seiji had started at his school eight days earlier.

It was late that night when Takumu informed him that Dusk Taker hadn't appeared in Shinjuku that day, but rather in Shibuya. The area might have been different, but what he did was exactly the same as the previous day. No midlevel Burst Linkers were able to fight back on first contact with Nomi, who held the most powerful cards imaginable: flight, healing, super flame, etc.

The tag team managed a win rate of 100 percent for the second day in a row, scoring a vast number of points. As a result, Dusk Taker was at level six. Lime Bell had reached level four.

This was no longer a phenomenon that fit in the duel framework. It would have been more fitting to call it an invasion of the existing Accelerated World.

Around the time the sky of Shibuya was red with the flames of war, Haruyuki was still leaning up against the railway of his balcony, intently ponderous.

The playback of his memories went past the mortal combat with Nomi on Tuesday and instead focused in on the scene in Akihabara the previous day and its mysterious Burst Linker, Rust Jigsaw. What *he* was doing was also an invasion of the existing system. He was using the special privilege of list-blocking to earn easy points in the Akihabara BG local net.

So it wasn't necessarily so far-fetched to think that there was some kind of connection between Rust Jigsaw and Dusk Taker. At the very least, they were likely using the same logic to block the list. He again felt a keen regret at losing Rust Jigsaw's real self in the crowd.

Tasting once again the bitterness he had chewed so thoroughly on since the day before, Haruyuki called to mind the figure he had glimpsed from behind. The gray team jacket. The pale neck with the sharp Neurolinker tan. Receding quickly into the distance, rubbing that neck as if in pain.

The boy waved his right hand just as he was on the verge of disappearing from Haruyuki's sight, as if to say that the passersby in front of him were in his way—

The playback of his memories stopped dead on this moment.

He rewound a few frames.

With the outstretched fingers of his right hand, the boy quickly pushed through the air, right around chest level.

Why was this scene bugging him so much? He tightened his

grip on the railing of the balcony and mustered every bit of processing power he had. The feeling he got in puzzle games, that faint clicking in the core of his mind when he touched on a clue that led to a solution, came over him in waves.

Think. Think. Replaying the boy's back over and over and over, Haruyuki unconsciously made the same motion.

Raise his right hand, sweep it to the right.

This movement felt strangely familiar. He waved his right hand again. Wave his right hand. Wave.

This— It wasn't to shoo the person in front of him out of the way. It was the movement to close a window on a virtual desktop.

But the boy hadn't been wearing a Neurolinker. In which case, maybe some kind of retina-projection wearable device? No, in the movie of his memory, there was absolutely no trace of any equipment like that.

So the boy was looking at a holowindow with no Neurolinker and no other device?

Impossible. As far as Haruyuki knew, no supersmall contact lens monitors had been developed, and there was no device that could be embedded in the eye.

Just when he was about to abandon this line of thinking with the idea that he was mistaken, words Nomi had said to him abruptly came back to life in his mind.

"You don't think that the only portable devices in this world are Neurolinkers, do you?"

That was what he had said as he pointed to the small digital camera he had used to secretly film Haruyuki in front of the Umesato shower rooms. It had meant nothing more than that. So why was it bugging him so much now?

"Device…A device other than a Neurolinker," he murmured, touching the aluminum silver device around his own neck.

A VR machine that was not a Neurolinker. They did in fact exist. Around 2020, before Haruyuki was born, you put this enormous headgear on your head. However, the machines of that time were only for full dives. Neurolinkers were the first to actually implement AR of the sort where you could operate a virtual desktop while going about your daily life in the real world—

"No." Haruyuki furrowed his brow. "No, that's not right, is it? The first thing to implement AR was..." He stopped and let his gaze wander through space.

Something in among his vague memories was jabbing at him. Between the initial headgear and the current Neurolinker, there had to have been another kind of device.

After struggling for a while, Haruyuki moved a quiet finger and tapped on the drive icon on his virtual desktop. He dove steadily into the countless data folders within his Neurolinker's local memory. At a very deep level, a folder with the simple name of *F* appeared.

F was for *father*. Here he had saved all the information, or rather memories, he had relating to his real father, a man he had not heard from once since he'd left them way back when. Very few photos. Sound files. Text memos. And a data folder on his father's work that Haruyuki had copied from the home server right before his mother would have deleted it completely.

His father had worked at a key network-related company. He'd almost never made it home, and even when he was home on a rare day off, his vision would be full of work materials; he never bothered to look at anything else.

Remembering that there should have been something about the development history of a VR device among these materials his father had left on the home server, Haruyuki pushed aside the prickly emotions stabbing at his heart as he waded intently through the folder. Finally, he found the file he was looking for and opened it. He traced the chronological text with a finger and scrolled through it.

The first headgear-type VR machine realizing the full-dive technology had come onto the market in May of 2022. The first generation of the current Neurolinkers was released in April of 2031.

The instant his eyes took in the name of a certain device printed between these two in small letters, his heart jumped into his throat and his breathing stopped. The skin covering his body suddenly froze, and Haruyuki grabbed on to the railing as hard as he could with both hands.

No way. Ridiculous. Impossible. But...

It could happen, if you used this. Looking at a virtual desktop without a Neurolinker...and connecting to a local net without one, too.

Lips trembling, he released the words into the air in a hoarse voice.

"...Brain...implant chip..."

Brain implant chip. *BIC* for short.

A wild child existing only for the briefest of moments in the history of wearable VR machines.

The device itself was a small neuroelectronic chip implanted between the surface of the cerebrum and the dura mater. With self-growing terminals placed on the sensory area of the brain surface, the owner was able to use AR displays like the virtual desktop and even do full dives without equipping any external devices whatsoever. In a certain sense, it was the ultimate VR machine, much more so than the Neurolinker. It was developed and put on the market in 2029. However, only a few years later, it was banned within the country.

Because, unlike the Neurolinker, you could never power down a BIC, much less take it off. If, hypothetically, a black hat hacker got into your system, you'd face some extreme difficulties in fighting back. Conversely, if you were to use it maliciously, you could get around rules in a variety of ways. The prime example of this was a high school or university entrance exam, or any kind of certification test really. At the time, Neurolinkers did not yet exist, so the basic principle for entrance exams was no VR machines, but if you had a BIC implant, you could easily get full marks in memorization-type subjects. It was essentially the same as bringing every dictionary and reference book ever printed in with you.

Cases of desperate parents implanting BICs in their test-taking children popped up all over the country, and once the phenomenon spread to the bar exam and the civil servant test, the government was forced to regulate the production and use of BICs. As of the present day in 2047, BICs were illegal VR machines.

Which was exactly why Haruyuki hadn't even considered the possibility when Nomi started at Umesato. Now, however, he had to assume no other conclusion was possible. General use of BICs was restricted, but their manufacture continued for specialized applications, and he had heard that there were even hospitals that would implant "dark chips" diverted into the black market. He had absolutely no idea how a junior high school kid would manage that, but if there was one person who could probably do it, it was Nomi.

Seiji Nomi/Dusk Taker—and probably Rust Jigsaw, too—had a second VR machine on the surface of his brain. It wasn't that Nomi was blocking the matching list while connected to the Umesato local net. He had never connected a Neurolinker with Brain Burst in it to the net.

In other words, he used his Neurolinker as a normal standalone. In so doing, he avoided the supposedly unavoidable duels that were the risk that went hand in hand with the privilege of Brain Burst's power of acceleration, for he could also connect to the network with the BIC. Take the kendo match with Takumu, for instance: While Nomi used the BIC in his head to connect to the local net, he used his unconnected Neurolinker to physically accelerate and dodge Takumu's *shinai*. It was only natural that his name wasn't on the matching list when they looked.

Except for that one moment when he was connected through his Neurolinker rather than the BIC and had used acceleration to get top marks on his social studies test—

"Right...That's right...," Haruyuki squeezed out hoarsely, killing all of the countless windows still displayed in his field of vision with a wave of his hand.

Finally. He had finally gotten it. The only correct answer.

And this information was lethal for Seiji Nomi. You could check for the existence of a BIC with an X-ray scanner. If a chip was discovered in Nomi's brain, his acceptance at Umesato Junior High would definitely be rescinded.

If Haruyuki played this card, he could drag Nomi down to the same place as he was in. To a battlefield without privileges. In which case, there was only one thing left for him to do. Duel him, fight with every bit of strength he could muster—and win.

He stared out at the night sky over the center of Tokyo; Dusk Taker was no doubt soaring through it right about then. "Nomi... This time for sure, I'm finishing this," he said briefly, each word a bullet.

9

April 19.

Friday.

On lunch break that day, just one day before Kuroyukihime's return to Tokyo, Haruyuki proceeded toward the student cafeteria, cut through the rows of long tables, and headed straight for the very back.

His objective was the lounge, a place where, on top of the unspoken rule that only eighth and ninth graders could use it, many of the tables were reserved seats for council members and the champions' club. Haruyuki had, up to that point, not once set foot in it when Kuroyukihime was not there.

However, for now at least, he mustered up the courage to slip through the white gates and walked over to one of the round tables. The students sitting there, having lunch as they chatted pleasantly, noticed Haruyuki's approach and lifted their faces.

As the stars of the swimming and softball teams showered him with the dubious gaze reserved for the obviously out of place, Haruyuki turned toward the lone seventh-grade student, small of stature, back still turned, and began to speak in a low voice. "Nomi. I need to talk to you. Come to the place we first spoke."

And then he turned on his heel without waiting for a reply.

*   *   *

As he waited for Nomi under the gloom of the stand of trees in the courtyard, free from the watchful eyes of the social cameras, Haruyuki recalled the day he had first met the grade seven here.

The lowerclassman, cute like a girl, had declared to Haruyuki with a bright voice and a broad smile that the fight was over. And just as he said, from that moment on, the more Haruyuki struggled, the worse he made his own situation. He struck out at Nomi and was instead beaten down himself; on top of being stepped on, he had his flying ability stolen in a direct duel. Although an upset victory had been within his reach in the rematch after he learned the Incarnate System in the Unlimited Neutral Field, he was forced to even greater defeat because of Chiyuri's unexpected appearance.

Nomi's war even pushed into the real world, where Haruyuki was pushed up against the wall thanks to Nomi spreading the rumor that Haruyuki was the secret camera criminal. In the Accelerated World, Nomi was using Haruyuki's wings and Chiyuri's person to earn vast quantities of points and level up. If this kept up, the Black King, Black Lotus, most likely Nomi's final target as Takumu had said, might even be exposed to danger.

However...

It ends here, Nomi.

He heard branches breaking under footfalls approaching him from behind, and Haruyuki slowly turned around. He stared at the innocent yet cunning smile of the lowerclassman, who appeared from the shadow of a thick oak's trunk.

"That's game over. Seiji Nomi—I mean, Dusk Taker."

"...What did you say?" Smile still playing on his lips, Nomi cocked his head slightly. "Does this then mean that you're admitting your complete defeat? Are you saying, *I give up, so please don't torment me anymore?*"

"No. I mean that this game with you is finished," Haruyuki

replied in a low voice, putting every ounce of force his body had into his eyes, to meet his opponent's teasing gaze.

Nomi's smile gradually faded, and a faint line of displeasure dug in between his eyebrows. "Arita, you really are slow on the uptake, aren't you? I'll concede that you worked hard, learning a stingy little Incarnate attack and finding that firecracker thing you call an Enhanced Armament, but it should be clear by now that this served you absolutely no purpose. All you and Mayuzumi can do now is watch enviously from the sidelines. I will defeat the Black King and rule this school—no, the entire Suginami area."

Nomi's voice was cold, a slicing knife, and Haruyuki shook his head hard to brush the words away. "No. I won't let you do that." He took a step forward and announced curtly, "The reason you don't show up on the matching list is because you have a second VR machine in that head of yours. By which I mean…an illegal brain implant chip."

The sudden change that came over Nomi's face confirmed the correctness of Haruyuki's guess. Both eyes flew open before narrowing grimly. His bared teeth squeaked and several thin lines ran along the bridge of his nose. But he didn't make a move to open his mouth to try and speak, so Haruyuki pushed further.

"If I'm wrong, then go ahead and take off your Neurolinker right now. I know the school register tag I can see won't disappear even if you do."

Nomi and Haruyuki both knew there was no point in him feigning ignorance and saying he had no obligation to do any such thing. If Haruyuki sent in an anonymous tip to the school authorities, Nomi would end up getting a brain scan at the hospital with a member of the school management staff as a witness. It would be completely and entirely impossible to falsify the result. Nomi would then be deemed to have been admitted to the school under false pretenses, and in addition to being expelled, he would be forced to undergo treatment to inactivate the BIC. The damage would be equivalent to or greater than what would happen to Haruyuki if he was "outed" as the secret video criminal.

Not even trying to hide his rage, Nomi glared at Haruyuki. "...Here I thought you were a pig, and the truth is you're a rat, hmm?" he spat in a hoarse voice. "Endlessly darting about, sniffing at everything..."

"Then you should have crushed me at the start. The fact that you didn't is your mistake."

Nomi gradually suppressed the heat of his anger at Haruyuki's retort, and the sneer returned to his lips. "Well, I will give you that. So? What do you plan to do? Is it your wish to fire our missiles and be destroyed together? We'll both be expelled. I'll be sent to the hospital and you to juvenile detention. Moreover, at some point we'll both be attacked in the real and lose Brain Burst. Are you saying that that is the ending you're choosing?"

"If it comes to that. I'm not afraid of that." But clenching fists cold with sweat, Haruyuki opened his mouth to suggest the ending he had spent the whole night thinking up. "Nomi. We each hold a trump card, you with my video, me with your secret. If there is a way to resolve this other than using these cards and destroying each other in the real...it's a duel."

"A duel?"

"Yeah. You and I are both Burst Linkers, after all. Connect to the local net right now through your Neurolinker, not your BIC. Turn off the once-a-day limit and just keep fighting me. Until one of us admits defeat or loses all his burst points. Although I'll tell you right from the start, I have no intention of surrendering until my last point is gone."

And then even if I do lose, after that, it's Taku. And then Kuroyukihime will fight you.

Nomi had to have heard these unspoken words, added on in Haruyuki's heart.

Once more, albeit for a very brief moment, deep anger and irritation rose up onto the face of Seiji Nomi. "Duel. Burst Linker.

Both terms that I despise. No, the very mentality that would seriously use those words is so detestable I can hardly stand it. But... if that is what you desire, then I suppose I have no choice." His expression reverted to his usual faint smile as he leaned back against the oak and flipped a finger up. "But if it's going to be like this, then I have one suggestion."

"...Suggestion?"

"Don't you think it's ridiculous to fight accelerated duel after duel, dozens of times, even hundreds of times if it goes poorly, until one of us loses all his points? And assuming one of us surrenders, what kind of guarantee does that offer?"

"So what are you saying we should do?"

"Let's finish it in one go. The 'final battle' you do so like," Nomi said, gruesome grin cut into his face. "In the Unlimited Neutral Field, there's a way to wager all the burst points of the players on a single match. Two or more duelers charge all their points into an item, and then the last player left standing gets the item and the points. So? Don't you think this is a rather smart way of deciding things?"

Haruyuki stared hard at Nomi's smiling face for several seconds and then shook his head slightly. "Unfortunately, Nomi, I can't trust you that much. I'm sure this is no surprise to you or anything. In the Unlimited Neutral Field, I can't rule out the possibility that you'll ambush me with your friends in the place of the battle."

Nomi spread his hands in a "what am I going to do with you?" sort of way. "I think I'm the one at risk of that! But in that case, allow me to give you two guarantees. The first is that you are welcome to bring Cyan Pile—Mayuzumi. I'll fight you each in turn. And the second is that you can go ahead and postpone the time of the battle immediately before it is to start by however many minutes as many times as you like. That way, it would, in reality, be impossible to ambush someone."

Haruyuki held his breath and thought quickly.

In the Unlimited Neutral Field, time passed at a thousand times faster than in the real world. So for instance, if they initially set a dive for five PM, if he postponed it by ten minutes a few seconds in advance of that, a week of time would pass inside. If he did this several times, the lapsed time would balloon, making it impossible to keep waiting and not go insane. And if you repeatedly broke away with dives in small increments, you would have to use ten burst points each time. No one but a king-class player could sustain that kind of point loss.

The talk of ambushes in the Unlimited Neutral Field made him remember the Yellow Legion's scheme against Red King Niko during the whole Chrome Disaster thing three months earlier, but it wasn't like they had been sitting there waiting for months, not knowing when Niko would show up. In the process of transferring the Enhanced Armament, they had cracked the real of Disaster's true self Cherry Rook, and they had guessed at what time Niko would dive by monitoring *his* movements. Without means like that, setting up an ambush in the Unlimited Neutral Field was impossible—or you would think, anyway.

However, Haruyuki was well aware that his knowledge of the Accelerated World was still far from great, so of course, he didn't give an immediate answer. "If that's what you want to do, I can talk it over with Takumu, yeah?"

"Of course you can. Please do! Go ahead! You go and discuss it to your heart's content." Grinning, Nomi took a step back. "Once you make a decision, please get in touch with me at this address. I'd also like time to prepare mentally." He flicked an anonymous mailing address at Haruyuki, then whirled around and left the courtyard. Haruyuki held his breath and stared at his receding back.

He had a bad feeling. He had assumed this would play out with him hitting Nomi with the single word *BIC* and then they would just jump into the duel straightaway. He felt like Nomi was trying to wrest back control by getting this time now.

After checking that Nomi had disappeared into the school

building, Haruyuki leaned up against a nearby tree and uttered in neurospeak, *"What do you think, Taku?"*

"It's risky," Takumu replied immediately. He had been listening to the whole conversation with Nomi online.

Haruyuki had already told Takumu all about the BIC things he had realized the night before. They had also decided on how to finish things with Seiji Nomi, the idea that first Haruyuki, and then Takumu, would intently challenge him to duels on the local net until Nomi ran out of burst points.

Naturally, it wasn't as though they hadn't considered the possibility that both of them would lose all of their points going up against the level-six Dusk Taker. But if they were defeated in a normal fight—well, that was that. *Once you dive into the battlefield, there is only the fight.* That was precisely the thinking of their master, Kuroyukihime.

However, neither of them had anticipated Nomi's proposal. Takumu repeated once more in a tense thought, *"It's too risky, Haru. We don't know what could happen in the Unlimited Neutral Field. Especially when our opponent is Nomi."*

"So then we ax his proposal?"

Here, Takumu fell silent. Finally, he started in a darker tone, *"But like Nomi says, even supposing he does surrender, we have no guarantees...That still leaves the possibility of him setting up a new trap someday."*

"Hey, Taku. Can you think of any way to set up an ambush in the Unlimited Neutral Field and get around the indefinite postponement of the specified time?"

"Maybe a huge number of burst points," Takumu replied slowly, after another few seconds of silence. *"A huge amount of endurance. There shouldn't be anything other than that. The problem is whether or not Nomi has any friends who would be willing to make such an enormous sacrifice."*

This time, Haruyuki thought for a while before speaking. *"Hmm. There's a good chance he belongs to some kind of organization. The kind that'd make its members have a procedure to get a*

BIC implanted. *That Rust Jigsaw I fought in Akihabara's probably one of them. Neither of them have a tag on their avatar name, so I guess it's not a Legion.*"

"*So like a bunch of guys who efficiently earn burst points with the brain chip and then use them in the real world? Those 'acceleration users' Nomi talked about before, no doubt.*"

"*Right. So would these guys basically be infinitely wasteful with their points and time to help Nomi out of this jam he's in?*" Biting his lip, Haruyuki soon continued. "*No, I can't believe they would be. That bit Nomi said about there being no such thing as freely given friendship is the truth for him. To put it the other way, if he did have friends like that, I'm sure Nomi...would be a better real Burst Linker.*"

These words of his were without any foundation, but Takumu replied quickly with an assenting thought. "*Yeah. You're right. That's exactly it. This is a fight between you and me, Burst Linkers, and Nomi, acceleration user. That's the ground on which our pride stands...Yeah, that's right...*"

For a moment, the shared thought was a white light flowing through the voice call circuit.

Haruyuki nodded sharply and sent a strong thought. "*Okay, then. I'll say yes. The first set time'll be once you and Nomi are done with practice and have gotten back home. So let's say...eight tonight. If we postpone this a minimum of even ten times, that's more than an hour, which should take care of the possibility of an ambush.*"

"*Roger.*"

His shoulders relaxed at the prompt response and Haruyuki added, "*And to be honest, I'm kinda glad to get a one-off fight.*"

"*Heh-heh. That's 'cause you're the overconcentrating type, Haru. I'm counting on you to finish him quickly for me.*"

"*But that'd suck for you after you went to all the trouble of the Incarnate training.*"

They laughed together for a minute, and after a quick "See you after school" back and forth, Haruyuki ended the call.

I'm so glad I have Taku with me. He felt it deep down, and he was thankful from the bottom of his heart that he hadn't chosen to strike the final blow when he and Cyan Pile fought for the first time six months earlier.

After school. Seven thirty PM.

He finished cleaning up the living room and had just pulled his usual frozen pizza out of the freezer to heat up when the doorbell rang. He glanced at the holowindow that popped up, confirmed that it was Takumu's face there, and raced to the entryway. He pressed the UNLOCK button and said to the opening door, "Hey! Right on—"

Before he could finish with *time*, Haruyuki reeled back, mouth hanging open.

Standing behind Takumu with a stern look was another familiar face.

"Ch-Chiyu?!"

Why now, here?

Not even giving him the time to voice this question, Chiyuri, in her street clothes, murmured, "I'm coming in," expressionlessly and stepped up into the hallway. She slid by Haruyuki and walked into the living room.

He stared dumbfounded after her before turning back to Takumu. "Wh-why?"

"I didn't call her. She was just in the elevator with me," Takumu muttered, also having a hard time understanding it. He exhaled a thin breath and closed the door before asking if he could come in with a tilt of his head.

Nodding repeatedly, Haruyuki went back down the hallway with Takumu.

Chiyuri, standing in the kitchen rather than the living room, lifted up the frozen pizza box he had left in the sink. "As usual, eating stuff like this," she said with a small smile. She returned the box to the freezer and held up a bag she had brought with her. "I got Mom to make lasagna again. For the three of us."

She paused for a moment. "Don't worry. It's not poisoned or anything."

The instant the joke reached his ears, a sharp pain pierced his chest squarely in the center and he twisted his face up. *Why do things have to be like this between us?* The thought spun around in the back of his mind. When he averted his gaze, he saw Takumu's eyes also stiffen under his glasses.

Looking away, Chiyuri quickly pulled a heat-resistant container out of the bag and split its contents over three plates. With one plate in her left hand and two adroitly balanced in her right, she headed into the living room. "C'mon, sit down." Smiling, she placed the plate with the slightly larger piece in front of Haruyuki and a plate with a piece about the same size as her own in front of Takumu. She took forks from the cutlery basket in the middle of the dining table and handed them to the two boys.

Compared with last week's Chiyuri, each of these movements was dull, as if her arms were bound by some unseen rope, and Haruyuki couldn't bear to watch anymore.

He accepted the fork and fixed his gaze on his plate. "Thanks," he said in a small voice. "So let's eat."

"Yeah, let's eat," Takumu agreed.

At Chiyuri's "Go ahead," the two began to eat her mother's special lasagna. It was delicious. It was even a cut above the one they had been treated to the previous week. However, the deliciousness just made the pain in Haruyuki's heart all the starker. He felt like he would start crying if he stopped chewing, so Haruyuki moved fork to mouth intently, almost cradling his plate.

Within ten minutes, all three plates were empty. Chiyuri went to do the dishes and then sat back down at the table. She finally opened her mouth to break the silence at 7:50 PM. "Nomi told me to come. To the place of the final battle."

"Wh—"

"Huh?!"

Haruyuki and Takumu spoke at the same time.

After a momentary blank space, his thoughts started spinning at high speed. "H-he did? Right, you're already level four now. So you can go to the Unlimited Neutral Field, too." Foolishly, Haruyuki hadn't even considered the possibility that Chiyuri might show up, too. But he knew Nomi wouldn't hesitate to use Lime Bell to ambush them.

"B-but…how was Nomi planning to tell you the right time?" Takumu's question was totally natural. Haruyuki and Takumu could change the specified time at will and shake off any Burst Linkers lying in wait. Chiyuri was no exception.

Chiyuri dropped her head, as if trying to escape the two sets of eyes pointed her way. "Nomi told me," she muttered. "He told me to meet you guys directly and say I was betraying him. To make you trust me like this and dive at the same time as you guys. He told me to heal him once the duel started."

"…What are you…" Haruyuki clenched his teeth abruptly.

How far will that coward go?! Rage shot through his brain, while an even greater confusion bubbled up in him—what was Chiyuri's intention in confessing all this?

As if sensing his doubt, Chiyuri continued thinly, "But I guess that's too much, huh? After everything that's happened, I'm not especially persuasive. So I…To tell the truth, I wanted to ask you both a favor."

"Ask us…?"

She looked at Haruyuki and Takumu in turn, large eyes veiled with tears. "Please take me with you," she said, enunciating each word. "I have to go. If you say no…Although if that's what you say, there's nothing I can do about it. In that case, I'll just dive into the Unlimited Neutral Field right here and now and wait on the other side until you come. I'll wait however many months, years it takes."

"…Chiyu, you…" He squeezed the words from his choked throat. Naturally, this declaration hit him hard, but hearing the words "Unlimited Neutral Field" come so smoothly from her mouth was even more of a shock. She should still have been a total beginner; a mere week earlier, she hadn't know the first thing about Brain Burst. The question welled up in his heart for the hundredth, thousandth time since this whole thing started.

Why, why? Chiyu, why are you doing all this?! Why are you so stuck on Brain Burst when you were pushing against it so hard before? What do you keep earning points for?!

And yes, Haruyuki couldn't stop himself from even this thought: *What if this is a trap? What if she's betraying us a second time, and this is a strategy to get herself into the final battle and steal our points?*

He honestly didn't know if he could win this fight against Dusk Taker, even one-on-one, but adding in Lime Bell's healing ability against him, his chances of victory essentially disappeared. Just like in the fight on Tuesday.

He didn't know. He couldn't manage to get a handle on what Chiyuri was actually up to.

Breaking the heavy silence was Takumu's quiet voice. "Okay, Chi. Come with us."

"T-Taku..."

Takumu turned toward Haruyuki and smiled gently. "Haru. Six months ago, you saved me in that first fight in the hospital. I'm sure you had your doubts. There was a very real possibility that I was just saying whatever to stay alive, and once the fight was over, I'd immediately try to hunt Black Lotus, still in her coma. But...you forgave me. No, you trusted me. I'll never, ever forget that...which is why..." He took a deep breath, throat trembling, and declared resolutely, "I trust Chi. I hate it that no matter how much I think about it, I can't figure out her real motives... but whatever happens because of what she does, I'll accept it."

In the once-again-silent room, Haruyuki watched Chiyuri's lips move soundlessly. It was just the slight movement of a tremor, but words did in fact reach his ears.

Thank you, Taku.

Haruyuki squeezed his eyes shut tightly. On the screen of his eyelids, the tears she had shown him in her room the day before came back to life.

I move of my own free will.

That's what she had said as tears poured down her face. In which case, the little stuff didn't matter. It was just like Takumu said: Either he trusted her or he didn't. That was the only issue. And the answer was obvious. He had already decided that years before, back when Chiyuri and Haruyuki didn't really talk for real.

"Got it." Haruyuki bobbed his head up and down. "We go. The three of us."

As the clock struck eight, Haruyuki sent the first text mail to Nomi. Dive time 8:05 PM. The place: in front of Koenji Station in the Unlimited Neutral Field.

Of course, both of these would be successively changed going forward. He would send the new instructions mere seconds before the specified time, so even supposing Nomi did have someone lying in wait, it would be impossible for him to communicate the change. The sole risk was that Nomi had his ambush personnel with him in the real, like Haruyuki and his friends, so that they could dive at the same time, but he couldn't believe that Nomi had any friends he trusted that much. To remove this possibility as well, they had considered meeting Nomi on this side as well and then diving, but this proposal was abandoned with the reasoning that leaving their unconscious bodies alone in front of Nomi was even riskier.

Haruyuki kept sending mail after mail, changing the time and place at irregular intervals. The tension he felt while on standby was uncomfortable, like being left for an extensive period in the dentist's waiting room. However, it was probably nothing compared to the irritation Nomi must have been feeling, so he endured it. Nomi couldn't know exactly how many minutes, how many times they planned to drag this thing out.

9:12 PM.

After postponing the fight a full fifteen times or more, Haruyuki finally said, "Okay. We dive in one minute."

"Roger," Takumu replied, and Chiyuri nodded.

A single fight with their cumulative points on the line. No matter how drawn out it got, it wouldn't take more than an hour. In other words, in real time, everything would be over in a mere 3.6 seconds.

Kuroyukihime. Haruyuki's heart called out to her in distant Okinawa. *If I lose, you'll probably be super angry and pretty sad, too. But I know you'll understand in the end. It's exactly because I'm trying to be your knight that I have to do this.*

Five seconds before 9:13.

Haruyuki hit the SEND button on the final mail.

The text: "Place: Umesato Junior High School grounds. Time: Now."

"Here we go!!" Haruyuki shouted, and then the three of them called out the command with one voice.

"Unlimited Burst!!"

10

Night.

An enormous pale disc glittered and glimmered in the black sky. The surface of the earth, the buildings, everything was white as though the color had been drained out. The world wasn't colorless, but more like the shade of dried bone. Square houses cast neat shadows on the broad road. In the distance, the Shinjuku center, transformed into chalk towers carving out spirals, pierced the night sky and soared upward.

"A Moonlight stage?" Takumu—Cyan Pile murmured after looking around at the virtual world of western Tokyo.

Haruyuki quickly listed the characteristics from his memory. "It's bright, but you basically can't see anything in the shadows. Noise carries from far away. Few Enemies. There are no trap-type terrain effects."

"Surprise attacks from a hiding place in open spaces are basically impossible. We were right to choose the school." After nodding at one another, they glanced behind them.

In the empty white space that had originally been the Arita living room stood a quiet Lime Bell, shining a vivid emerald green in the light of the moon. She didn't look any different from when he'd seen her on Tuesday. But in a mere two days, she had been in an incredible number of duels and won all of them, meaning that she had already reached level four, just like Haruyuki and Takumu. They had been at level four for a while, though, so there was probably still a fair gap in the total number of points they had earned, given that Haruyuki and Takumu were on the verge of reaching level five and Chiyuri had barely leveled up to four, but at the very least, their potential should have been the same.

During the short period of this dizzying climb, Chiyuri, as Nomi's healer/bait, had no doubt been exposed to all kinds of attacks from countless Burst Linkers. Haruyuki keenly understood just how difficult and painful that experience must have been.

But she came to stand in front of them in a movement that revealed no exhaustion whatsoever. "Let's go," she said briefly. And then without hesitation, she tossed herself from the terrace, which was the equivalent of the twenty-third floor of the former condo. She fluttered down to the ground using the terraces below and the decorative objects as footholds, all without a trace of a newbie's awkwardness.

Haruyuki and Takumu looked at each other again, and after unconsciously grinning wryly, they flew down the same way. The three avoided the route they usually took to school and trotted down a back road. As they kept an eye out, the two boys smashed objects as they went along to build up their special-attack gauges.

They didn't enter the school from the front but first came out on the roof of the family restaurant on the other side of Oume Kaido and checked out the location of the final battle from the shadows.

Umesato Junior High School had been transformed into something like a medieval European palace. In what was perhaps a gothic style, enormous columns were lined up along the front, and several sculptures of angels and demons jutted out from the walls.

Those can't all be duel avatars, can they? He rubbed his eyes and, after checking that they were all, in fact, stone, he turned to the school once again.

The expansive grounds had become a garden covered by thin tiles in complex patterns. There was not a single object on the field, just the long, thin shadows cast by the lance-like towers—formerly the main pillars of the baseball fence.

"Doesn't look like anyone's hiding here," Haruyuki murmured, and Takumu nodded.

"Yeah. But Nomi's not here, either...Maybe he was a half second behind us on the dive."

"If he doesn't come in five minutes, we'll port out for a bit through Koenji Station...Wait, hold up a sec." The faint sound of the wind reached Haruyuki's ears. The stage was completely windless, so something was moving in the sky. A flying Enemy—or a flying duel avatar. Whirling his head up toward the southwestern sky, Haruyuki froze solid the instant he saw it.

A shadow approached within the night sky aglitter with tiny stars, and then shined white in the moonlight. Slim body. Claws on both hands. And stretching out from his back: devil wings.

Dusk Taker.

"No...mi...," he groaned unconsciously, and, as if drawn by that voice, the avatar began its descent.

Arms crossed, drawing an elegant spiral in the air, he came down in the center of the schoolyard, an almost-silent landing. Just seeing this, Haruyuki knew that Nomi had already completely mastered the flight ability.

The avatar with the marauding attribute slowly folded his wings and stopped moving. Once again, the world was filled with silence.

Haruyuki's senses couldn't pick up any changes. There were no movements of secret approach, no footfalls crawling up from his blind spot, nothing.

After waiting a full minute and more, Haruyuki whispered, "Let's go."

Next to him, Takumu nodded. They stood up at the same time and jumped down onto the street. Dusk Taker jerked his head up at the sound of their feet.

Staring over at him, Haruyuki and his friends entered the Umesato campus through the school gates and headed for the schoolyard, going around the edge of the school. The three avatars' feet *clack*ed against the hard tile. The light of the moon carved sharp shadows behind them.

Rather than entering the courtyard, Chiyuri walked along the southern wall of the school and stood quietly in the shadows. Haruyuki and Takumu moved straight ahead toward the wide-open space of the center, stopping when they were about twenty meters from Dusk Taker. Haruyuki silently shot his gaze toward him.

After a few seconds of this, Nomi uncrossed the arms folded in front of his chest and spread them lightly to the sides. "I suppose I am the one who said it was fine to postpone as many times as you wanted!" Tinged with a metallic effect, the boy's voice echoed lightly in the pale world. "But, honestly, I didn't expect you to drag it out like that, Arita! I'm not sure if I should call you cautious or suspicious."

"By now I've learned that with you as my opponent, I can never be too suspicious."

To Haruyuki's retort, Nomi gave a short chuckle before thrusting his right hand out. Pinched between the tips of his fingers was a single card. It resembled the one the Yellow King had used before to play a video of the past, but this one was red like blood. Haruyuki had heard that the majority of special items sold in the Unlimited Neutral Field Shop were card-shaped.

Nomi waved the card at Haruyuki and Takumu. "The name of this card is Sudden Death Duel. It's fairly expensive, but I'll make it my treat." He laughed once again. "First, I'll charge it with all the points I have. The remaining two fighter slots are set to team, so please, both of you wager your points as well. At the point when my HP gauge becomes zero, if you are both still alive, all the charged points will be evenly split between the two of you. If there's only one of you, then he gets them all. And at the point when I defeat both of you, I get the points."

"In other words, if the both of us survive, there's no need for us to fight each other, right?"

"Precisely. Call it a little forethought on my part. The key critical factor here is..." Nomi brandished the card once more and said, "The battle won't stop until someone dies. And the person who dies will lose Brain Burst. No holds barred, hmm? Oh, and just so you know. If you leave through a portal, it will be treated as defeat at that moment. You'll be faced with a forced uninstall the moment you return to reality."

"Got it." Nodding, Haruyuki looked at Takumu. Cyan Pile also jerked his head up and down, eyes shining fiercely beneath the slits lined up on his mask. "Okay, guess that's fine."

At Haruyuki's voice, Nomi nodded slowly and touched the card with the fingertips of his left hand. He performed several operations and the card gleamed a brief, vivid bright red. Then he tossed it at Takumu, who caught it, touching it as he did, and the card shone once again. Takumu tossed it to Haruyuki, and he pinched it in the fingers of his right hand. Taking a deep breath, he clicked with his left and touched the CHARGE button in the center of the holowindow that popped up.

After an explanation of the sudden-death rules scrolled past in a blunt font, a YES/NO confirmation dialog popped up. YES.

When the normally extremely curt Brain Burst system asked, ARE YOU SURE?, Haruyuki truly understood the fact that he was on the brink of death. Despite the fact that he was technically cut off from his real flesh-and-blood body, a chill ran up his spine. At the same time as his limbs went numb, a virtual adrenaline pumped into his veins.

However, of course: YES.

The card flashed a remarkably dazzling red, pulled away from Haruyuki's hand, and rose up slightly in the sky. Around it, the digital numbers of a countdown slowly rolled down.

If news of this final battle had made it into the Accelerated World, they would've no doubt been instantly surrounded by the largest Gallery ever assembled. Although it had been six months since Haruyuki became a Burst Linker, before now, he had never even heard of a sudden-death battle with all your points on the line.

No. That wasn't right. He had heard of something like it.

Black Lotus, the Black King and a master of the sword, who Haruyuki loved and respected more than anyone. Because of a special rule that applied only to level-nine Burst Linkers, she carried the risk of sudden death with her into every fight. For instance, in the Territories every weekend: If another king were to show up, meticulously prepared, in the worst case she would lose that duel, and she would immediately lose Brain Burst forever.

Kuroyukihime. You've been living all this time under this heavy cloud, he murmured in his heart, and a second later, the countdown reached zero.

Flaming letters announced the start of the duel.

Dusk Taker threw out the talons of both hands.

Haruyuki crouched and readied his sword hands around him.

But Nomi's wings stayed folded up, and he didn't seem to be generating the purple pulsation. Maybe he wanted a ground fight with no Incarnate first?

Bring it! Haruyuki cried in his head and kicked off the ground. A fierce dash would cover the twenty meters between them at once. The figure of his enemy rapidly grew larger before his eyes. He cut across the shadows of the poles stretching out over the white schoolyard. One, two—

It happened when he stepped on the third pole.

Something sprang up, spurting forth from the slim shadow not more than ten centimeters wide: A darkness that shouldn't have been able to hide anything closed in on Haruyuki from both sides. Squares, sides about a meter long: Two matte jet-black panels shot up as if on a spring mechanism the instant Haruyuki stepped on the pole's shadow and boxed him in with terrifying force. Even with Silver Crow's speed, he couldn't avoid them. It was all he could do to stick out his hands and try to stop their advance.

Clang! The metallic impact echoed in the night, and sparks flew from the joints of his arms. A slice was taken from his HP gauge, the only one he could see.

"Ngh!" he involuntarily cried out at the sharp pain. Although the panels were extremely thin, no more than a few millimeters thick, they exerted an incredible pressure, like he was being clamped by an enormous vise. Very much unable to spread his arms out, he changed the orientation of his hands and intently fought back with his elbows and the backs of his hands. But the panels instantly imprisoned Haruyuki in a gap of about fifty centimeters before finally stopping.

Listening to the creaking of his own avatar, Haruyuki forced himself to shake off his astonishment and think. *There are no traps in a Moonlight stage. So does that mean Dusk Taker has some special attack I didn't know about?! No, if that were it, there would definitely have been some kind of motion or shout when he activated it. And if he had this kind of powerful attack, he would've used it the last time we fought. In which case—*

The jet-black panels were not Nomi's. And, of course, they weren't Lime Bell's. Which meant there was someone else on this battlefield.

No, impossible. There was no way anyone could ambush this fight after they had postponed it so close to the start so many times. His racing brain had reached this conclusion when he sensed a ghostly presence and his conclusion was immediately overturned.

The northern edge of the white schoolyard was sunken into the black shadow created by the four-story school building. He could see the tiny figure of Lime Bell still crouched against the wall there. Wordlessly, Haruyuki and Takumu behind him stared at the silent appearance of the fifth avatar far ahead of her, from the very front edge of the school's shadow.

Bizarre.

That was the only word to describe it. Haruyuki had never before seen a more bizarre-looking duel avatar in the Accelerated World.

The entire body was made of thin panels lined up perpendicularly, almost as if someone had built up layer upon layer of square sheets of paper to form the shapes of body parts. There was a gap of about a centimeter between each panel, so that although a clear silhouette was obvious from the side, from the front, the avatar looked like nothing more than an arrangement of thin vertical lines. The dozens of panels were a lusterless black, as though they had all been painted with ink.

But more than the avatar's shape, the color had the larger impact on Haruyuki. The layered avatar was clearly and obviously a perfect black. It had none of the hints of silver, like Chrome Disaster, or purple, like Dusk Taker, or the other blackish avatars he had seen. This black was complete, absorbing all wavelengths of light, rejecting all color.

"...Who are you...?" Haruyuki murmured hoarsely.

However, the avatar said nothing in reply, instead tilting its square head and returning Haruyuki's stare from behind several openings. Instantly, the pressure from the panels pinching his body increased. Silver Crow's armor squealed in a deeply unpleasant way.

Here, Haruyuki finally noticed that the layered avatar had no right arm. In its place, a hazy gray light shimmered around the shoulder. He didn't understand the logic behind it, but it was clear from the color and shape that that right arm was made up of the two panels currently confining him.

One other thing was also clear.

This black avatar was the ambush Nomi had prepared. The ambush Haruyuki and Takumu had examined and carefully eliminated every single possibility of.

"...Why...? How...? There should have been no way to know the time..." The groan from behind was Takumu, stunned.

Even at this, the layered avatar maintained its silence.

It was Dusk Taker, a few meters in front of Haruyuki, who began chuckling instead.

Dropping from his fighting stance, the dusk-colored avatar sneered once more. "Heh-heh! Honestly. You all do let me have *so* much fun with you. I like it, this shocked look of yours. This is a show I'd even pay to see. Which reminds me, didn't you say something earlier? That you'd learned you could never be too suspicious? Unfortunately, you don't appear to have studied hard enough, hmm? Hah-hah, ha-ha-ha-ha!!"

Laughter barking loudly, he threw both hands out. "And you're both about to lose all of your points, so there's no real point in doing anything for you now. Although, as a farewell gift, I suppose I could clear a few things up for you. I obviously couldn't predict the time you would pick, and this one over there wouldn't exactly wait months on this side for us to show up. Of course."

He moved the talons of his right hand farther and tapped the lens-shaped visor of his own head. "You already know that *we* have brain implant chips. The BIC connects growth terminals to the sensory area of the brain for a bioelectronic interface. Depending on the programming, it's possible to reach the deepest parts of the brain."

"D-deepest parts?" Haruyuki murmured, and Nomi nodded exaggeratedly.

"Yes. Naturally, it's very dangerous. I myself haven't gone that far. But this person here, despite appearances, is relatively daring. The terminals stretch all the way to his brain's mental clock control area."

Mental clock.

These words were the supertechnological foundation used to realize the acceleration of Haruyuki and the other Burst Linkers. The Brain Burst program accelerated thought by increasing the user's base clock, which was based on a standard of the user's heart rate, a thousand times within the brain. As long as you were diving in the Normal Duel Field or in the Unlimited Neutral

Field, the amplification was fixed and could not be manipulated in any way.

In other words, with Haruyuki's and Takumu's postponement of the time of the final battle by more than an hour, nearly two months of subjective time had passed in this world. Nomi didn't have any friends who would patiently wait all that time to help him with an ambush. Or he shouldn't have. And yet.

"I'll say it again. He has been on a dive in this Unlimited Neutral Field since eight o'clock in the real world. However, he definitely hasn't been sitting around waiting inside for a few months. Do you understand? By inactivating the mental clock control area of his brain with the BIC, he can stop the acceleration of his thoughts at will. He is, you see, *the sole deceleration user in the Accelerated World!*"

"...De...celeration..."

Haruyuki couldn't tell if the voice came from his own throat or if it was Takumu's. He was speechless.

"...Really now." A new voice at last reached his ears, the gentle voice of an older boy, somehow seeming warm even through the electronic effect peculiar to the duel avatar. It sounded a lot like that of the young, bespectacled man who had been the only teacher in Haruyuki's elementary school days who he had ever liked.

With Haruyuki restrained by the terrible pressure, the layered avatar spoke in a soft voice, without a hint of tension. "Look, Taker. I can't help but think that all this chatting and running about is what got you into a sudden-death situation in the first place."

"Ha-ha! I guess we differ in opinion there. It's simply that you think silence is a weapon, and I think eloquence is. Say, what do you think? Their stunned faces? Don't they look like our technological strength has already robbed them of the will to fight?"

"I don't know about that. The little one there is really trying for some reason. He's hard, and I can't crush him any further."

"Oooh, that's a metal color for you. Even a weak one."

"Which is to say..." The layered avatar signaled the chuckling Nomi with a finger on his left hand. "I've got my hands full holding him. It'd be a big help if you'd hurry up and take care of the big kid behind him."

"Understood, understood. I don't intend to have you work for any more than the remuneration I've already provided. Avatar like that, I'll be done in three minutes—no, thirty seconds."

Nomi's contemptuous words finally reignited the fire in Haruyuki's heart.

Avatar like that? You, who's never won an honest fight against Taku! You're calling him an "avatar like that"?! Gritting his teeth, Haruyuki let his eyes race momentarily over the panels at his sides. *This is no time to let these flimsy plates hold me forever. There're two enemies and there're two of us. I'll leave Nomi to Taku, and I'll...take down this guy!*

Haruyuki focused all his awareness, including these thoughts, in one spot between his eyebrows. A metallic high frequency came out of nowhere, and Silver Crow's body began to shake. He felt his consciousness connecting with the imagination circuits hidden within the Brain Burst program.

For this entire time, that gray aura had been coiled about the right shoulder of the layered avatar restraining Haruyuki. Niko had said that a continuous light-emitting phenomenon, i.e., Overlay, was proof that the Incarnate System was being used. In other words, these panels were the avatar's Incarnate attack. In which case, he would also fight, digging up every bit of strength he had.

Silver Crow's sharp fingertips began to glow with a white light. This soon moved up from his wrist to cover his arm to the elbow in a thin layer of light. Haruyuki took a deep breath and shouted the Incarnate attack name he had so recently come up with.

"Laser...Sword!!"

And then he crossed both arms and plunged the tip of his right hand into the left panel and the tip of his left hand into the right. With a high-pitched *screech*, the lengthening light swords crashed into the jet-black panels, sending dazzling sparks flying. The places where his swords had bitten in turned red hot immediately, as if bathed in the fire of a plasma arc. This glow spread out over the surface of the thin panel in the blink of an eye and shook them violently.

I'll rip them apart!! he cried in his heart, and focused in on that image. At that moment.

"Whoops. Now, this, this is an issue." He heard the gentle voice. Followed by, "Static Pressure."

An attack name call.

Abruptly, the two panels rumbled.

Previously mere millimeters thick, the panels grew wider before his eyes. Five centimeters, then ten centimeters, until at some point, they were more appropriately referred to as *lumps* rather than *panels*. The two massive rectangular solids, black as if they had been cut out of the night itself, engulfed Haruyuki in a pressure far greater than what it had been.

"Hngh!" Groaning, he pushed his own will to the limits and fought back with his light swords. But although he had been on the verge of melting the squares, the instant they turned from panels to lumps, the red-hot areas were halved.

The gray aura wafting around the shoulder of the layered avatar grew denser. Haruyuki was more than sure now that this attack wasn't a system-regulated special attack but rather an Incarnate attack brought about by the enemy avatar's image.

Through the conflict of their imagination output, Haruyuki felt like he could touch what was unfolding within the layered avatar.

Darkness.

Not the starving emptiness that threatened to devour everything like Nomi's Incarnate. What existed inside him rejected all interference and had no energy; thus, it gave none and it took none. No, it wasn't even an active refusal. It was isolation. It was an absolute alienation, a state that seemed impossible for a human heart.

The instant he felt this, Haruyuki reflexively feared their two wills touching. The light swords of his hands weakened momentarily and flickered. That was enough. The two impossibly heavy and hard objects ate in at his shoulders, rendering him completely immobile.

"Hey, you." Once again, he heard the voice of the layered avatar. "As a favor, maybe you could stay quiet like that. I was only hired to keep you from moving temporarily. I'm not interested in fighting you."

What...So it's all about you?! he shouted back sharply in his heart, and his light swords surged back to life. But it took everything he had just to marginally ease the intense pressure of the black lumps; he didn't get anywhere close to pushing them away.

Totally bound and unable to move, Haruyuki watched the other two duel avatars in the fight walking slowly toward each other.

From the west: Dusk Taker, arms too long for his small physique dangling at his sides.

From the east: Cyan Pile, the tip of his Pile Driver right arm glittering sharply.

They stood in the middle of the white schoolyard and faced each other. The crackle of impending battle abruptly flooded the field, and the air grew thicker. Trembling with a prickly tension, Haruyuki could not speak, nor even pray.

"Ooh," Nomi said abruptly, flapping both hands at the wrists. "It seems you came prepared in your own way. Well, maybe I'll get to have a little fun, then."

He lifted both hands and brought his fingertips together in front of his chest. The whine of vibration began to hum through the air, and a fluctuating purple light jetted out into space. It was Nomi's Incarnate attack, what Haruyuki and Takumu called the Nihilistic Fluctuation. Haruyuki thought he would quickly take to the sky and attack with his long-distance flame power, but Nomi apparently intended to fight on the ground, perhaps to show his disdain for Cyan Pile.

"Does that technique have a name?" Takumu asked, sounding relaxed.

"Haa!" Nomi responded with a laugh like a long sigh. "I do not give names to my techniques! I'm told that, without a name, it takes a moment longer to activate, but I'll have no part of that sort of gamer business! And, really..." He threw his arms out to the sides. The pulsing light left hazy lines lingering in space. "Is there any point in asking something like that? When you're about to lose Brain Burst?"

"Of course there is. I at least want to remember the opponent for whom I performed last rites," Takumu returned coolly, readying the Enhanced Armament of his right arm sideways across his chest.

Haruyuki knew that under the guidance of Red King Niko, Takumu had spent a week training his Incarnate. However, he hadn't gone so far as to ask what kind of attack it was or if it had even reached the level where it could be used in a real fight. Pinched between the two lumps, Haruyuki's avatar squealed, but that couldn't stop him from staring intently at Takumu.

Cyan Pile lifted his left arm and moved in a way Haruyuki could not have predicted. With the five fingers of his left hand, he tightly clasped the sharp tip of the stake peeking out of his Enhanced Armament.

Taku, what the—?! Haruyuki opened his eyes wide.

That spike—Takumu's wounded psyche—was born from the memories of the cruel bullying he had been subjected to at his kendo lessons when he was in elementary school. It was the wooden *shinai* that had been stabbed at his own throat time after time after time, and also a lethal weapon to stab the throats of those who had tortured him.

Why would he grab the tip of it himself?

Takumu answered Haruyuki's question with action.

"Cyan Blade!!"

Ga-shk! After an attack call like thunder, the spike was ejected. Haruyuki half expected the tip to blow Takumu's hand away, but what broke into pieces and flew off was the launcher, the Pile Driver of his right arm itself. Still gripped in his left hand, the spike became a pale light and remained after the Driver was gone. Takumu drew it above his head in a large half circle, and then slapped his liberated right hand into that rod of light before bringing it down with a *snap* in front of him.

The light scattered, and appearing from within it was a close-range cutting weapon with a firm and elegant construction.

A sword.

A meter and a half long, the single edge of the katana was a perfect straight sword, with a lone deep blue line running along the peak side. The blade was colored a light blue, and the entire thing was enveloped in a faint phosphorescence of the same shade.

With this beautiful weapon readied before him, Cyan Pile became, in line with the color of his armor, nothing other than a complete close-range duel avatar. So complete, he was more swordsman than avatar.

...*Taku*, Haruyuki whispered in a voice that was not a voice.

Perhaps hearing his thought, Takumu looked at him momentarily and nodded. Facing forward once again, he slid his right foot forward. With this motion, the move of a skilled kendo player, he readied his sword below chest level. From his feet, an even more intense air of battle-readiness surged up from his feet, shaking the aura surrounding Nomi's hands.

"I see," Nomi murmured. He sounded unfazed as he took in this new development, and his contemptuous laugh soon followed. "Heh-heh, I see now. You were really torn up at losing the match to me after all, hmm? So you materialized this shoddy little sword. But, well, if it's a sword fight you want, I suppose it can't be helped. I'll play along with you for a little while."

And then Nomi also grabbed at something with both hands and snapped into the standard *chudan* midlevel ready-posture.

Haruyuki watched, half understanding, half stunned, as the purple fluctuation slithered out and took on the form of a long sword. Nomi had changed the fluctuation's previous long talon shape. Haruyuki supposed if your Incarnate was a close-range weapon, you could change it into a variety of forms, depending on the image.

Although outwardly, they were duel avatars, it was two swordsmen who faced each other, in exactly the same ready positions they had taken in the final match of the kendo team tournament the previous week. Here, however, there was no judge. There was also no defensive gear. And at stake were their lives as Burst Linkers.

The tips of both players' toes slid forward, and they began to close the distance between them. Midway between the tips of their two swords, white sparks actually bounced thinly and burned the air. The battle had already started. Takumu and Nomi were fighting each other in a war to overwrite the world with the stronger imagination.

Taku, believe in yourself!! Haruyuki shouted in his heart.

"Sehyaaaaa!!"

"Sheeeeeh!!"

The two *kiai* battle cries rang out in the moonlit night of the battlefield, and both avatars kicked at the ground at the same time. Tracing out vivid blue and purple trajectories, the two swords slammed into each other.

Skreeeenk! The sound of the impact was fierce. Takumu's will, materialized as the cutting power that was the essential nature of the sword, bounced back from Nomi's will, which tried to erase all things. The two swords violently repelled each other and their owners swung them downward simultaneously. Once again, thunder and sparks. And then again.

Here, the two avatars put some distance between them and faced each other once more in the *chudan* stance.

A teasing voice slipped out from beneath Dusk Taker's mask. "My goodness, this is a surprise. For a hasty stopgap, you do fairly well with it, hmm?"

"Naturally. In a fair kendo match, I am stronger than you, after all."

Nomi greeted Takumu's retort with a throaty laugh. "I wonder about that, Mayuzumi. Do you think I hadn't noticed? No matter how you try to hide it, it's blindingly obvious! You…have a fatal weakness!"

As he shouted, Nomi stepped sharply in. The sword he gripped with both hands stretched out even farther. Adding his own thrust to the extended blade, Dusk Taker released a savage lunge at Cyan Pile's throat. "Sheeeeeh!!"

Takumu's arms sprang up in a convulsion to protect his throat with the blade of the blue sword. But in that instant, Nomi's sword bent like a fencing foil and the lunge changed its aim.

Vzzzm! The tip of the purple sword cut into Cyan Pile's defenseless right arm with an earsplitting noise. Nomi followed through, pushing the sword ahead of him. As if chasing him, a single line of pale sparks arced out from Takumu's wound.

"Hngh!" Groaning, Takumu immediately pulled himself back up and went after Nomi. *Kote, kote, men*: He threw a succession of barely visible blows at Nomi's forearms and mask. But the purple sword writhed like a living creature to repel each attack.

"Come now, shouldn't you be protecting your neck?" Once again, Nomi thrust his howling blade forward. Taking advantage of the very tiny window when Takumu stiffened, this time, the sword ripped into his left side.

Come on, Taku!! Haruyuki cried in his heart as he resisted the black vise with all his might.

Takumu's psychic wound. The memory of the bullying he endured in his kendo class when he was in elementary school. It had been humiliating to have his arms pinned down, to be used as a practice dummy for lunges, but more than humiliating, it had been incredibly terrifying.

But Takumu didn't quit kendo. He said it was because he didn't even have the willpower to quit, but that couldn't have been it. He was able to keep going because he loved kendo. His love was greater than his fear. That feeling…

Believe in it, Taku!!

There was no way he could hear Haruyuki. But Takumu righted himself as he started to stagger and yanked upward the sword in both hands. Past the *chudan* position, past the height of his neck, far above his head. An aura bluer than the moonlight enveloped the sword—held ready in something beyond the high *jodan* position—along with Cyan Pile's arms, up to his shoulders.

Nomi glared down at Takumu, taking in this fixed position, the Overlay of his will shimmering. "Quite the transparent bluff, isn't it? Oh, all right, if you're that interested in having a giant hole cut out of your windpipe..." Purplish-black light cascaded from Nomi's sword and arms. "I'll pierce it right through for you, just as you wish!"

Dusk Taker's charge was so fast that Haruyuki's eyes almost lost him. Moving ahead in a blur, he launched a savage lunge squarely at Takumu's throat. No feints this time.

Takumu didn't dodge or guard. Instead, he stepped forward. The approaching sword tip, and the force of the special attack latent within it, hit him hard in his thick left shoulder, gouging a deep hole from his armor. Narrow trails of pale sparks gushed out.

"Ngh!" A quiet voice slipped out from under the mask, withstanding the pain. But this was immediately followed by a *kiai* battle cry that shook the air.

"Hnnyaaaaah!!" He swung the Cyan Blade straight down.

Nomi's reaction was, of course, to jump to the right, but, unable to avoid the blow, he took the sword tip on the left side of his chest. Although the cut was fairly shallow, reddish-purple sparks still bounced and dazzled.

"Tch!" Nomi clicked his tongue as he tried to put some distance between them, and Takumu rained another blow down on him. The purple sword barely intercepted the blue blade just as it was about to make contact with Nomi's mask.

The two moved, swords locked, pushing against each other. Sparks jetted from where their blades met, brightly illuminating their masks.

The equilibrium was momentary. Cyan Pile had the larger

physique and greater physical strength, and he pushed his blade harder and harder. The outcome was not dependent on the Incarnate System. This was a simple power imbalance between a close-range type and one who mixed both close and long.

Finally, Dusk Taker's knee crunched into the ground. His blade slipped, and Takumu's Cyan Blade drew in on Nomi's left shoulder. Thin cracks caused by the enormous pressure raced through the white tiles covering the schoolyard. The two masks were so close, they were practically touching.

Abruptly, a certain foreboding shivered through the back of Haruyuki's brain.

Taku! Run!

An instant before he could shout these words, Nomi cried sharply, "Demonic Commandeer!!"

Zrrt! A concentrated darkness came swirling from Dusk Taker's lens-shaped visor, hit Cyan Pile's mask, and penetrated it, shuddering almost like some kind of animal. The blue avatar reeled and stopped.

Demonic Commandeer.

The sole fixed special attack Dusk Taker had. Using up the entire gauge when activated, the effect was to steal one of the target duel avatar's abilities, special attacks, or Enhanced Armament. Nomi let the battle unfold into a close-range fight without using the wings as a trap.

Cyan Pile didn't have any systematic abilities. And of his three special attacks, two of them basically came entirely from the Enhanced Armament. Which meant if he got hit with Demonic Commandeer, there was a 75 percent chance that the Pile Driver would be taken. If that happened, the Cyan Blade, the transformation of the spike through his will, would disappear.

The instant of stillness that blanketed the field felt like an eternity to Haruyuki.

The darkness that should have flowed back out from Cyan Pile's mask and returned to Dusk Taker—

Didn't.

Instead...

"Aaaaah!" With a roar, Takumu brought the sword he gripped with both hands down in a straight line.

Nomi's left arm was severed below the shoulder, and the undulating purple light scattered into the night. The avatar was thrown to the ground, bounced violently, and tumbled nearly ten meters backward.

Of course, he was quick to get back on his feet and ready his sword of nothingness with his right hand alone. However, in perhaps a sign that he was shaken, the tip of that blade shook very slightly.

"You're too greedy," Cyan Pile said, brilliantly shining blue sword readied straight ahead of him. "Way, way too greedy."

Haruyuki didn't get what he meant right away. Takumu probably wasn't intending to explain himself, though, as he continued quietly.

"I've always thought it was weird. That you didn't take Lime Bell's healing ability, I mean. If you had, armed with flight, firepower, and healing, you'd have been the end all and be all, beyond even the kings. But you didn't because..." His eyes glittered keenly beneath the slits as he declared, "*Insufficient capacity.* A special attack as ridiculously powerful as stealing other people's abilities, there's no way it wouldn't be restricted somehow. There's an upper limit to the total abilities, the total potential you can steal and keep with your Demonic Commandeer. Which is why you wouldn't have enough room to steal both of the super-rare abilities of flight and healing, even if you deleted all your other powers. Isn't that right?"

Dusk Taker pressed his right hand over the cross-section of his severed left arm and remained silent. He was no doubt suffering fierce pain, double what players felt in the Normal Duel Field. Was he unable to move? Or maybe he was so angry, he had forgotten the pain?

Takumu carefully readied his sword and slowly closed the distance between them. His quiet voice once again flowed across the field.

"The person who guided me in the Incarnate said the majority of Cyan Pile's potential is taken up by this Pile Driver. I'm sure you figured you had enough empty space right now to be able to take something like my Enhanced Armament. Unfortunately for you, you figured wrong."

"Heh-heh-heh, I see now." Dusk Taker finally uttered his usual contemptuous laugh, but perhaps reflecting his feelings, his voice was tinged with a dark, distorted effect. "I see. I know I said this before, but that flimsy stick of yours must have been made with some quite painful memories, hmm? A metaphor for the *shinai* maybe? Did something bad happen to you on the kendo team, hmm? Perhaps you, so cool and handsome, were subjected to ugly bullying? Ha-ha! Ridiculous! You're not the little pig over there or something!!"

Taku, this chatter's a trap! Don't listen to him! Haruyuki cried soundlessly, fighting desperately against the black vise mercilessly crushing him.

Perhaps because of Takumu's own surging anger, the light housed in his blade wavered slightly. But he quickly regained control and replied calmly, "My memories are really no big deal. Nothing compared to the wounds you produced that avatar with. You're a marauder because there's nothing left inside of you. Because you've had everything taken from you, and you're nothing but an empty hole. You must've realized it by now. You can steal other people's powers—no, other people's *hope*, their *friendship*, their *love*, but those things will never truly be yours, not in any real sense."

Silence once again.

Bathed in the blue moonlight, the avatar the color of darkness hung his head. Finally, he staggered to his feet feebly. Still clutching his left shoulder, he slowly brought his face up. His whole body trembled and shivered violently.

"Fu-hu-hu." A choked laugh slipped out from the spherical visor. "Hu-hu, hch-hch-heh…Ha-ha-ha-ha-ha…A-ha-ha-ha-ha-ha-ha-ha!!"

Tossing his head back, Dusk Taker laughed loudly and heartily. "A-ha-ha-ha-ha-ha!! Nothing?! Empty?! Ha-ha-ha! That's…Well, that's him!!"

He laughed again for a moment before he started talking, the words bursting out of him. "You two are so clever, you must have had it figured out from the yearbook. My 'guardian' is my own brother, three years older than me. He's the real marauder. With his huge body and his violence, he took my candy and toys when I was little, and then when I got a little older, he took my allowance and my New Year's money. In the end, he even took the girl who was my only friend. He really was the perfect marauder. Heh-heh-heh."

He shook his head two, three times, laughing in a sort of amazement. The gloomy monologue continued.

"The first thing he ever gave me was, of course, Brain Burst. Foolishly, I was delighted, even moved. Because no sooner had the first lecture ended than he was telling me to come and pay him ten points every week. I was so disappointed. But if I refused, he'd have really let me have it in the real world. I went afar to depopulated areas and dueled desperately, honestly collecting the points to pay to my brother. Like a dog. Oh, and in the process, he stole from me the last thing I had. My pride as a human being."

No. I don't want to hear this. Haruyuki held his breath and tried to shut out the pain he felt just listening to Nomi, almost as if his words themselves were some kind of attack. *I don't want to hear this story. I actually don't need to hear it.*

Taku, just hit him with the finishing blow. End this. We don't have to sit here and listen to this story. How are we even supposed to know if it's true or not? I mean, it has to be a lie. It's a strategy to shake us up.

However, Haruyuki couldn't stop the certain knowledge that

what Nomi was saying was true—and that Takumu couldn't cut into him like this.

Dusk Taker turned toward Cyan Pile, who had stopped moving, and continued talking. "But, you see, even stuck as I was, I saved points for myself bit by bit and leveled up. And then one day, this avatar, which had had no real power, came to have its first special attack. And that was Demonic Commandeer. During that same period, I obtained two significant powers: the BIC and knowledge of the Incarnate System. The Incarnate training was quite difficult. My guide told me over and over that I was wasting my time. But I endured it, my hatred of my brother feeding me. And then, yes, the moment finally came. The moment when I took back everything he—my brother—had ever taken from me."

Keh-heh-heh-heh. The laugh and its resentful echo fell in drops in the field.

"I called my brother to the Unlimited Neutral Field and first took his abilities. Once that was done—he was so surprised—I tortured him to death with my Incarnate power. His HP slipped away a little too readily, so the *second time* I got more creative. Each time he was revived after an hour, my method of killing him got better. I can't begin to put into words the feelings and pleasure of that time! Eventually, his points were exhausted, and when he came at me weeping and wailing, about to lose Brain Burst after one more death...Just remembering it even now, the laughter...hm-hm, heh-heh-heh, a-ha-ha-ha-ha-ha!"

He clutched his stomach and laughed briefly before jerking his head up. "Nothing?! Empty?!" he shouted. "That, you see, isn't me; that's him now!! A former acceleration user, bereft of Brain Burst. There's nothing more pathetic and miserable! I'm not like him...I have everything. In the Accelerated World and in the real world. And this illusion of friendship and bonds you all believe in..." The eyes beneath his visor glinted sharply. "I'll take that from you, too, and leave nothing behind!!"

Nomi made a flourish with his right hand. From the stump of

his shoulder where his arm had been cut off, black snakes shot out ferociously fast. Three tentacles, the Enhanced Armament he had equipped during his first fight with Haruyuki. He had secretly given the "equip" command and then waited for it to regenerate.

The ever-extending tentacles did not roar in assault at Takumu standing in front of Nomi. Nor did they lash out at Silver Crow, pinned in the vise.

They reached for Chiyuri—Lime Bell, silent this whole time, quietly sunk into the shadows of the distant school building.

"Wha..." Takumu couldn't stop the short, stunned cry from slipping out, but he was, of course, quick to brandish his sword to cut the tentacles.

But a second before he could, the tentacles, snapping back like rubber, pushed under the blade of the avatar the color of fresh leaves they held captive.

His entire body squealing at the strain, Cyan Pile stopped his slashing attack. The tip of his blade just barely touched the brim of Lime Bell's pointed hat, sending a trail of sparks flying.

The three tentacles immediately coiled themselves around Chiyuri and squeezed cruelly.

"Ngh!" The slender avatar threw her head back, the groan of pain slipping from between her teeth joined by Nomi's stifled laughter.

"Heh-heh-heh-heh. Did you think I only called her here for her healing capacity? Ridiculous! I've long been aware that Lime Bell is your Achilles' heel. You have to effectively use anything you can use...That's the secret to the duel!"

"...You. Bastard...," Takumu snarled, tip of his sword shaking, as Chiyuri tried to say something to him. However, several layers of tentacle immediately coiled over her mouth and kept her silent.

"Now then, please throw your sword down and remove that Enhanced Armament," Nomi coolly instructed.

"Lime Bell isn't part of the sudden-death duel," Takumu countered in a voice like a creak. "She's no good as a hostage."

"Oh? Is that so?" Head cocked.

Dusk Taker casually grabbed Lime Bell near her right elbow, his right hand dripping with purple fluctuation.

Skrrk. An extremely, extremely unpleasant sound echoed in the air. The sound of the yellow-green arm being torn off at the elbow.

"Hnnngh!!" Lime Bell's entire body convulsed and a sound-less scream surged out of her. She threw her head back two, three times as far as it would go. Each time, an ocean of green sparks spurt forth from the stump.

Haruyuki's vision was dyed a sudden red. An overwhelming rage swept through him, and in a trance, he struggled to break free. However, the black vise didn't budge, almost as if sneering at his anger. In fact, the instant the light sword output he had been using to resist the pressure was disturbed by his anger, the vise pressed even more fiercely down on his shoulders.

"You...bastaaaaaaard!!" It was Takumu who yelled instead. The large avatar took a step forward when something hit his chest with a clang. Lime Bell's torn-off arm. It bounced back and broke into countless polygon fragments in midair before disappearing.

"Do you understand, Mayuzumi? This is her first time diving into the Unlimited Neutral Field. This world where the sensation of pain is twice that of the lower field."

Takumu didn't need to be told. At that moment, Chiyuri was no doubt feeling pain equivalent to having her flesh-and-blood arm ripped off in the real world. Perhaps because of the severity of the shock, the thin avatar continued to ripple with tiny convulsions.

Cyan Pile was frozen in place, and before him, Nomi lifted his right hand once again. "And by doing this, I also increase her special-attack gauge so she can heal me."

He thrust the tip of his sharp index finger into Chiyuri's side. *Thrk.*

The green avatar recoiled fiercely. Even through the layers of tentacle coiled around her, they could clearly hear a thin scream. When Nomi pulled his finger out, a thin stream of sparks erupted from the cruel wound.

Thrk. One more time. And again.

"Stop!!" Takumu shouted in a cracking voice, immediately before Nomi could dig out a fourth hole. His entire body was shaking. The extra light wrapped around Takumu's sword and arms flickered irregularly, like a poorly connected lightbulb.

No, Taku, Haruyuki wanted to shout. But he could say nothing. He knew too well that Takumu—and if it had been him, he, too—had no other choice.

"...Please, just stop..." Cyan Pile groaned. The Cyan Blade fell from his hands and clattered to the ground.

Immediately, it turned to light and melted away. The luminescence flowed through space, was sucked into Cyan Pile's right arm, and turned back into the original stake.

When Takumu whispered the "unequip" command, the Enhanced Armament also disappeared. Once he saw this, Dusk Taker waved his left arm extravagantly and left Chiyuri somewhere off on the edge of the field. He didn't even glance at Lime Bell, who huddled into herself against the pain.

The dark avatar charged at Cyan Pile and buried the talons of his right hand into the sturdy stomach. A wet noise joined the black arm as it broke out through his back. Leaving a torrent of pale sparks, Nomi yanked his arm back out.

Takumu staggered and dropped heavily to his knees before ceasing to move, head hanging.

"It's because you believe in the lie of 'bonds.'" Nomi's voice was quiet, almost as if he really were feeling pity. "Or rather, it's because you act like you believe this, that you will lose. If you really trusted each other, you would have cut through her and right into me. Isn't that right?"

No...no, no!!

Haruyuki struggled, crazed. Sparks flew from the joints of his arms as he fought to free himself from the vise and save Takumu. Resisting with all his might, he howled in a voice that was not a voice.

What do you know?! There's no way you could understand how strongly Takumu feels about Chiyuri!! If he had cut Chiyuri with you there, that wouldn't be trust, just calculation!!

But the black lumps at his sides indifferently applied more pressure, as if trying to crush even his anger.

Why can't I move?! Why can't I even scream?! I have to move now; what has this all been for—

"Sorry, boy." He heard a muted whisper from behind. The layered avatar, who had been silent all this time. "This attack stops you from talking as well as moving. So you can't say anything and you can't use voice commands. I'd like to at least let you say a few words of farewell to your friend there...Sorry."

At these words, which sounded sincerely apologetic, Haruyuki's anger flamed even higher and swept through his avatar.

Thmp. His back ached. *Thmp. Thmp.*

A throbbing like lightning pulsed in regular intervals between his shoulder blades. He felt like he could hear a voice. But, perhaps obstructed by the vise, it couldn't reach all the way into Haruyuki's awareness.

If he couldn't talk, then he could only fight back with his will— his Laser Sword—but the pulsing anger prevented him from concentrating.

In the schoolyard, Dusk Taker had just raised his right hand at Cyan Pile, who was on his knees. The Nihilistic Fluctuation once again transformed into a thin sword. He sliced it through the air twice with a *whoosh.*

With a leaden sound, Cyan Pile's arms were severed at the base and fell to the ground. Bundles of lightning cascaded from his shoulders.

Haruyuki could hear his voice.

Haru, I'm sorry.

I can't fight anymore. I'm really sorry...

The tears welling up beneath Haruyuki's silver mask blurred his vision. In the distorted screen, he watched Dusk Taker raise his sword high to bring down the final blow.

Here.

It ends here? This is my...This is Takumu's Brain Burst ending?

This thought crystallized in his heart like a single droplet at absolute zero, and the flames of his rage turned to frost and scattered. His limbs went cold. The light of his hands burned up and disappeared. All the sensations of his body receded. The sign of avatar shutdown he had experienced so many times.

Oh, so that's it? Zero fill. And this is a thing the Incarnate System makes happen, too. Negative imagination puts out the flames of your heart and turns your avatar into a cold lump.

What does it matter figuring that out now?

No, wait.

If zero fill is the negative will that all Burst Linkers can use, then the opposite must be true, too. Moving an avatar who can't move with positive imagination. Like, say, even when he's stuck in a vise with absolute strength. Like when, battered and broken, he stood up again next to the bed of black thorns she was sleeping in.

A small flame sprang to life in Haruyuki's chest with a *pop*. But not the black flame of rage he had felt toward Nomi so many times now. Something better called *determination*. It was the pure power of heart he had learned from Kuroyukihime, and Niko, and Blood Leopard, and Sky Raker.

The meager heat began to melt the ice binding his body. The connection to his four limbs came back to life. From the thin seams and joints of Silver Crow's mirrored armor came abruptly a blue luminescence akin to a high-temperature flame—Overlay.

However, unaware even of this, Haruyuki placed the palms of his hands flat against the vise on either side.

"Ngh..." A low moan slipped from his throat. Mustering every ounce of strength, he tried to open the gap. His avatar creaked and squealed, and an intense pain assaulted his elbows and shoulders. He heard a succession of high-pitched metallic *pops*, the sound of thin cracks racing up the armor of his arms. Blue light shone through those thin lines as well.

"Hng…Ah…Ah!" Clusters of pure pain exploded throughout his nervous system, and his consciousness was colored white. However, Haruyuki didn't stop putting all his strength into his arms. His crumbling armor peeled off and scattered around his feet, and the blue aura wrapped around his slightly exposed dark gray body like a flame.

The black lumps of absolute hardness and pressure, however, didn't so much as shudder. But Haruyuki believed.

Not in his own power.

He believed that the power of the people who had supported and guided him this far could not bend to the power of someone who believed that the Accelerated World was nothing more than a tool.

"Ah…Ah! Aaaaah!!" With his howl, every bit of armor on his upper body other than his helmet crumbled and blew away.

Blue flashes condensed, exploded, and colored the world.

Haruyuki felt it, just barely, for a mere instant: the constraint of the black vise weakening.

He kicked at the ground with everything he had. He scraped his shoulders on the walls and his HP gauge turned to sparks and scattered. He put all his energy into running the distance of a single step that might as well be infinite, and finally, Haruyuki slipped out of the restraint.

He fell to the ground. After a single somersault, he was back on his feet. Still running hard, he pulled in his right hand. Concentrated his will. Roared.

"Unh…Naaaaaaah!!"

The arm about to cut off Cyan Pile's head stopped, and with an air of surprise, Dusk Taker turned. Haruyuki mustered what mental strength remained to him and launched his Laser Sword.

Schwiiing! The tip of the light blade reached through space more than five meters and severed in half two of the three tentacles of Nomi's left hand.

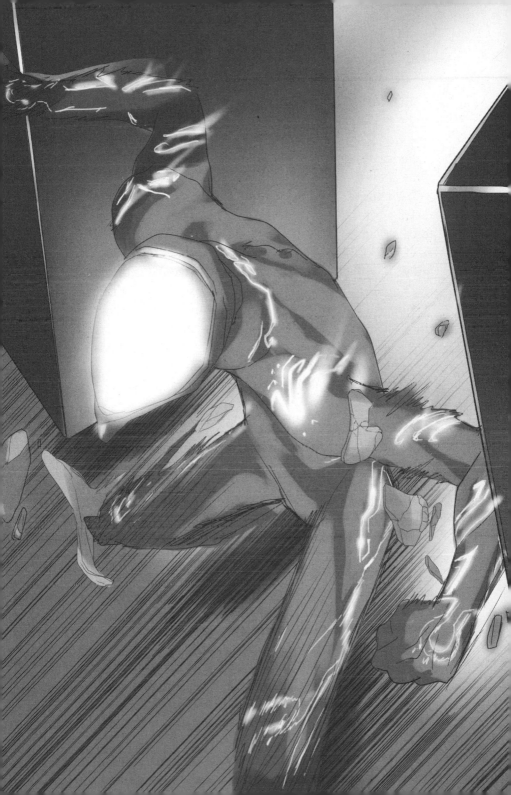

That was all he could manage. The strength drained from his body, his feet tangled together, and Haruyuki fell facedown onto the ground.

Perhaps because he had mustered such a strong image, his consciousness flickered and registered Nomi's voice from a distance.

"Goodness! Please don't scare me like that, Arita." He paused briefly. "Aren't you lying down on the job a bit, letting your prey escape from your vise?"

"Unthinkable, really," the layered avatar responded, also far away. "I was at full power. I really have to hand it to this little guy: He's quite the trooper. That said, it seems he's about finished."

Haruyuki stared hollowly as the thin panels rose up around him once more. Shifting his gaze, in the center of his upside-down world, he could see Dusk Taker brandishing his purple sword to at last strike the final blow against Takumu. He could no longer think. His mental powers were so exhausted, he couldn't even feel despair.

"Well, then…farewell, Cyan Pile."

The nihilistic blade slid through space.

The afterimages of several half circles lingering in the air, the blade slid toward the nape of the blue avatar's neck—

Haruyuki closed his eyes, and just as he was on the verge of cutting loose of his consciousness.

Klink.

A crisp sound.

Nomi's blade, about to touch Takumu's neck, was severed at the base and melted into nothingness.

Incarnate can't be cut without another Incarnate attack.

It wasn't Haruyuki. And there was no reason for the layered avatar holding him to interfere with Nomi. Which meant another new Burst Linker on the battlefield.

Haruyuki opened his eyes wide and lifted his head as if guided by something to stare up into the night sky before him.

The magnificent palace was a dim white. On top of the spire in the center that had originally been the stairs at Umesato Junior High was a silhouette shouldering the enormous blue full moon. A mounted figure.

The sturdy black horse's mane fluttered in the wind, eyes glittering white, and four hooves enveloped in blue flames. A slim rider straddled its back neatly.

Black crystal armor sleekly reflecting the light of the moon. Sharp V-shaped mask. Black lotus skirt encircling a slender body. Both arms long, razor-edge swords. The legs also swords. A sage brilliance that seemed to cut through even the moonlight pouring down.

"...Aah."

A quiet voice, almost a sigh, spilled from Haruyuki's mouth. And again. "Aaaah..." He felt like if he said anything more, the rider and mount would turn into a hallucination and disappear.

But the rider nodded slightly, as if hearing his whispers as he lay on his side off in the distance, and lightly spurred the mount on with her right foot.

The horse raised its front legs high into the air, and then clapped its hooves down. Neighing fiercely, blue flames erupting from its nostrils, it began to run through the air. The duel avatars on the ground watched soundlessly while the mount and rider arrived at a point directly above the schoolyard, carving out a pale arc in the night sky.

Here, the rider made her body dance lightly. She opened up the long swords of her hands and approached the ground, almost sliding. Right before she landed, she kicked her legs out, straight down. With a ringing echo, the avatar dropped to the white ground on the tip of her right sword leg.

The black horse in the sky finished the arc and disappeared, as if melting, as soon as it started to dash off into the south-western sky.

After seeing it off, the jet-black avatar was quick to look straight at Haruyuki, to whom she nodded again. She turned to the raised face of Cyan Pile before her eyes shifted to the distant layered avatar and the still-fallen Lime Bell in turn. Finally, the avatar stared at Dusk Taker. Violet-blue eyes glittered visibly beneath the mirrored mask.

"...Im...possible." Nomi's rasping voice. "Impossible. Why... How are you...Why are you here?"

The same stunned question was living inside Haruyuki. But much greater than that was the overwhelming emotion that filled and overfilled his heart, and he could say nothing. Still on the ground, he could only stare raptly at the beautiful black crystal duel avatar.

Nomi groaned once more. "Impossible. Did you come back from Okinawa by yourself for this battle alone? No, even if you had, you couldn't have made it in time. This can't be...Why— How are you here?! Black King...Black Lotus!!"

Yes, the jet-black avatar could have been none other than Black Lotus, the Black King, occupying one of the seats of the Seven Kings of Pure Color, leader of the Nega Nebulus Legion.

However, her real-world self, Kuroyukihime, vice president of the student council and ninth-grade student at Umesato Junior High, was currently supposed to be on a school trip in Okinawa. And Haruyuki and Takumu had only decided on the time for this final battle a little more than an hour earlier in real-world time. Assuming she had managed to find out about it somehow, she wouldn't have been able to get back to Tokyo from Okinawa.

Nomi's howling showering her, Kuroyukihime shook her mask coolly and spoke for the first time. "You're Dusk Taker? You seem quite proud of your ingenuity. But you're still soft. There are countless ways of fighting in the Accelerated World, ways you haven't even dreamed of."

Even as her voice was silky smooth, her words had a razor-sharp edge to them and cut through the virtual space. Nomi inched a half step backward.

"I haven't come back to Tokyo; there's no need for that. Let me remind you of the basic rules of Brain Burst. In the Normal Duel Field, there is a time limit of eighteen hundred seconds and movement restrictions due to the area boundaries. However, in the Unlimited Neutral Field, there is neither. Which is why it's *unlimited*. Understand?" Brandishing the sword of her right hand, Kuroyukihime declared crisply, "*In this world, Okinawa and Tokyo are connected!* Hmm, seems you finally get it. That's right. *I dove into this field in Okinawa and ran to Tokyo.* Although I did have to tame that divine-level Enemy earlier. And it took about fifteen hours to get here. Still, in the real world, it didn't even take a single minute."

"...Wh-what..." Nomi gasped in amazement, and Haruyuki felt the shock run through his own body as well.

He had visited the Unlimited Neutral Field many times before, and had in fact wondered more than once just how far this world spread out. But it was just an idle thought; he had never even considered trying to check. But the answer turned out to be quite simple: As far as the social network cameras ran, so too the medium for the Accelerated World reached. Put another way, the whole of Japan, from Hokkaido in the north to Okinawa in the south.

But who on earth would think to cross this expansive world all alone? This was no safe, touristy VR world. It was a place of death filled with swaggering Enemies so large they could easily kick around several dozen Burst Linkers.

Except for this one person here.

"Kuro...yuki...hime," Haruyuki whispered. Beneath his cracked mask, hot tears welled up and spilled over.

She turned her eyes once more to Haruyuki, and for the first time, he felt the hint of a smile from her. However, she soon checked that and shifted her gaze to the layered avatar, the owner of the vise restraining Silver Crow.

Ting! came a sharp metallic sound as pale sparks lit up the darkness.

When the black panels holding him disappeared, Haruyuki was slow to grasp what had happened.

Not moving her avatar in the slightest, Kuroyukihime had launched a long-distance attack using Incarnate, with just the faint light housed in her right arm. The layered avatar had met this with his own Incarnate. Thus, the image of the vise imprisoning Haruyuki had been released and the prison had disappeared.

Ting! Tinnng! Light bounded through the sky three more times. The phenomenon was visually modest, but the attacks crashing into each other made their immensity known, and Haruyuki felt the field itself beneath him shake violently.

The force was such that it made it hard to breathe, and he was not surprised at all that Kuroyukihime, a king, could use an Incarnate Attack. After all, Niko, who was also level nine but had had a considerably shorter career, was able to demonstrate an attack of awe-inspiring power. But the power of the layered avatar fighting her attack head-on was also bottomless.

"Your name?" Black Lotus asked briefly when she paused in her attack, as if the exchange of volleys just finishing up were a formal greeting.

Twenty or so meters away, the layered avatar inclined the thin panels of his head hesitatingly. The same gentle voice, a dead ringer for the young teacher's, flowed out. "Giving my name here would really be pointless. But a king such as yourself has come all this way to be with us. I suppose it would be rude to not at least introduce myself."

There was a whistling sound as several black panels rose up from the avatar's feet and arranged themselves into his right arm, which had been missing until then. There was no mistake: They were the vise that had been restraining Haruyuki all this time.

The avatar brought this right arm to his chest and bent at the waist to bow. His voice rang out again. "I'm the vice president of the group the Acceleration Research Society...My name is Black Vise. It is a pleasure to make your acquaintance."

From possibly the moment Haruyuki had seen the armor, he had had a faint premonition. But actually hearing the name, he still couldn't help feeling an enormous blow.

Black. The pure color black.

The color he had been convinced crowned only Black Lotus herself. In fact, up to that point, Haruyuki had never once heard of any doubling of the color names given to any of the Burst Linkers in the Accelerated World.

In contrast with Haruyuki and his stunned eyes opened wide, Kuroyukihime herself didn't seem the slightest bit ruffled. She simply sighed lightly. "Hmph, not a Legion but a 'group,' hmm? Quite elaborate, no?"

"Apologies. Society policy."

"Obviously, I'm no fan of the name. And I do need to thank you for inflicting such severe pain on my Legion member. Two-fold, naturally." Her bluish-purple eyes emitted a dangerous light. An aura the same color took up residence in the swords of both hands.

In response, the layered avatar—Black Vise—spread his hands in a gesture that showed no hint of tension. "Well, this is a problem. The one who injured your friend for the most part was not me but Taker. Although, well, I suppose I'm in no position to ask you to let it go."

A pale black aura came to life in one of his slowly lowered arms, followed by several panels being soundlessly released, to sink as if sliding into the shadows at his feet.

"Kuro..."

Watch out! Haruyuki started to shout. However, by that time, two panels had already flown up from Kuroyukihime's feet and snapped up around her so quickly he could barely see them.

Clang! The panels crashed into her arms. The thin sheets imme-diately increased in volume, transforming into enormous lumps.

It was Black Vise's Incarnate Attack, Static Pressure. Having himself been mercilessly subjected to the terrifying assault, which completely prevented any movement or speech on the part of the captured avatar, Haruyuki forgot the pain coursing through his own body and tried to shout again. But before he could—

Clink! A crisp echo through the field.

Blue lines traversed the two jet-black lumps.

Haruyuki stared in amazement as the lumps slid to the sides from the center and fell heavily to the ground. Kuroyukihime, appearing from inside with her arms out slightly, said, as if nothing had happened, "Unfortunately, physical restraint does not work on me."

The severed cuboids turned back into panels and sank into the ground. This time, the sword of Kuroyukihime's right arm emitted a red flame with a roar.

"Vorpal Strike!!" Coldly uttering the attack name, she launched an intense emptiness.

The motion was very similar to that of Black Lotus's special attack Death by Piercing, but the range was wildly different. The red lance spilling from the sword howled metallically and lunged at the distant Black Vise.

The layered avatar, dyed a glossless black, raised his left arm straight ahead, gray aura swirling. "Layered Armor."

The panels of his arm leapt off, each transforming into a large square. The ten or so flat squares lined up horizontally, leaving gaps, and stood in the way of the red lance, protecting the main body of the avatar.

The thundering roar of the impact shook the world.

The lance pierced 90 percent of the way through the protective panels the layers created and then stopped but did not disappear. The air squealed and creaked as the weapon shone brightly, trying to pierce the remaining panels.

The two Burst Linkers named Black, hands thrust out, fought each other's will.

Despite the extremity of the situation, Kuroyukihime glanced over at Haruyuki and ordered in a stern yet gentle voice, "Now, stand up, Silver Crow. I'll keep this one in check. You defeat your enemy—Dusk Taker."

A second earlier, Haruyuki had thought that there was not a shred of fighting power left within him. But the words of his beloved sword master pierced his heart, almost as if they were even another form of the will, and reignited the fire that was about to extinguish.

"Right," he responded in a hoarse but determined voice. He bent the knees of his battered avatar, thrust his hands into the ground, and stood, albeit wobblingly. Just over 30 percent left in his HP gauge. He turned his face toward Dusk Taker, a way off, and Cyan Pile next to him.

Consciousness perhaps inhibited by the intense pain of having his stomach pierced and both arms gone, Takumu's head was still hanging heavily. There was no light from the eyes beneath the mask. But he was still there. He was alive.

Dusk Taker, as if finally waking from the shock, slowly raised his right hand to cover the visor of his face. "Heh. Heh. Heh-heh." The sneering laugh Haruyuki had heard countless times already slipped thinly from between his fingers. "Heh-heh. Honestly. You truly are disgusting people. Do you intend to keep playing make-believe with your friendship, your bonds, your what-have-you forever? You say you ran from Okinawa? Heh-heh, the height of madness. Really."

Vmm! He waved his hand. A hazy fluctuation entangled itself around the talons.

"But, well, this does save me some trouble, doesn't it? Once I destroy the puppet here and that little bug, then it's just Black Lotus. You might call yourself a king, but there's no way you can take on the both of us. In fact, this is some unparalleled good fortune. In one hour, at a single time, I'll torment you plenty and kill you all. Until your points are entirely gone. Heh-heh, keh-heh-heh-heh."

Haruyuki was essentially ignoring the mocking voice. His

consciousness was turned only toward the badly injured Takumu and Chiyuri, still collapsed in the distance. The scene of Nomi trampling the pair flashed up on the screen in the back of his mind. Chiyuri, arm ripped off, screaming. Takumu, stomach gouged out, fallen. What they felt was not just a virtual pain. It was the pain of their friendship and love being used and stomped all over. It was the despair of the thing they cherished more than anything being sullied and destroyed.

As Haruyuki clenched both hands into fists, his entire body trembling, Nomi turned toward him and said consolingly, "But please be reassured. I'll save her, Lime Bell, at least. And not for the reason this puppet here said, because I can't take her healing power. I do it in deference to the lady's loyalty. Her devotion is indeed praiseworthy. I'll make sure to lavish attention on her. Ha-ha-ha-ha!"

From between teeth gritted so hard they were about to crumble, Haruyuki squeezed his words out. "Nomi. You're wrong."

"About what? And since when?" The twilight-colored avatar cocked his head.

Haruyuki glared at him. "Everything. Right from the start," he declared softly. "When you started at Umesato, you could've just challenged any one of us to a duel like a normal person and said, *Hey, nice to meet you.* All you had to do was say, *I want to join the Legion.* Then you could've gotten what you really wanted. Companions, friendship, bonds."

Dusk Taker froze in place. An entirely different voice, lower, colder, came from beneath his visor. "What did you say? Me? Companions?"

"Yeah. You're just like Taku and me. You were tortured and scarred mentally, and then you became a Burst Linker. You should've learned through duels that the real bonds we've been looking for exist in the Accelerated World. Why couldn't you believe in that? Why would you turn to the fake power of a BIC? I know you must've had the opposite choice."

A few seconds of silence followed, and then a terrifying aura abruptly gushed from Nomi's entire body. Haruyuki knew that it was an incredibly angry pulsation, and that its source was the feelings locked up in the very depths of Nomi's heart.

"So in other words, is this what you're saying?" Nomi asked in a voice that was not a voice. "That you forgive me. That you pity me, so you'll be my friend. That in your boundless mercy, you are reaching out a hand of salvation to me. Is that it?"

"Oh no." Haruyuki immediately shook his head. "I'm totally not doing that. You and I will never understand each other at this point. Let's settle this, Seiji Nomi."

Naturally, there was anger toward Nomi inside of Haruyuki. But a simple feeling far stronger than that became a super-heated blue flame and filled his body: determination. It was the resolute intention to put an end to all of this, right here, right now. The flame burned so hotly, without wavering in the slightest, that it was almost static. Like the cold stars twinkling in the night sky.

In contrast, Nomi's body radiated a raging tornado of anger and he laughed briefly one more time. "Heh-heh. That's a relief. You narrowly missed being unable to forgive your pathetic self in the real world, once I take care of your avatar here…I suppose we could settle this now, Haruyuki Arita. This world doesn't need two fliers, after all."

He raised his right hand, clenched it into a fist, and yanked it back. The black wings on his back, folded up all this time, flapped wide open.

Haruyuki also lifted his right hand high up in the sky, opened his palm, and cried: "Equip Gale Thruster!"

Chk! A large sky-blue star sparkled in the inky sky before becoming two laser beams shooting down at the ground. They hit Haruyuki's back, but, still glittering, the light stopped there and took shape, finally producing the beautiful Enhanced Armament.

Dusk Taker spread his wings even farther and flapped them hard.

The boosters on Silver Crow's back started to whine, the high-pitched noise of operation.

The only two flying duel avatars in the Accelerated World locked eyes for a brief instant and stilled.

Nomi was the first to kick off the ground, but by the smallest of margins. Dragging the remaining tentacle of his left arm like a tail, the membrane wings beat the air, and a clearly demonic silhouette rose up in a straight line.

Haruyuki carefully watched that trajectory, hips dropped in a low ready position.

"Go!!" At the same time as his sharp call, he opened the boosters all the way. Blue jets of fire scorched the white earth. An almost terrifying propulsive force shot the small avatar up into the air, and he immediately chased after the dark shadow.

Glancing down, Nomi flapped just one wing forcefully. Turning sharply, he brandished his right hand. "Sheeeeh!!" he howled, and the purple fluctuation stretched out into long talons, carving out five arcs in the night sky.

In return, Haruyuki readied the fingers of his right hand. "Laser...Sword!!"

The sword of white light met the purple talons from directly below and collided fiercely. Their weapons were crossed for an instant. The tip of the light sword and the ends of the talons all severed, the pair faced each other and fought with what remained of their Incarnate weapons.

A thick gash raked Dusk Taker's chest, but five thin scars etched into Silver Crow's, sending dichromatic sparks flying. Gritting his teeth against the pain, Haruyuki continued to ascend, and when the energy gauge for the boosters was exhausted, he opened his hands and dropped in free fall.

The price he paid for the overwhelming propulsive power of the Gale Thruster, the Enhanced Armament he had been given by Sky Raker, was that it used up the entire gauge once it was ignited. He couldn't break the jet propulsion up into chunks and hover by adjusting the power. Once he reached the pinnacle of the ascent trajectory, all he could do was control the direction of descent with the booster stabilizers. Normally, you would have to wait nearly ten minutes for the gauge to be full again.

But Haruyuki was able to overwrite the system with the message that he could fly, using the Movement Expansion Incarnate. Of course, he was nowhere near the level where he could fly with that alone. But at the moment, with the Gale Thruster on his back, he could use the power of his imagination to get the system to reduce the gauge-charging time to the bare minimum.

He might have been far from mastering the Incarnate System, but by combining the image of flight—which was in his bones thanks to all his experience in the sky—with the system-type propulsive power of the Gale Thruster, Haruyuki could fly.

The problem was it took almost five seconds to activate the Incarnate to recover the gauge.

And Nomi, who had watched him do the Incarnate charge in the previous fight, knew that, too.

As he fell, Haruyuki spread his hands far out to his sides and visualized the clear image of flapping the wings on his back through the sky. Following Niko's advice to reduce the activation time, he figured he had better give this Incarnate a name, too. But he felt a serious resistance to giving the desire to fly an "attack name" and fixing the image.

Because this was a wish that had been secreted away in the depths of his heart for a long, long time—it was the core that produced this avatar, Silver Crow—what else could he call it but *hope*?

Thus, Haruyuki simply prayed silently. *I can fly. Even if my wings have been stolen, no matter how much pain I'm suffering, no matter how many times I'm made to crawl, I will still aim for the sky.*

This prayer was, to Nomi, however, a serious opening.

"You think I'm going to let you?!" Dusk Taker called fiercely and worked his black wings madly, charging in a straight line.

Haruyuki mustered all his mental stretch to ignore the ominous flapping and completed his image. In his heart, a clear blue sky unfolded. The excess light became illusory wings and was released, pouring into the booster sitting there and becoming a fuel called *determination*.

Skrrk! He felt an intense impact and five talons dug deeply into his chest, crisscrossing his earlier wound.

"Hng!" Sparks cascaded down to the ground as he groaned. Haruyuki popped his eyes open and grabbed on to the tentacle of Dusk Taker's left arm as he tried to fly away.

The wings, being the materialization of the flying ability, definitely had a much higher degree of freedom than the boosters. But they had a weak point: In compensation for that high maneuverability, they lacked stability.

Yanked by his own tentacle in Haruyuki's hand, Nomi abruptly lost his balance and fell into a half tailspin. Using that force, Haruyuki whirled around with all his might and severed the tentacle in one stroke of his light sword. Centrifugal force was added to his propulsive force, and Dusk Taker shot through the sky horizontally.

"Tcch!" A cry of anger slipping from between his lips, Nomi frantically flapped his wings to regain balance. But control did not return so easily.

Haruyuki turned his body in Nomi's direction, took a deep breath, and yelled, "Flyyyyy!!"

The Gale Thruster responded with the throaty sound of flames.

Haruyuki charged through the dark night, a blue shooting star. The light of the ground and the stars in the sky all melted away in circles around him; his eyes saw only the clear form of Dusk Taker. He drew his right hand in. Lined up his fingers. There was no longer any need to shout the attack name. The pure thought *pierce* turned into light and moved into his hand, quavering violently.

"Aaaaaah!!"

Riding this howl, Haruyuki released a platinum luminescence into the center of the radial light.

"Sheeeaaah!!" Recovered, Nomi met him with the talons of his right hand and a battle yell.

An explosive shock wave roared through the world, piercing with its resonance.

The tip of the light sword was held fast deep within the five talons of nothingness, effectively stopping it. But right hands extended, the point where the two avatars met grew powerfully hot, clashing vibrations singeing their masks.

"Ugh, ah, yaah!!" Haruyuki throttled the energy of the gauge jetting out from the boosters, attempting to break Nomi's defense. The thunder on his back grew infinitely louder. The flames reached out endlessly, dyeing the sky blue.

A little more. I can reach him if I just push a little harder. My sword will reach the ultimate enemy. A little more...Just a little...!!

Even with his accelerated senses, he could see the energy gauge in the top left of his field of view dropping rapidly. Once the gauge was exhausted, Nomi would no doubt slice him up with those claws and not allow him the window he needed to Incarnate-charge. He had to break through before that!

"Ah...Aaah!!"

His overheated brain burned his vision into whiteness. But he had already wrung his imagination dry and nearly pierced the wall before him.

Skrrk. Skrrk. The silver light pushed into the nothingness. His gauge emptied mercilessly.

Perhaps because he had been so focused on the extremely concentrated attack, the field itself rippled and shuddered. The light sword pushed into the center of this ripple, bit by small bit.

It hit him. The tip of his sword finally touched the palm of Nomi's actual hand.

And the final pixel glittering in the energy gauge disappeared.

The thunder of combustion wavered, and the jet of flames flickered.

A wild smile rose up on the lips beneath Dusk Taker's visor.

And then—

"Now, Corvus. A little more."

He heard a voice, and a pale hand came to support his right arm.

"Come on, fight. Just a little more."

Another voice rang in his ears, and someone pushed on his shoulder.

"Ungh…Ah…Aaaaaah!!" Haruyuki howled, focusing his remaining power on the single point of his right hand. Although it was for a mere moment, an enormous flame jetted from the boosters, despite the empty gauge.

This final propulsive force shot him forward and the sword of light finally broke through the wall of nothingness. The five talons scattered into purple phosphorescence and evaporated.

"What—" As if to drown Nomi's gasp:

Kreeeeeeen!!

The superextended sword of light cut Dusk Taker's right arm perfectly in two, and the pieces fell apart into countless fragments.

"Ngaaah!!"

Haruyuki's consciousness was exhausted, to the point where it was a mystery that he could still move. Even in this half-autopilot state, however, with an overarm stroke, he plunged his left hand into the chest of his enemy as hard as he could, before he could drop from the heights of the sky.

The light of his Incarnate was so weak it was barely visible, but he felt a powerful resistance nonetheless as his arm pierced the darkness avatar, the tip coming out through its back.

"Hng!…Nnnngh!" Scattering reddish-purple sparks, Nomi groaned and his upper body reeled.

One more hit!!

If he hit Dusk Taker with one more serious blow, his HP gauge would be finished.

But Haruyuki would almost certainly die with him. He didn't have enough power left to control his descent, much less charge the Gale Thruster one more time. He had just the barest amount of HP left; if he crashed into the ground from this height, he would vanish in short order.

But even if I do, that's okay.

As long as we both go down and all of our points are given to Cyan Pile, as long as Takumu takes up this dream of mine, my fighting won't have been in vain.

Whipping up his awareness, which threatened to disappear, Haruyuki raised his right hand high above him. Setting his aim on the black visor of his enemy, who had also nearly lost consciousness, he readied the final blow—

But the instant he went to strike, he heard a voice.

"Citron Call!!"

A voice he had heard so much and so often, maybe more than his own mother's, the voice he had been listening to the longest. They laughed together, played, sometimes fought, quickly made up. That voice—

Mesmerized, Haruyuki looked at the ground. A pillar of beautiful emerald-green light soared up from the avatar the color of fresh leaves standing quietly in the schoolyard and enveloped Dusk Taker.

The ringing of infinite bells spread out through the night sky.

As if it were the blessing of an angel, the light restored the dusk-colored avatar. The cracked and scorched armor regained its sheen. Lost arms were regenerated.

An instantaneous and painfully deep despair blanketed Haruyuki.

In the depths of the black spherical mask, reddish-purple eyes blinked and shone brightly once again.

"Heh-heh, ha-ha-ha-ha!" The shrill laugh. "Ha-ha-ha! A-ha-ha-ha-ha-ha-ha!!"

The regenerated arms opened wide, wider, and Dusk Taker screamed, "See? Isn't that loyalty absolutely worthy of praise?! So...this is power! This is ruling!! Friendship?! Bonds?! As if I need those!! Rule through pillage!! That alone is absolute power!! Ha-ha-ha-ha…Ha-ha-ha-ha-ha-ha-ha-ha-ha!!" The twisted, loud laughter became an aura and scattered purple electricity racing through the sky.

"Now…it's time…to settle thiiiiis!!" The Nihilistic Fluctuation reached out from ten sinisterly tapered fingers. On the verge of splitting apart Haruyuki's body—

Something happened.

The *pop* of an intense glimmer.

The devil wings sprouting from Dusk Taker's back, spread out to both sides, were shining. Cracks raced through them as though they had been transformed into ultrathin glass. They began to crumble noisily.

And then disappeared.

"Wha—" Nomi gasped, eyelids flying all the way up. "Wh-wh-why are my wings dis—"

Before he could finish, the two avatars shuddered heavily. The flying power that had been keeping them in midair had disappeared, and they began to fall, still entangled.

But Haruyuki soon felt something trying to pull him back. It was hot. A modest, living heat sitting at the tips of his shoulder blades. The speed of Silver Crow's descent alone eased, and his left hand, still piercing Dusk Taker, was pulled free.

The twilight avatar, hands still spread out in mute amazement, fell backward toward the earth.

In contrast, Haruyuki slowed even more, until he finally felt a sense of buoyancy and came to a stop.

It wasn't Gale Thruster. That gauge was completely empty, and the Enhanced Armament remained silent.

Right. This feeling. A yearning that made him want to cry, an exaltation.

"Ah. Ah…" As the sound slipped out of him, tears welled up in both eyes.

The heat in his shoulder blades gradually became hotter. The energy grew and swirled, seeking an outlet. Almost as if his bones were waking up the memory of the organ formerly attached there.

Guided by something, Haruyuki raised his hands and crossed them in front of his body. He clenched his fists. He put his power into it.

"Welcome home. Thank you," he murmured and threw his arms out to the sides.

Claaaang!!

A sound more beautiful than any other filled the night sky.

Even without being able to see directly, Haruyuki knew. Ten metal fins had been deployed on his back on both sides of the booster, shining silver in the reflected moonlight. Platinum wings. The power to reach the heavens, the reason for Silver Crow's existence.

He was finally back. To his original form. To being the sole flying duel avatar in the Accelerated World, a power nurtured and created by his own mental scars.

This conviction and emotion overflowed in his heart—and then something else happened.

The Gale Thruster fused with the wings and the gauge glittered as if linked to them, automatically refilling. He felt like it was telling him to fly.

Haruyuki nodded, and, drawing his right hand into his chest, he turned his body straight down.

In the center of the endlessly unfolding white field, he could see the tiny shadow of Dusk Taker yet falling. He might have lost his wings, but his HP would have been recovered with the power of Citron Call. He might have been able to endure a crash from extremely high up.

But I'm ending this.

Haruyuki spread his silver wings. The fins began to vibrate lightly. A familiar propulsive force enveloped his body. At the same time, the Gale Thruster ignited. Blue flames were reflected

by the silver wings, glittering gorgeously. He held his breath at the awe-inspiring surge of energy.

"Goooooooo!!" Haruyuki shouted

A platinum aura radiated from his wings. The blue jet of flames gushed out farther. At once, Haruyuki broke through the wall of air and flew.

He was likely moving faster than any avatar had ever moved since the beginnings of the Accelerated World. With the propulsive force of the wings and the booster, plus the pull of the virtual gravity, Haruyuki charged ahead, a single bolt of lightning.

Even accelerated as he was, the rest happened in an instant.

With the Incarnate sword in his right hand as the tip, Silver Crow transformed into an arrow of light and closed in on the falling Dusk Taker, touched him, and then plunged through him.

Pop! The dusky avatar flew apart in pieces, spinning from the center of his body. Pushing past where their weapons had crossed without touching these polygon fragments, Haruyuki straightened out his wings and pointed his booster straight down.

The propulsion counterbalanced the ferocity of his descent, and he decelerated before coming to a stop. The soles of his feet grasped the surface of the earth. Crumbling to his knees, Haruyuki heard a heavy crash a moment later. He fought the sudden exhaustion that washed over him and lifted his head.

Looking out at the Umesato Junior High schoolyard near where he had landed revealed a black lump tumbling along.

Dusk Taker. But all that was left of him was his head, chest, and the short tentacles that had started to regenerate from his left shoulder. The eyes beneath his visor were very dim and flickered irregularly. If he had anything left in his HP gauge, it had to be less than 10 percent.

Haruyuki dragged himself to his feet. After he had taken one, two steps, he heard a voice.

"Wh…y…Why…My wings. Disappeared…," Nomi moaned, as if this were an even bigger shock than having his body blown away.

It wasn't Haruyuki who answered.

"That's…because my power isn't healing."

He jerked his head up, and there was Chiyuri—Lime Bell. She was holding her side and the deep holes that had been gouged out of it with her severed right arm.

And standing beside her was Cyan Pile, missing both arms. He could also see Black Lotus and Black Vise facing each other, both on guard, holding themselves in ready positions, but they seemed to have stopped their Incarnate attacks.

"Wh…what?" Nomi muttered hoarsely. "If it's not…a healing ability, then what are you saying it is?"

"Ever since I became a Burst Linker, I thought it was weird," Chiyuri replied quietly after a brief silence. "Like, why would I be given this healing power? But, well…after I healed you for the first time in fifth period on Tuesday, I was talking with Haru and Taku, and I figured it out. Haru said it wasn't just your wounds and HP that were healed; even the machine in your right arm came back. I thought that was pretty strange. That's not healing; it's more like repair. And then…I understood."

Taking a deep breath, the fresh green avatar announced crisply, "My power's not healing. It's turning back time. Time for the avatar it hits goes backward. Which is why…I thought, if I used this power, I could for sure get Haru's wings back. I could rewind time to before Dusk Taker stole Silver Crow's ability and make it like the whole thing never happened."

So that's it. Haruyuki felt a keen pain throb deep in his heart. Tears blurred his vision once again. *And I doubted her. I couldn't trust my old friend when she was trying so hard for me. I'm an idiot. A super, total idiot.*

Hanging his head low, Haruyuki heard a deeply resentful voice rise up from the ground below.

"What…You betrayed me? You betrayed *me*, Lime Bell?" Having lost his body and being near death, Nomi shouted as though his anger gave him power. "After I let you win, after I gave you vast oceans of points, you betray *me*?!"

"No, I didn't. I didn't betray you at all," Chiyuri responded, sounding like she had gotten back just a little of her usual contrary spirit. "The first time I healed you was because you threatened me with the video. And I obeyed you after that to level up and extend the amount of time I could go back...and also for this one chance today. I've never once been your friend!"

A brief silence fell once again.

The dusk-colored avatar shook the ruins of his body and abruptly laughed quietly. "Heh. Heh-heh-heh. Honestly...this one, that one, idiots all of you. I'm sick of looking at your faces; I'm leaving. I'll spread all of your real identities and let someone else finish you off. I'm going to transfer schools and build my own kingdom. Now then, what are you doing, Vise? Hurry up and get me out of here."

Haruyuki jerked his face up and looked over at the layered avatar facing off with Black Lotus in the distance.

"Well, this puts me in a bit of a spot," the jet-black avatar said gently, slowly cocking his head to one side. "Given the situation, that is a very difficult request to respond to, Taker."

"Well then, make the effort. If I'm gone and I'm the main force, then the Research Society itself is in a bit of a spot, isn't it? The BIC information might even be leaked."

"Oh no, I don't think that's a concern. Our BICs have been customized to automatically inactivate the instant they detect when we lose Brain Burst. The chip ends up dissolving into the cerebrospinal fluid and disappears, so tracing us is impossible. And, well...Taker, you of all people should know that former acceleration users are no longer able to interfere in this world in any way."

Haruyuki couldn't even begin to understand the meaning of what Black Vise was saying.

But Nomi raised his head with a start and glared at the moon directly above. "Dammit! Dammit!! Daaaaaammiiiiiit!!" he howled for a while, before snarling at them again. "I won't accept that! I will not allow this to happen! Anyone! Anyone's fine! Come here! Help me! If you do, I'll give you points!!"

That's enough.

The moment Haruyuki had this thought, Takumu looked at him and said, "Should we end this, Haru?"

"Yeah." Nodding, Haruyuki started to walk. To put an end to it all.

As soon as Dusk Taker saw Silver Crow approaching, he began to scream, "S-stop! Okay! From now on, I'll pay tribute in points to you! That's not a bad deal, right?! And I'll even join your Legion for you!!"

As he walked, Haruyuki raised his right hand. A white luminescence grew out of his readied fingers.

"Stop! No! I don't want to lose it! My power! My acceleration!! No, no…Noooooooooo!!" His torso recoiling as he twisted himself inside out, Dusk Taker tried to gain some distance by scrabbling at the earth with his short tentacles.

With a frozen heart, Haruyuki brandished the sword of light high. It flashed down without hesitation.

The air shook and a thin line of light raced along the decorative tiles, stretching out to swallow up Dusk Taker, who was crawling along in front of it. The twilight avatar was soundlessly split in two, straight down the center.

Immediately, an enormous pillar of reddish-purple flame shot up. From inside the flames, countless ribbons of light were released into the sky, only to melt into the air and disappear. The ribbons were woven from detailed digital code; it was a phenomenon that accompanied the final annihilation of a Burst Linker, something he had seen only once before.

In that moment, the marauder who had reigned over Umesato Junior High and held Haruyuki and his friends under his overwhelmingly heavy boot was gone forever from the Accelerated World.

As he stood there stock-still, the system font announcing the conclusion of the sudden-death duel shone redly in Haruyuki's vision. A large quantity of burst points was added to his stock, followed by a message to the effect that he could now advance to level five.

However, he felt no exultation in the victory or even a sense of achievement, just the recognition that it was all over. He dragged his battered body a few steps toward Chiyuri and Takumu.

"Now then."

He heard a resolute voice: Kuroyukihime, who had until that point held the mysterious Burst Linker Black Vise in complete check with an Incarnate battle.

"I have a great many things to ask you, but you don't look like you have any intention of talking. In which case, let's finish this already."

At this, the layered avatar shook his head emphatically.

"No, in these few minutes, I've seen to the point of unpleasantness the actual power of a king. I really don't have a chance of winning. I'll simply quietly take my leave here." His voice was calm, as if he thought nothing of the fact that his companion had completely disappeared before his eyes.

Kuroyukihime gracefully raised the sword of her right hand. "Say what you will; I'm under no obligation to let you go," she whispered in a voice like knives. "I'll cut you down where you stand and use the hour until you regenerate to carefully consider how to properly deal with you."

"Ooh! Scary!" Black Vise batted her words aside lightly as he shrugged. "But my greatest ability is fleeing. Oh, but before that, one thing. I harbor not a shred of ill will toward you all in the Black Legion. I came here because Taker asked me to and paid for my services in advance. Naturally, I received absolutely no information about any of you in the real, and if possible, I would like to have nothing to do with you ever again."

"Too late," Kuroyukihime retorted coolly, and the sword of her right arm was clad in a red aura, the left in blue.

Taking a step forward, there, ahead of her, abruptly, bizarrely, Black Vise clapped together the countless thin panels making up his body. Where he had stood, there was now a single black panel—nothing more than a shadow. From Haruyuki's position, he could just barely make out the shape, but head-on, it was essentially invisible.

"Well then, you all take care." Immediately, the thin panel sank down, melting into the shadows of the schoolyard spreading out at their feet. A whistling sound followed as the avatar sped away.

"Hngh!!" With a slight battle cry, Kuroyukihime waved her right arm straight up into the air.

A red line raced along the ground, bit into the school, and began to climb.

"Uh, ah?!" Haruyuki cried out in surprise as he watched as the southwestern corner of the chalk palace—where the staff room and the principal's office were in the real world—was cut off and crumbled in a heap. Mixed in with the many white objects smashed and scattering, a single small black panel shot off and stabbed into the schoolyard in the distance before turning into an arm and rolling across the ground.

But that was it. The arm soon broke into an infinite number of polygon fragments, scattered, and disappeared.

"So he got away, then." Kuroyukihime lowered her sword.

"Kuroyukihime!!" Haruyuki cried out and began to walk after her, staring at her too beautiful, too brave, and ephemeral form for a while.

He made his avatar—armor blown off its upper body, scarred with countless wounds—run earnestly. Hearing his footfalls, Kuroyukihime whirled around. He stopped before her and clenched both hands tightly.

"Kuroyukihime...Kuroyukihime...I...I..." He couldn't say anything else.

She stared for a moment at the Gale Thruster, the Enhanced Armament fused with the wings glittering on his back. Her violet-blue eyes lit up and she nodded deeply. Raising the sword of her right hand, she patted Haruyuki's shoulder with the blade's ridge. "Well done. I'll have you tell me the details after I return to Tokyo tomorrow. For now, rest and relax."

She then shifted her gaze behind Haruyuki, where Cyan Pile and Lime Bell had also come to stand.

"Takumu, you fought well. Good job. And…Kurashima, or rather, Chiyuri." Here, Kuroyukihime did something unexpected. Turning toward Lime Bell, she lowered her head.

However, the real surprise was the words that followed. "Thank you, really. If you hadn't notified me, I wouldn't have been able to run over here."

"Wh—"

"What?!"

Haruyuki and Takumu cried out in surprise in unison.

"Y-you told her…Chiyu, you?! *Kuroyukihime?!*"

"I did!" Waving the bell of her left hand, Chiyuri shouted in her usual spirited way. "What did you think I came all the way over to your house for, huh? Obviously I came to set the actual fight time and tell Kuroyukihime!"

"Wh-whoa…H-hold on…" Groaning, Haruyuki worked hard to turn the gears of his exhausted brain.

After Haruyuki had sent Nomi the final postponement message immediately before diving into the Unlimited Neutral Field, he had indeed said, "Okay. We dive in one minute."

The instant Chiyuri had heard that, she had pushed the SEND button on a message to Kuroyukihime that was already saved on her virtual desktop. Kuroyukihime, receiving it in Okinawa, had immediately dived into the Unlimited Neutral Field, captured a flying horse Enemy, and raced toward Tokyo for fifteen hours. So that was what happened.

Chiyuri kept going as Haruyuki and Takumu exchanged dumbfounded looks. "I was worried about leaving things to you two stubborn jerks, so I sent Kuroyukihime a mail when you decided on the final battle and told her everything. And then she told me she would run in the field, so I should fix the exact time.

At your house, Haru, I was actually really annoyed! I just wanted you to pick a time already!!"

"S-sorry," he muttered, and then he shook his head hard.

He turned to Kuroyukihime and lowered his head as deeply as he could. "Thank you so much. To take fifteen hours and come to help us…When I saw you on the roof, I was overwhelmed…I was so happy."

"Maybe I put on too much of a show." Kuroyukihime shrugged, and Haruyuki held back his tears to return her smile.

Next he looked at Chiyuri and lowered his head once more. "Thanks, Chiyu. If it had been just Taku and me, we totally would have lost. Thank you…so much." His throat was blocked and his voice shook.

"Honestly." Chiyuri's own voice was also secretly damp. But his old friend continued in a more cheerful tone, "And I'm worried about it being just the two of you from now on, too. Guess I got no choice…I'll join your Nega Nebulus."

"Huh?!"

"Ch-Chi!"

Paying no further attention to the two boys, Chiyuri turned back to Kuroyukihime and tilted her head shyly. Kuroyukihime nodded decisively and did some quick operations on her Brain Burst console. Without the slightest hesitation, Chiyuri pressed the Legion entry application that popped up in her vision.

The two girl-type avatars, one jet-black, the other the color of fresh grass, took a step toward each other.

Sword and bell met with a ringing *clang*.

Haruyuki could only stare silently as Takumu's muttering next to him reached his ears. "What were we so worried about?"

"Seriously. But…this is great. Really great…Really…" Haruyuki stretched out his arm unconsciously and clasped Cyan Pile's shoulder.

Under the blue moonlight of the Accelerated World, the four Burst Linkers stood like this for a while.

Eventually, however, Kuroyukihime lifted her face and ordered her subordinates in a refreshingly clear voice, "Now. Go home. To the real world."

They left the Unlimited Neutral Field through the portal at Koenji station, and Haruyuki returned to his own living room in the real world.

Although the final battle had gone from one unexpected development to the next, it hadn't even taken a full hour altogether. In other words, on this side, it had all happened in a mere three seconds.

However, the instant he returned to his flesh-and-blood body, Haruyuki slumped over onto the table at the enormous sense of exhaustion he felt. Still, he managed to get it in check and lift his face. His blurry eyes focused on Chiyuri, similarly blinking rapidly.

For a mere instant, they exchanged glances. That alone made something hot well up in his heart, and his eyes started to blur dangerously again, so he hurried to open his mouth. "You could've told us."

"Seriously," Takumu said, bobbing his head up and down next to him. "If you had just told us that you contacted Master—no, wait, that you joined up with Nomi to get Haru's wings back, we could've gotten through all this with a little less agony."

The two boys were so full of self-reproach at having doubted their childhood friend, their voices were unintentionally resentful, and Chiyuri sighed deeply before responding with exasperation.

"Now, look! I told you before! I had one chance to rewind Dusk Taker's time with Citron Call! So there was no way I could let Nomi get the slightest idea about what I was up to. I mean, I didn't think he had, but what if Nomi had planted some eavesdropping app or device on me? The second I explained it all to you, the whole thing would be blown!"

Gulping, Haruyuki looked at Takumu, and then murmured in amazement, "Y-you thought that far ahead...even though it's you—"

"Hey! What exactly is that supposed to mean?!" she shouted,

and knocked her chair back as she stood with the intent to come around the table and punch him. But before she could, she fell back into her seat, exhausted, as though standing up had given her a head rush.

Haruyuki and Takumu hurriedly stood and dropped down in front of her.

"Ch-Chi! You okay?!" At Takumu's voice, she nodded lightly, head still hanging.

"I worked really hard, you know," Chiyuri whispered abruptly, tiny tremors in her voice.

Plip! A single droplet of water fell to the laminate floor.

"...It was so incredibly tough...but I kept trying. I worked so hard..."

Plip, plip. The drops falling one after another glittered beautifully like gems on the wood.

Pierced straight through, Haruyuki said gently in a voice that was definitely shaking, "Aah...thank you. Really, thanks, Chiyu."

Heaving a large sob, Chiyuri lifted a face stained with tears and leapt at their necks. She yanked Takumu in on the left and Haruyuki on the right and pushed all of their heads together. "I love you...I love you both!!"

His childhood friend then began to cry like a child, loud and suffering, and Haruyuki squeezed her back tightly. He couldn't maintain his own control then, and tears welled up in his eyes. Something shone on Takumu's cheeks, too, under his glasses.

The three friends—born in the same year, raised in the same place—stayed like this, letting their tears flow.

11

"A win rate of a hundred percent!"

Haruyuki clenched his right hand tightly, and then his shoulders fell as he continued, "Or it *was*. If only we hadn't gotten taken down in that last fight..."

The following day, Saturday April 20, a bright evening. The place was the same as the previous day, the Arita living room.

Every week at that time was the crown jewel of the fighting game Brain Burst: the Territory Battles between Legions. Haruyuki and the other members of Nega Nebulus had been expecting some difficult fights that week given that they were going in with a battle formation that lacked their Master Black Lotus, but they ended up with an almost-complete win ratio.

It was because Lime Bell jumped right in, even though she had just joined the Legion the day before. Her healing ability might have turned out to be the ability to reverse time, but it could also definitely be used as a sham means of recovering HP. The only issue was, if she went back too far, repeatedly cycling through heal, hit, heal, they were back in damage territory, but she managed to keep this straight somehow with an expert's knack.

Thus, Haruyuki and his friends adopted the strategy of always keeping either Silver Crow or Cyan Pile with Lime Bell for protection, while the other attacked and returned to the base for healing. This worked very well, and he thought that they were going to have a total Territories victory for the first time in a long time. But…

The long-distance, three-person team that challenged them last didn't approach their base at all and showered the lone person who came to attack with concentrated firepower. The remaining two were forced to gradually advance, and when the three of them were all together, their enemies blasted with multiple special attacks and wiped out all at once.

"Well, it happens. Just winning as much as we did with a team that was thrown together's more than enough," Takumu said, sipping his large drink, and Haruyuki pursed his lips.

"Yeah, I know. In the end, they got us right in our weak spot, the fact that we don't have any long-distance firepower, and we lost."

"And that weak point's not going to change when Master comes home, either."

"If it's without Incarnate, then yeah."

They both simultaneously remembered Kuroyukihime's long-range technique and how it severed the distant Umesato school building in a single blow, shivers running up their spines.

Chiyuri wasn't there—perhaps embarrassed about all the crying she did the day before, she said she would dive from her own place—so it was just the two of them. After popping into his mouth a fry from the hamburger meal he had bought in the shopping mall on the first floor, Haruyuki cleared his throat and changed the subject.

"Anyway, nice work in there. And…Taku. That…Have you had any contact?" He left out the "from Nomi" part.

"No, none." Takumu shook his head slightly. "I'm a little worried about it, though. I mean, it's Nomi. He might have proposed the battle, but I seriously can't believe he'd give up, even if he did lose."

"Me, either."

The air suddenly heavy, they both fell silent.

"That avatar that showed up there, Black Vise," Haruyuki said as he chewed on the end of another fry. "He said something weird. About how former acceleration users who had lost Brain Burst couldn't interfere with the Accelerated World. Wonder what that was supposed to mean."

"Huh? Isn't it just that they can't accelerate, so they can't fight?"

"That's what I thought, too, at the time. But, like, that kind of goes without saying. You don't really need to go out of your way to push the point. Hey, Taku. Maybe you don't want to talk about it, but..." He glanced over at his friend sitting next to him on the sofa. "Your 'guardian'...the captain of the kendo team at your old school...He had a forced uninstall with the Blue King's Judgment Blow, right?"

"Yeah, that's what I heard."

"Did you guys talk after that? Like about Brain Burst."

At this, Takumu furrowed his brow in an interesting shape and appeared to think for a minute. "I was in a pretty big hurry to transfer schools after all that...I went to say my good-byes to the kendo team, but our teammates were there, too, so naturally, I didn't say anything about Brain Burst. And, I dunno, he seemed to be surprisingly over it, so I didn't dare bring it all back for him."

"Over it...?" Haruyuki muttered, and thought for a minute; he felt like he had heard something similar before. He soon hit on it.

Cherry Rook, Red King Niko's guardian. After using the Armor of Catastrophe to run wild in the Accelerated World, he had been judged for his crimes by Niko's hand and lost Brain Burst. Later, Niko had said he was back to his old self and was talking to her for real again. He had said that even though he was moving, he planned to keep playing other net games together with her. Somehow, this was similar to what Takumu had told him just now.

But there was no way either of these cases fit Nomi in any way. Nomi's resentful screaming immediately before he left the Accelerated World stuck in Haruyuki's ears even now. He had been prepared for the fairly likely eventuality of some kind of vengeance. But Haruyuki, Takumu, Chiyuri—none of them had had any contact from him.

"Guess our only choice is to go talk to him in person on Monday," Takumu said slowly, and Haruyuki nodded slightly.

"Guess so. There's the video thing, too…"

Now that he was no longer a Burst Linker, Nomi had nothing left to lose in the Accelerated World. If he decided to, he could reveal that video he secretly took to get his revenge and also disseminate the real identities of Haruyuki and his friends to other Burst Linkers. The only counterattack they had was the brain implant chip in Nomi's head, but Black Vise had said something worrying about that.

If you lost Brain Burst, the BIC would automatically cease functioning and melt away.

The BIC body was a synthetic protein micromachine assembly. Depending on the programming, it could be detached/dissolved, in which case, it would no longer be detectable with a scan. In other words, it stopped being a reason for Nomi to be expelled.

Which is why Haruyuki and his friends couldn't just cut off contact with Nomi. They still had to go to him and negotiate, to force him to delete the video. It was seriously depressing.

Finishing off his drink, Takumu dumped the ice in the kitchen, carefully washed the recycled materials cup, and threw it in the special bag. "Okay, then, on Monday at school. You want me to come with you when you go see Nomi?"

"No, I'll be fine. I'll go by myself, thanks. G'night." He saw Takumu off at the door and went back to the living room to clean up, sighing. He looked at the clock on his virtual desktop, and then stared out the window at the night sky.

She's still on the plane right now. Or maybe she's landed at the airport already, he wondered idly, and then shook his pudgy head and switched tracks. He'd get to see her on Monday at school. He'd waited a whole week; he could handle another day and a half.

He had wrestled his emotions back under control, so that when the doorbell rang minutes later, he assumed Takumu had forgotten something. Not wanting to bother with the hassle of the intercom window, he went back to the entryway. "Coming," he said as he unlocked the door.

"What? You forget some—" The *thing* got stuck in his throat, and his heart stopped. Without even being aware of this, Haruyuki opened his eyes so wide, they almost popped out.

Standing there, paper bag in one hand, carrier bag with motor assist dangling from the other, was a girl in the Umesato Junior High school uniform. In the slight breeze that wafted down the corridor, her dark red ribbon and long black hair fluttered, and he caught the faint scent of the tropics.

"How many seconds are you going to stay frozen?" she asked, and Haruyuki's brain finally restarted.

Bwah! After several at-best-ragged breaths, Haruyuki squeezed out a hoarse voice. "K-K-Ku-Kuro—Kuroyukihime?! Wh-wh-wh—"

"Some hello. And after I came straight here from Haneda to bring you a souvenir."

The expression on the face of the older student—Kuroyukihime, cheeks puffed out adorably—made Haruyuki jump to attention. Quickly, he swept his right hand back like a traffic control robot. "Oh! C-c-come in! Please come in!"

"Thanks. I'd be glad to." Nodding crisply, Kuroyukihime walked into the entryway, left her shoes and carrier bag there, and stepped up into the hallway. She moved briskly past Haruyuki and went into the living room.

Chasing after her, feet tangling underneath him, Haruyuki no longer had any idea of what he should do and shot his eyes around and around his apartment before saying, "Uh, um, my mom never gets home until late."

"I know. That's why I came."

"Y-you did? Uh, so…R-right, t-t-t-tea!"

Calm down! Calm down and deal with this! he told himself as he started toward the kitchen, and Kuroyukihime reached into the paper bag with a quick "Oh yes."

"Perhaps you could also warm this up in the microwave for me." She pulled out an enormous yellowish-brown sphere. Haruyuki accepted the object that was maybe fifteen centimeters in diameter and stared at it intently.

The characters printed on the clear packaging in a somehow Okinawa-like font read ANDAGI BOMB.

"Is this *sata andagi*?"

"Mmm. You did put in a request, didn't you, saying you'd like one thirty centimeters round? As expected, there were none that big, so you'll have to make do with this."

"N-no, this is plenty big. I'm kind of surprised."

"Right? I was surprised, too, when I came across it."

Ha-ha-ha!

Haruyuki stared long and hard at Kuroyukihime's laughing face, and finally felt his nervousness dissipate. At the same time, his eyes got a little misty, so he hurriedly whirled around and escaped to the kitchen.

He pulled the enormous Okinawa-style doughnut from the bag and warmed it in the microwave. He brought a bottle of oolong tea and two glasses to the table, rolled the now-heated *andagi* onto a plate, and after a moment's thought, took it and a small knife out with him.

Already seated at the dining table, Kuroyukihime took the knife from the plate, and as adroit with a blade as would be expected, she split the *andagi* into two perfect halves. "Here." She pushed one half toward Haruyuki, steam rising up from the golden cross-section.

"Th-thanks." He took it from her and bit into the edge. Enjoying both the crunchy surface and the moist insides, he thought to himself, *I get it. There's a reason it's this big.*

"I-it's delicious. Really delicious."

"Is it? Good."

Here, Haruyuki finally stumbled onto the question of why he had even asked for a giant *andagi* in the first place. Munching on it, he tried desperately to remember his own actions, as the smile on the face of Kuroyukihime across the table from him grew even broader, beautiful like a narcissus.

"Now then, Haruyuki," she said.

"Y-yes?"

"Shall I tell you what I'm feeling right now?"

"O-okay."

"Forty-nine percent the desire to praise you for a job well done. Fifty percent the desire to punch you."

And the last one percent?

This was perhaps not the time to ask such questions, and he straightened his back. A rather large lump got caught in his throat and after somehow managing to swallow it, Haruyuki thrust his head downward.

"I-I'm so sorry! I take responsibility for everything. I didn't want to bother you on your trip, but then I ended up relying on you in the end…And, I mean, I made you run fifteen hours from Okinawa and everything…"

"Look, you." The smile changed to a dangerous look suddenly, and Kuroyukihime produced an extremely displeased voice. "I'm not mad about having to fight. Just the opposite. Why didn't you call me right from the start? If you had said even a word about the situation, I would've flown home from Okinawa right away!"

"Th-that's…I mean, you only get one school trip your whole life, don't you—"

"Either way, it wasn't that much fun! And I suppose you won't understand the reason for that, either, unless I tell you!" She said it with such force that if she had been her duel avatar, there was no doubt she would've sliced the table in two with the sharpness. She frowned sullenly, but, fortunately, she soon sighed, dropped most of the swords in her voice, and continued. "Well, that's fine. In any case, you'll tell me now. Everything from start to finish— don't leave out a single byte of information!"

And then Haruyuki told her everything as he chewed on the giant doughnut. The long, long story from the appearance of Seiji Nomi to the first battle with Dusk Taker, the training in the

Unlimited Neutral Field, and the events leading up to the previous day's battle.

When he had finished the nearly hour-long explanation, Kuroyukihime lowered her long lashes and sighed softly. A few seconds later, she opened her mouth. "Haruyuki. When you summoned that Enhanced Armament—Gale Thruster— I thought my heart would stop."

Drinking his oolong tea, Haruyuki jerked his face up. However, no words came out.

Sky Raker, the recluse of the Accelerated World, had given Haruyuki the Gale Thruster. She had been a core member of the initial Nega Nebulus and also Kuroyukihime's friend. Seeking the sky as if possessed, Sky Raker had asked Kuroyukihime to cut her own legs off for her. Kuroyukihime had agreed—and after that, she had apparently thrown herself into the bloody battle with the other kings.

But right now, Kuroyukihime's face was calm, a somehow plaintive smile rising to her lips. "So unexpected…that she would be the one to initiate you into the Incarnate System."

"…I'm sorry. I didn't get your permission. I just went off on my own."

"No." Kuroyukihime shook her head gently at his apologies. "She's likely more qualified for it than I am. Of all the high-level Linkers who have mastered Incarnate, Raker is probably the one who most believes in the possibilities of that system. And…I no doubt could not have been that complete of a demon toward you."

A giggle tumbled from her lips and Haruyuki gave her a big nod.

"Sh-she was amazing. She pushed me off of the top of the old Tokyo Tower."

"Ha-ha-ha! That's so like her." She laughed fondly for a moment before abruptly falling silent.

She dropped her gaze to fix it on a single point on the table, but then finally stood up, chair clattering slightly. She moved to the front of the large window on the southern side of the apartment and stared wordlessly at the night outside.

For a while, Haruyuki watched her back with the long black hair flowing down it, but then resolved himself and stood up as well. He walked over to her and looked outside with her.

"The Incarnate System is extremely enormous," she said slowly, after a few seconds. "Thus, it enthralls everyone who touches it. They master the depths of the power, charging forward to make it their own. But, well...this is what I think. If it were a simple program bug, the administrator wouldn't just leave it, they'd do something about it. Thus, the power is not an irregular system generated accidentally but rather...part of Brain Burst from the start. Perhaps as some sort of trap."

"A-a trap...?"

"Mmm. To lure us Burst Linkers in and draw our minds to another dimension somewhere..."

The meaning of her words was a complete mystery to Haruyuki. Still, he furrowed his brow and tried to understand somehow. Kuroyukihime glanced at him and then touched her left hand gently to his cheek.

"No, don't bother yourself about it. All you need to do is simply move straight ahead the way you are. Mmm...Perhaps you...You might be able to surpass that deep darkness and approach the true light at the heart..."

Laughing softly, Kuroyukihime brought her right hand up to his face as well. Her expression and tone shifted. "Now. Shall I tell you the remaining one percent of my feelings?"

Haruyuki's entire body stiffened with a gasp. *Something more than* punch?! *So then, some kind of leg technique?! Or maybe a submission hold?!*

As Haruyuki's mind raced with absurd thoughts, Kuroyukihime wrapped both arms around his neck and pulled him firmly toward her chest. Held tightly, his brain quickly over-revved at the pressure from all directions and the sensation of contact against his face; the gears whined and shrieked.

A voice arrived at his no doubt burning red left ear from so close that the lips uttering it were practically touching him.

"I wanted to do this. Ever since I got Chiyuri's mail telling me you had had your wings stolen…and that despite that, you were trying so hard to stand up to your enemy. All this time, I've wanted to do this."

Kuroyukihime hugged Haruyuki even harder, with a power that seemed impossible for those thin arms, and whispered in a trembling voice, "You really did do great. It must have been so hard…I'm sorry I couldn't be there for you. I…I'm a failure as a guardian."

A hot droplet touched his left cheek with a *plop*.

Haruyuki opened his eyes. The glossy hair swinging in his field of vision blurred and mixed with the light. Unconsciously, he raised his arms and wrapped his hands around her slim waist. He forced out shudderingly, "M-me, too. I'm sorry for making you worry."

"I was worried," she told him, half shouting, and her shoulders shook in tiny earthquakes. "I was so worried. I don't know what I would've done if I had lost you…I was scared. I was really scared!"

Throat blocked, Haruyuki couldn't say anything more. So he chanted in his heart earnestly, *I'm here. I'll always be with you. I'll never disappear.*

For the next minute or two, thin sobs escaped her, but at last, she took a deep breath and finally relaxed her hold slightly. "I have to give you your reward," she said suddenly.

"Huh, re…?" Haruyuki blinked repeatedly.

"You defended wonderfully in the Territories, didn't you? I told you, if you ferociously defended Suginami, I would let you ask me for anything as a reward."

Having such a thing whispered in his ear, Haruyuki's consciousness was plunged once again into the red zone.

However…

Rude thoughts like directing with a thirty-centimeter cable or bathing suit pictures were instantly swept away.

Being here like this right now.

This person continuing to exist for him in this world. What else could he want?

I'm going to get a lot stronger and someday become a knight who can protect you from any enemy. So until then, please be by my side, watching over and guiding me.

The instant he made this wish, his mouth began to move half automatically.

"Then please be with me." He gave voice to the feelings welling up deep in his heart just as they were. "Please be with me forever. That's it...That's all I want."

Even after you graduate. As my mentor. As my Legion Master. And as my guardian, he was about to add in the back of his mind when Kuroyukihime's body, so gentle against Haruyuki's head, stiffened intensely with a *snap*.

She suddenly ended the embrace, dashed back nearly two meters, hit the sofa, and fell onto it. Although her face was kind of a mess with the tears, she had opened her eyes wide as if she'd forgotten all about that, and was flapping her mouth. Finally, her face burst into rapid flames from her neck up to her forehead. Her voice, turned inside out, rang out at a high pitch.

"Wh-wh-wh-what are you even talking about?!"

"Huh? Um, what? I—I. Just. It's. Nothing."

Not understanding what was happening, he opened and closed his own mouth at the same high speed, and after a full ten seconds or so had passed, Kuroyukihime's face started to return to its usual paleness, from the top to the bottom. *Haaah.* Letting loose a very long sigh, she shook her head back and forth repeatedly.

"Understood," she murmured suddenly. She stood and walked over to Haruyuki once more, placing her right hand on his head. "I promise you. I will be by your side. Forever and into the future."

So said Kuroyukihime, brushing aside her hair, the biggest smile slipping onto her lips.

12

"Arita, hit me!! Please, hit me!!" The shaved head in front of him cried for the *n*th time as it was thrust forward.

The owner of both head and voice was Ishio from the basketball team, the same student who had called Haruyuki up to the roof a few days earlier and punched him.

"N-no, it's fine. I get it." Haruyuki also repeated the same words for the *n*th time as he desperately looked for a way out.

But the place was the teacher's podium in grade eight, class C, the time Monday morning homeroom, and with forty students filling the room on his right, there was no escape route. On top of that, his homeroom teacher was standing on the other side of Ishio, arms crossed with a meek look on his face. So this was what it meant to have your back pushed against the wall.

Ishio brought his face even closer and, making an upside-down *V* of his eyebrows, argued vehemently, "No! I'll never forgive myself unless you hit me!! I just jumped to the conclusion that you were the one who tried to take the secret video, even though I had no proof of that. And on top of that, I even hit you! Seriously, the school should be kicking me out or something! But you didn't say anything to the teacher. I can't leave things like this!!"

Then go and hit yourself! Haruyuki yelled inwardly and, looking for rescue, glanced at Chiyuri and then Takumu. But the two merely grinned. They were thoroughly enjoying this. That the "secret camera incident," in which a small digital camera had been discovered in a locker in the girls' shower room, had reached this sudden turn was all due to Kuroyukihime.

The strategy she had implemented with the skill and sagacity of nothing other than a networking wizard was simple and immediately effective. She had slipped into the school's lost and found list a record with the exact same manufacturer, product number, and serial number as the discovered camera.

Naturally, Haruyuki asked if it was okay for her to do that, but Kuroyukihime was quick to reply that a camera that had, from the start, had nothing to do with him would now have even less to do with him.

When even the serial numbers matched, there could be no room to doubt that that camera was actually one that had turned up lost two years earlier. And Haruyuki hadn't been at the school two years earlier. The suspicion that he had set it up and turned it on was instantly erased. The moment Sugeno made this announcement during homeroom, Ishio had stood up and dragged Haruyuki in front of the podium—and that was how he ended up in this situation now.

"C'mon, hit me! Please!" Ishio shouted again.

Haruyuki stared, groaning in his heart, *You're saying all this here, but you know, the classroom is totally covered by social cameras. You're just making new proof that you broke the school rules. And you, Sugeno! You should be stopping him! Why are you just watching with that weird look?!*

But Ishio seemed to already be resolved not to shut it down unless Haruyuki threw a punch at him.

Swallowing a sigh, Haruyuki whispered, "O-okay, if it's not your face. Your stomach." *And from this angle, the cameras won't pick up a body blow,* he added to himself mentally.

Ishio grinned broadly, as if delighted, and got up with an "All right!"

Carefully measuring the visual field of the cameras, Haruyuki clenched his right hand. He launched an awkward punch, and his round fist slammed into toned stomach muscles and bounced back.

After a momentary grimace, Ishio was quick to grin again. "You're a good guy," he said, and returned to his seat.

The punch hadn't even been close to payback, although Haruyuki had put pretty much all he had into it. Grumbling in his mind, he heaved a sigh of relief and also went to sit down.

"Arita." He heard Sugeno's solemn voice from behind. "I'm really sorry. Come and hit me, too! It's okay!"

Give me a break!! Haruyuki yelled, not quite out loud.

However...

This did not bring the whole matter to a conclusion. A bigger and much weightier task still awaited Haruyuki: the negotiations with Seiji Nomi. Until he took care of the secret video of the shower room that Nomi had saved, Haruyuki wouldn't be able to attend school with any kind of peace of mind.

It was no sooner lunch break than he was headed up to the third floor, where the seventh-grade classrooms were. He waited near the stairs, and a few minutes after he arrived, he saw the familiar longish hair in a group that was no doubt headed toward the lounge. Seiji Nomi was walking with several classmates, chatting cheerfully. As they approached, Haruyuki's palms started to sweat and his heart raced.

Three days ago, I fought the ultimate battle with this guy, all our hatred going up against each other. And I mercilessly took his Brain Burst. I completely wiped out the power of acceleration when he was so fixated on it.

Nomi grew steadily closer as these thoughts raced through Haruyuki's mind. He batted eyelashes long like a girl's, and his eyes caught sight of Haruyuki standing in a corner of the hallway.

And then he passed right on by.

Haruyuki stopped breathing. He had been expecting to be glared at or cursed out, but to be ignored...

No, this was different from being ignored. It was almost like Nomi didn't know him. As if he were just another student at the same school, one of hundreds.

Haruyuki unconsciously took a step forward and called out to Nomi as he passed. "Uh, um!"

Stopping and looking at Haruyuki again, Nomi cocked his head with a puzzled look on his face.

"Um...Nomi...right?"

"Mm-hmm. Did you need something?"

What? What is going on?

Working hard to contain his confusion, Haruyuki moved his mouth stiffly. "Um, I, uh, wanted to talk to you."

A suspicious look came over the other boy's face again, and then Nomi turned to his friends and told them to go on ahead to the cafeteria. He looked once again at Haruyuki.

"What is it?"

"Uh...umm..."

It didn't seem like an act. The small-statured freshman before him was simply staring curiously at the upperclassman who had called out to stop him. There was not a trace of any other emotion on his neat features.

No way. Is it a different person? Like his twin brother or something? Haruyuki thought, and figured he might as well introduce himself.

"Um, I'm Arita. Eighth grade. Haruyuki Arita."

Nomi didn't even twitch an eyebrow. "...Arita." Frowning, he had the air of trying to remember something. "Oh, oh, right. We've played that net game together."

"...Th-that's...right."

Weird. Something is totally, incredibly weird.

Looking up at Haruyuki standing there, Seiji Nomi appeared to be searching his memory even more intently. He said:

*   *   *

"Let's see…That game…*What was it called again…*"

The awesome terror Haruyuki felt in that instant was, without doubt, the greatest fear he'd felt since becoming a Burst Linker. Horrified cold shivers, fiercer than when he had faced Chrome Disaster and the Armor of Catastrophe, fiercer than when Dusk Taker had stolen his wings, raced up his spine in great numbers.

His memory's gone!

He could no longer believe it was anything else. By some means or another, essentially all memories relating to Brain Burst had been erased from the mind of Seiji Nomi.

He didn't remember. Not that he had been the "marauder" Dusk Taker. Not the desperate battles he had fought against Haruyuki and his friends. Not even the existence of the Accelerated World.

Taking some cue from the expression on Haruyuki's face, Nomi smiled as if troubled. "Oh, did you maybe come to invite me to play? I'm sorry, but I don't really have much interest in net games anymore."

Haruyuki could only stare at the lowerclassman and the seemingly sincere look of apology on his face.

Immediately before the suspicion took back control of Nomi's face, Haruyuki forced himself to smile and made his mouth move. "Oh. You don't? Then…that's okay. Um, and that video of mine…"

"What? Video? I'm sorry, what was it again?"

"Nah, sorry. It's nothing."

When Haruyuki shook his head shortly, Nomi smiled again and bowed his own neatly. "It is? Well, then I'll be on my way."

And then the boy formerly known as Dusk Taker whirled his lithe body around and hurried down the hallway until he disappeared from view.

Reeling backward a few steps, Haruyuki leaned a back covered in cold sweat up against the wall of the hallway and closed his eyes tightly.

Former acceleration users are no longer able to interfere in the Accelerated World in any way.

Haruyuki now finally understood what the mysterious avatar Black Vise had meant. Burst Linkers who lost Brain Burst lost all memories relating to the Accelerated World. Thus, they can do nothing. They don't try to do anything.

Having pushed his actual brother, his own guardian, into a forced uninstall, Seiji Nomi would have known this fact. The moment his avatar had scattered in the moonlit field, he had even acknowledged it. That his own memories would disappear. That even the idea "former Burst Linker" would be gone from his own awareness.

"This is...This...," Haruyuki muttered, face pale in front of a seventh-grade classroom, and the students stared at him curiously.

After school.

At the usual table in the cafeteria lounge, Haruyuki related his discovery to Takumu and Kuroyukihime. There wasn't another soul around.

Even just explaining it, he was forced to feel that fear again. He was anxious that maybe the Brain Burst program was monitoring every word he spoke, and the instant it detected key words like *uninstall*, *memory*, and *erase*, Haruyuki's own memories would be purged.

Thus, after making them all take off their Neurolinkers, Haruyuki told the story like a tongue twister. Even after they had heard everything, his audience of two didn't speak for a while.

After a full thirty seconds or so of silence, Kuroyukihime lifted her teacup and wet her lips before almost whispering, "You both must have thought it strange. How could the existence of the Accelerated World continue to be so perfectly hidden like this over seven and a half years?"

"...Yeah." Haruyuki nodded sharply. "If it were me, and I lost

Brain Burst, I'd be a total mess. There's a pretty good chance I'd expose everything on the net or to the media and try to bring the Accelerated World down with me."

"Hey now, is it all about you?" Kuroyukihime offered a faint, wry grin and set her cup down before continuing, "But, well, there are definitely some people who think like that. And some of them would move from thought to actual action. But for some reason, no one has. We guessed at several reasons for this. Because without proof, children can say whatever they want and the media won't believe them. Because a system deleting all Brain Burst information has made inroads into every network. And one reason I've heard at the rumor level…" Her black eyes narrowed sharply. Her voice became even more contained. "Because when Brain Burst is deleted, it takes your memories with it. But…I didn't—no, I couldn't believe that unless I saw it with my own eyes. However, here we are…This reason is, in fact, the truth."

Silence once again.

"But, Master. To begin with, is that even possible?" Takumu asked in a choked voice. Having come during the break in kendo practice, he was still in his kendo gear. "I mean, a single application, deleting a user's—no, a human being's memory…"

"I have heard that in theory, it's not impossible," Kuroyukihime replied, staring at the three devices in the center of the white table. "Strictly speaking, it isn't as though the Neurolinker accesses the brain as a living organism."

"Huh? Th-then what does it connect with…?" Haruyuki furrowed his brow.

Kuroyukihime shifted her gaze and stared into his eyes with her own obsidian ones. "I don't exactly understand it properly myself. There are these things called microtubules in the cells of the brain that entrap the light quanta that are the true nature of human consciousness. The Neurolinker reads the spin and vector that these quanta store as the data itself and writes over them. At this level, there's no difference in the data format, whether it be sensory or memory information."

"...So then, in the same way it shows us and makes us feel the virtual world, the Neurolinker can read our memories and overwrite them...Is that it?" Haruyuki said, almost moaning, and Kuroyukihime shook her head firmly.

"It's all hypothetical. And even if this were, in principle, possible, I can't imagine that a commercial item like the Neurolinker would be equipped with such a function. I can't imagine it, but..."

Seiji Nomi has, in fact, lost his memory.

None of them said it out loud, but they were certainly all thinking it.

"It's pointless to discuss this any further," Kuroyukihime said crisply, after another silence of indeterminate length. "If we want to know the answers, our only option is to reach level ten and ask the developer of Brain Burst."

"I—I guess so. And that was our goal right from the start..." Nodding, Haruyuki timidly asked Takumu, "So...how's Nomi looking?"

"Like a completely regular seventh-grade team member. The demon's been exorcised...and I guess that's it. He's always been so cheerful on the surface, so maybe no one other than us will be able to tell the difference." After a brief pause, Takumu muttered hoarsely, "Haru, I can't help wondering...who's normal now and who's not, us or Nomi..."

"It's obvious. We're the not-normal ones." The immediate response came from Kuroyukihime. Leaning back in her chair, she crossed her black tights–clad legs neatly, in a gesture that showed she had completely regained her usual solemnity. The Black King looked at each of her two subordinates in turn and added with a daring smile, "However, we chose this path. Yes?"

"Honestly, you're totally right, Master." Blinking rapidly, Takumu laughed quietly. "Yikes! I have to be getting back. Um... Regarding this and Chi..."

"Mmm. For the time being, we'll keep this to ourselves."

Bowing neatly, Takumu got up from his seat and plucked the

blue Neurolinker off the table before he trotted away, wide black *hakama* pants swinging.

Once they could no longer see him, Kuroyukihime stared at Haruyuki. "Even if I lose Brain Burst, even if all my memories of the Accelerated World are wiped away," she whispered, "you alone I won't forget. I definitely won't forget you."

Feeling a sudden tightness in his chest, Haruyuki earnestly returned her words. "I know. Me neither. I won't forget. Just you at least."

"Mmm. I believe you." Grinning, Kuroyukihime nodded exaggeratedly. "Now then, does this mean that this series of incidents is at an end?"

Haruyuki hesitated briefly and then shook his head slowly from side to side. "No. I still have one more promise to keep."

"Oh? What's that?" She cocked her head to one side.

"Please." Haruyuki bowed his head deeply. "Take me to meet with the person who lent me her wings…Sky Raker."

Five PM.

Haruyuki and Kuroyukihime walked out through the gates of Umesato Junior High together. Wordlessly, they strode along Oume Kaido and turned to the north midway along it. When they reached a narrow road, they headed for Koenji Station.

Kuroyukihime had sent a text mail, after a fair bit of hesitation, and the response had come ten minutes later. Just two lines of characters specifying a time and a place.

To go to this meeting place—the Southern Terrace at the south exit of Shinjuku Station—the pair boarded the Chuo Line at the station. Kuroyukihime was entirely silent. Haruyuki couldn't even begin to guess at the sort of thoughts going through her mind.

Now that he had his flying ability back, he needed to return the Enhanced Armament, the Gale Thruster, to Sky Raker. That was the promise he had made to her. But Haruyuki had thoughtlessly forgotten to ask for a way to contact her in the real world. Thus, he had asked Kuroyukihime, who probably knew an anonymous address at least.

Strictly speaking, he also had the option of asking Sky Raker's child, Ash Roller, again. However, he had dared to choose to rely on Kuroyukihime. And when she had announced that she was going home, he had pushed even further and gotten her to come with him.

The momentary look on Sky Raker's face the morning she had given him the Enhanced Armament was burned vividly into his memory. She had lost friendships to her foolishness—that's what the recluse of the Accelerated World had told Haruyuki.

He had absolutely no idea what had happened between her and Kuroyukihime, so maybe he had no right to say anything, no right to do anything. But he thought about it like this: Even supposing the friendship was really lost, was there any reason why they couldn't get it back again? After all, they both remembered each other. So many memories, all the times they had fought together, were etched into their hearts. Those memories had to still connect them.

The train slid smoothly into the platform. Haruyuki and Kuroyukihime took the escalator up with the many other riders and stepped out through the south exit opening up before them. Shinjuku Southern Terrace was an enormous, pyramid-shaped, multilevel shopping center. They slipped through the bustling groups of shoppers and got on the central escalator.

Kuroyukihime, as before, said nothing.

I should probably say something. I definitely should, Haruyuki thought, but could say nothing.

The giant flight of automatic stairs passed splashy panels of advertising as it carried the two upward until finally, they arrived at the peak of the pyramid. The open terrace on the top floor was a hundred meters above the ground. Of course, this was still no match for the surrounding skyscrapers, but it offered a clear view of the Shinjuku Station terminal, the countless rows of tracks, and the trains of many colors coming and going there.

The evenings being still chilly, the breezy place held very few people.

Haruyuki and Kuroyukihime moved to the northernmost railing and looked out at the evening scene below as they waited for the appointed time.

Five thirty PM.

The sound of small footsteps clacking reached Haruyuki's ears from behind. He took a deep breath and turned around. As did Kuroyukihime, after a slight pause.

Against the reddish-purple clouds, she was there, smiling. Her long, soft hair fluttered in the breeze. The hem of her uniform skirt flicked up, and she held it down with a pale hand. Legs wrapped in thigh-high stockings, she took another step.

Sky Raker, the recluse living in the old Tokyo Tower, a member of the first Nega Nebulus, and level-eight Burst Linker, turned first to Haruyuki. "Good evening, Corvus." And then she turned her gaze on Kuroyukihime next to him. The color of her smile changed slightly. "Good evening, Lotus."

Several emotions wrestled in his heart, and Haruyuki could do nothing but lower his head deeply. However, a smile very similar to Sky Raker's rose up to Kuroyukihime's lips. "It's been a while, Raker."

"...It really has. Three years in the real world. In the Accelerated World...I don't know anymore how long it's been."

"Ages."

They both laughed lightly and drew no closer to each other.

"Um...Raker. I'm returning them...Your wings."

Sky Raker nodded gently, a kind smile on her face. "So you got them back, hmm? Your silver wings—no, your hope."

"I did. All of it. Thanks to you." And then Haruyuki pulled from his pocket the XSB cable he had come prepared with and stuck one end in his own Neurolinker before holding out the other end. Sky Raker accepted it and connected it without hesitation to her own Neurolinker.

The retransfer of the Enhanced Armament through a direct

duel took place quickly, without a word of conversation. The transfer request window was opened and the request accepted; the draw application was similarly submitted and accepted. At that point, it was Burst Out.

When they returned to the real world after a moment, the Gale Thruster was back with its original owner. Plucking the cable out, Sky Raker handed it to Haruyuki and smiled once again. "I have it now...so then, I'll be on my way." She looked at Kuroyuki-hime and bowed lightly.

After taking one, two steps, servo motors whining faintly, Sky Raker moved her lips slightly. "Corvus. I know you will be able to fly up to the heights I couldn't reach. I'll be rooting for you... Good luck." She grinned and turned around, leaving a quick wink in her wake. She walked off with a sure step.

But Haruyuki definitely saw it.

A small drop of light spilling from her quickly blinking eyes, tracing out a silver trajectory in the air.

Bag dangling from the hands behind her back, Sky Raker grew distant on sure feet. Under the night sky, her figure gradually became a silhouette.

Abruptly, the until now completely silent Kuroyukihime took a few steps forward, almost staggering. But she stopped just ahead of Haruyuki and clenched both fists, as if she were trying to endure something.

Kuroyukihime.

Kuroyukihime!! Haruyuki shouted in his heart. *Please, Kuroyuki-hime. She's waiting for you to say something. She's waiting for your hand. So, come on...*

Come on!

Haruyuki squeezed out every ounce of his will and pushed at Kuroyukihime's back in front of him, without moving his hands.

Instantly.

She ran forward another few steps.

"Raker!!" Kuroyukihime shouted in a clear voice. The receding back shuddered and stopped. Kuroyukihime took a deep breath, shoulders shaking, and yelled once more. "Come home, Fuko! I need you!!"

Sky Raker dropped her head deeply. Her left leg started to take another step forward. But then stopped. Almost as if the CPU controlling the artificial leg were fighting against its owner's orders. As if it had a spirit and was following its own heart. Bit by small bit, the leg was pulled back.

Ever so slowly, Sky Raker turned around. She moved her lips and uttered in the faintest voice, "Sach." And then a silent question. *Are you sure?*

Kuroyukihime nodded firmly and shouted again, "Fuko!"

The girls began to run toward each other. They tossed their bags aside at the same time. Kuroyukihime was the slightly faster of the two, but Sky Raker had her arms out to catch her. She embraced the somewhat shorter girl with black hair, and the girl called "Fuko" twisted her face up sharply.

Large tears spilled over her cheeks. "Unh...Unhaaah..." Almost as if from the moment she had appeared on this terrace—no, as if she had been holding her heart back all the way from back when she went to live in seclusion on the old Tokyo Tower, Sky Raker buried her face in Kuroyukihime's hair and released all that buried emotion.

"Aah...Aaaaaaah!" Haruyuki could hear the quiet cries of Kuroyukihime mixed in with that sobbing voice.

Unable to watch the incredibly beautiful, incredibly precious sight any longer, Haruyuki turned his face upward to keep his own tears from spilling out.

In the middle of the sky, stretching out endlessly as it turned from blue to madder red, a plane flying far, far above drew out a thin trail of white clouds and glittered brightly.

END

AFTERWORD

Reki Kawahara here. Thank you for picking up my first book of this year.

And here it is, 2010. It's just too far in the future. I'm a bit stunned. It's an everyday thing for us that all these exist now, but when I was a kid, things like SD memory cards, Blu-ray discs, and touch-panel cell phones were straight out of science fiction. Incidentally, the first HDD I bought had a capacity of twenty megabytes, but apparently, this spring, an SD card with sixty-four gigabytes is going on sale…

These days, I'm feeling like I can't keep up with advances in technology, but since a full-dive-type VR machine doesn't seem likely to show up any time soon, I'm thinking I'll just keep trying until then. My dream is to become a net game wreck in my old age, so I hope you'll manage something by then, please, all you manufacturers out there.

Now, here we come to our usual apology corner.

I am so sorry for ending the previous book, *The Twilight Marauder*, on such an incredibly terrible note! The biggest reason for having that kind of ending was simply because it wasn't finished, but you could say it was also the tiniest bit on purpose.

For a long time, I've been vaguely dissatisfied with the pages in a book. As you read, the number of pages gradually decreases, and whether you like it or not, this phenomenon communicates the information, "Once you read this much, it'll be over." Taking movies as an example, it would be like having a bar with the remaining time displayed in the lower right of the screen the whole time! But maybe my getting stuck on something so matter-of-fact is just because I've been a reader and writer of novels online for so long. There, you never have any physical sense of when it's going to end. (LOL)

Anyway, about all I could think of to avoid the spoiler information coming from the paper book was to make the text smaller and smaller, or to make the paper gradually thinner, but I was pretty sure that if I asked my editor to let me do anything like that, he'd tell me "no way" with a smile and that would be the end of that. So I tried something relatively more practical: not ending the book.

I'm sure that those of you who read the third volume without any prior information were probably outraged when you got to the last page, and no doubt felt a certain amount of surprise. If that was indeed the case, my objective was achieved. Of course, splitting a story into two books without any forewarning is nothing other than a kind of betrayal, so I apologize humbly and sincerely. I really am terribly sorry! Apologies! I won't do it again! Probably!

And having written this far, I feel like this afterword won't fit in the usual two pages. So we'll take a serious turn and continue into the excuses corner.

Although the end of this volume does mention that the quanta inside microtubules in the brain create human consciousness, this is in fact a complete fabrication I made up from the words of the very real theory of quantum mind. The actual quantum mind theory is a totally different thing and exceedingly difficult, which means I can't understand a word of it. For those of you who are interested in the subject, a man called Roger Penrose has written a book on the topic, so please read that. And then please break it down and quietly explain it to me. (LOL)

And one more thing. Another new female character has arrived on the scene, but I'm sure you've all already given up in this regard! Right?! I, too, have given up, and Kuroyukihime must have also given up...

I am indebted once again to illustrator HIMA, who designs at minimum one new female character for me in every volume! And I once again deeply and unconscionably inconvenienced my editor, Miki, by being later than late with my manuscript. At a meeting we had the other day, Miki's head looked newly neat, so I said, "Oh, you cut your hair," and he said, "I finally got the time to go get it cut." I was honestly touched by that. I hope we can enjoy working together again this year as well! (That said, at the present moment, I'm already ten minutes past the deadline for this afterword...)

And in conclusion, I would ask that all of you who have read my books would continue to join me this year as well!

I wish you all a wonderful 2010.

Reki Kawahara
December 15, 2009

ACCEL WORLD, Volume 4
REKI KAWAHARA

Translation by Jocelyne Allen

This book is a work of fiction. Names, characters, places, and
incidents are the product of the author's imagination or are
used fictitiously. Any resemblance to actual events, locales, or
persons, living or dead, is coincidental.

ACCEL WORLD
©REKI KAWAHARA 2010
All rights reserved.
Edited by ASCII MEDIA WORKS
First published in 2010 by KADOKAWA
CORPORATION, Tokyo.
English translation rights arranged with KADOKAWA
CORPORATION, Tokyo,
through Tuttle-Mori Agency, Inc., Tokyo.

English translation © 2015 Hachette Book Group, Inc.

Yen On
Hachette Book Group
1290 Avenue of the Americas, New York, NY 10104

www.hachettebookgroup.com
www.yenpress.com

Yen On is an imprint of Hachette Book Group, Inc.
The Yen On name and logo are trademarks of Hachette
Book Group, Inc.

The publisher is not responsible for websites (or their content) that are not owned by the publisher.

First Yen On edition: July 2015

ISBN: 978-0-316-29638-0

10 9 8 7 6 5 4 3 2 1

RRD-C

Printed in the United States of America